Necklace of Honor: Callie's Big Summer

Darla Alford

Published by Darla Alford, 2023.

NECKLACE OF HONOR: CALLIE'S BIG SUMMER
First edition, March 1, 2023.

Copyright © 2023 Darla Alford.
Book design by BookCoverZone.com
Unless otherwise notes, all Scripture quotations are taken from the Holman Christian Standard Bible (R), Copyright (C) 1999, 2000, 2002, 2003, 2009 by Holman Bible Publishers. Used by permission. Holman Christian Standard Bible (R), Holman CSB (R), and HCSB (R) are federally registered trademarks of Holman Bible Publishers.
ISBN 979-8-218-15066-2 (Print)
Published by Darla Alford

Table of Contents

To Jeff,

My husband, best friend, and tireless supporter

From Darla with Love

Chapter 1
CALLIE

The bright moonbeam shimmied its way through the dark trees, illuminating everything in its path. Its glistening rays made the mountain river look like a gleaming silver snake winding through the rich, green shadows of the Smoky Mountains. The blue moonlight stretched across open ground, and the trees cast long, lazy shadows. The moon's glow revealed a rustic cabin. The isolated home, two miles from the nearest neighbor, was part of a cozy community called Halo Notch.

What the moonlight missed, however, was the dark silhouette of a young woman moving cat-like and silent along the warm, tin rooftop. She carried herself with practiced ease, for she had been there many times before. A whisper of coolness tickled the breeze that tugged at her chestnut-colored hair, sending a chill through her body. At a certain spot, she sat and inhaled the fragrant air of early June. She remained motionless, surveying the area for anything interesting.

Eventually, 12-year-old Callie positioned both feet flat on the toasty roof to enjoy its coziness. It was her favorite secret spot. She gazed up at the moon and admired the sparkling stars. Sometimes the moon seemed close enough to touch—especially in autumn when it was big and orange. When the sky was dark with the new moon, she sat outside and just listened to the sounds of the night. When it rained, she stayed inside and enjoyed the sound of the raindrops tapping on the tin. It sounded like someone slowly pouring dry rice all over her roof, and it made her feel drowsy and content.

A lone owl called out, capturing her attention. She listened intently, eager to focus on anything besides her worries, if only for a moment. The river's babbling became the background music for every other sound. Random breezes tickled the trees, and the young leaves squirmed. Callie became aware of the thud-thud of her heart and tried to relax her breathing. It was no use. The more she tried to breathe normally, the more out of sorts her lungs seemed to be. She yawned deeply, resolving to think about anything other than the terrible school year she had just completed.

Callie reached into her pocket and pulled out the report card she had retrieved from the mailbox earlier that day: "Callie Johnson, 7th Grade Final." She had the grades memorized. There was no need to look again. The D's and one F appeared ghostly in the moonlight. She wished they *had* been ghosts instead of the real thing. She had known they were going to be lower than ever—she had watched them fall steadily from A's and B's since the school year began. *At least I passed to the 8th grade*, she thought with some consolation. *Barely*.

Her thoughts hop scotched through events that caused her to quit trying at school. The girls who used to be her friends at her small school had turned against her after a new rich girl moved to town. Her old friends and the new girl had joined forces to form a gang of snobs who tormented anyone outside their little group. Callie sighed. *I must be their favorite target.* She cringed as she remembered the last thing her former best friend said to her: "You're such a tomboy and a loser—you'll never be one of us." Those words cut to the heart. Good friends became enemies as the battle lines divided the Haves and the Have-Nots. And Callie felt alone on the side of the Have-Nots.

It wasn't just a difference in income and status, however. Callie loved being outside—hiking, fishing, playing, and exploring. The girls at school obsessed about boys, gossiped, and acted like they were better than everyone else. They made fun of anything that might hurt Callie. They even laughed at her unique golden eye color.

The only friend her age who accepted Callie, no matter what, was a boy named Tommy. He only lived a few miles away, but he went to a different school. He had been her companion ever since they were babies. He was funny and easy-going, always ready to join Callie for an adventure or a lazy afternoon of fishing. *Too bad he'll be gone most of the summer*, she sighed, still upset about the news. The day before her school was even out, Tommy had gone off for the summer to work with his cousins at a horseback riding stable an hour away.

Still, Callie never tired of exploring the forest and enjoying its company. Sometimes she pretended she was a pioneer woman, guiding the way for explorers. At other times, she was a forest ranger, studying the habits of animals and protecting them from danger. In autumn, when the wind's frosty breezes signaled the coming winter, she was a hunter, supplying food for her family. She knew that her pretending days were ending, and it saddened her a little. Sometimes she couldn't decide which was better—being old enough to drive and to do what she wanted, or to stay a kid just a little longer. Her birthday was coming soon. *Thirteen will be good I guess. I'm already independent. I just wish Mom would let me drive since I already know how.*

She heard the lonely cry of a wolf howling at the moon. *Maybe he's howling just for me*, she considered. "I know how you feel," she said gloomily. She sat up straight and strained her ears to listen, trying to imagine where he might be.

Callie lived with her mother, Kate, and Grandpa, Kate's father. Callie's father, a carpenter, died in a tree-cutting accident when she was only three years old. *I wonder what he would think of me now*, she mused.

Callie smiled despite her bleak mood when she thought of the good-natured kidding and fun that her family had together. Mom and Grandpa were loving and kind Christians. Callie had gone to church since she was a baby, but she had never personally become a follower of Christ. It was a personal decision; a step she knew she hadn't taken. She had been thinking about Jesus' love for her, though, as she found herself humming songs she had sung at church.

Callie had no siblings, and no cousins that she knew of. In fact, she knew little about her family. Outside of her mother and grandfather, she might as well have had no other blood kin. Whenever she asked about her other grandparents—or anyone else—the subject was changed. It was mysterious and frustrating. She often found herself looking for little clues or imagining what the extended family must have been like.

At least she had 27-year-old Jake McLain, a family friend who was like a brother to her. He had been an important part of her life ever since she could remember. Grandpa would sometimes talk about a time "before Jake came," but Callie couldn't remember ever being without his quiet strength, Christian warmth, and dry humor. He was part of her everyday world—kidding with her, watching out for her, and including her on hikes and camping trips. He often ate supper with Callie's family or hosted barbeques for them at his cabin. Sometimes his Granny Grace came. Callie admired him for his work as a paramedic and loved to hear him talk about his mountain rescues. She only wished he could spend more time with her during the summer. *Oh well, I don't really mind doing things alone that much*, she sighed, not all that excited.

She hugged herself, securely enfolded by her father's old, soft sweatshirt that she wore over her T-shirt. She was thankful that her mother had kept some of his clothes. She imagined his strong arms sawing and hammering on the cabin he had built for them. Sometimes Callie felt his presence so strongly that she thought she could look up and he would be there; but of course, he never was. Because she was so young when he died, she had no real memory of him.

Eventually the wolf's howls faded away, and she thought about the home she loved so much. Beautiful mountains surrounded her. Giant boulders directed the dancing river's flow. Secret hideouts dotted the hills. There was even one behind a big waterfall not too far away. A nearby mountain had a hidden cave, complete with a huge cavern and bats.

As she was considering what she might explore on her own, she noticed a small bat flying from high up in the barn to her left. His wings flapped eagerly as his trusty sonar led him into the dark woods. Callie's lips parted into a big smile. Bats were kind of ugly, but she liked them anyway. *I hope he eats every single mosquito in Halo Notch,* she thought, knowing she wouldn't be so lucky. The girls at school couldn't understand her love for nature, either. But she didn't care. *I'm not changing for them,* she thought stubbornly.

She braided her hair for the night and secured it with the hair band she wore on her wrist. It was always pulled back in some form or fashion. Having hair in her face just slowed her down. She rubbed her eyes and yawned, thinking about her little black dog on her bed. *Shadow is probably already asleep,* she thought fondly. Sometimes she wished she had a bigger dog like a Golden Retriever or a pet wolf to join her on her adventures in the mountains. But she still loved her fluffy terrier. His little legs were too short to keep up with her as she ran through the woods, but he was always ready to cuddle whenever she was at home.

She was still deep in thought when she stood carefully and stretched. Slowly making her way back through the window, she touched down gently on the wood floor. Suddenly, she heard a strange noise. She spun around, catching the windowsill for balance. She almost laughed out loud when she realized it was Shadow, snoring on her bed. Callie quietly closed the window, leaving a small crack. She untied the ribbon that held her curtain back and said, "Goodnight" to the moon.

CALLIE FELT THE REPORT card in her pocket once again when she pulled off her father's sweatshirt for the night. Suddenly she realized that she wanted to talk to someone about her loneliness, the girls at school, her dread of a summer alone, and maybe even her thoughts about Jesus. *Oh well*, she thought as she re-adjusted her T-shirt, *Mom and Grandpa are asleep. I'll talk to someone later.* She crawled into her cozy bed and tried to snuggle down for the night.

Report card. Mean girls. Loneliness. Song lyrics. Her brain buzzed with thoughts that kept her awake. One moment, it was too cold. She tried to get comfortable. *Talk to somebody.* Then, it was too hot. Her pillow smelled funny. *Do something about it now.* She was hungry. *Get up.* She tossed and turned, trying a couple of times to move Shadow over. *He's such a bed hog!* Moment by moment passed, but Callie was still awake—and getting more aggravated by the second.

"I just want to sleep!" she said aloud to Shadow.

He raised his little head and wagged his tail, then flopped over and went back to sleep.

Finally, Callie threw off her covers and grabbed the report card, deciding to write "I'm sorry" on it and leave it on the table in the kitchen. As she was moving toward the door, however, she decided to at least try to talk to her mother that night.

CREAK—she opened Kate's door slowly and heard the steady rhythm of her mother's breathing. A small ray of moonlight revealed the outline of the sleeping woman. Her soft hair framed her lovely face. Callie cleared her throat. No response. She eased over to the bedside and started to wake her up but changed her mind. *She worked a double shift today. She's probably tired. Maybe Grandpa's awake. He'll know what to do.*

Callie backed out of her mother's room, slowly pulling the door closed. She stepped onto the ancient rug in the hall and descended the squeaky stairs. "Nobody could sneak around in this house," she whispered as she tried to avoid the loudest steps.

She heard a deep inhale, followed by a heavy, masculine snore. *Oh, great. Grandpa's asleep, too.* Even his snoring was warm and reassuring, though. She adored her grandfather. Kate strongly favored him in her facial features and her clear blue eyes. Callie loved those unusual crystal-clear eyes; many times, she wished that she had inherited them instead of her own golden eyes which came from no one she knew of. Her father's eyes had been more hazel.

Callie darted quickly to the small table at the foot of the stairs and searched the drawers for a pencil or pen. While digging in the drawer, she knocked the large family Bible to the floor, spilling its contents. Callie rolled her eyes at the noise and the mess of random slips of paper and church bulletins. When she tucked the papers back inside the old Bible, she noticed a sloppy handwritten note that said:

"Ha. Ha. I took the stupid charms from your precious NOH, and you'll never see them again. T."

"What on earth?!" Callie said a little too loudly despite her earlier efforts to be quiet. *This makes no sense. What's NOH? Who is T?* She almost dropped the Bible again as she paced, trying to make some connection.

She gripped the mysterious note and turned to go back to her room, almost forgetting her report card. Hurriedly, she tiptoed to the kitchen and placed the report card on the table. Trying to avoid the loudest steps, she snuck back up to her bedroom. Back in bed, she tried to figure out what the note could mean as her eyes grew heavy. Soon, she fell fast asleep, dreaming about adventure.

And the mysterious note rested silently on her bedside table, just waiting for its secrets to be unlocked.

Chapter 2

A PLATE OF SYRUP

The next morning Callie woke up later than usual, glad to be out of school. She felt sluggish after staying up so late worrying about everything. One look in the mirror confirmed the rough night she had. Sometime during the night her hair had gone from neatly braided to a rumpled mess.

Her heart-shaped face was tanned from her active life. Her eyes glistened with intelligence and curiosity despite her puffy, tired eyelids. She quickly re-braided her hair and held the end of the braid securely with one hand while rifling through her bed covers for the lost hair band with her free hand. Spotting the curtain's tieback ribbon out of the corner of her eye, she used it to finish off her signature hairstyle. She pushed back the curtain to lighten her room and was greeted by a lingering fog. Even though it was already June, the morning air was cool. Callie hoped that her t-shirt and shorts would be warm enough for her first day of summer break.

Shadow jumped around wanting to go outside. He led the way down the stairs but, not wanting to get too far ahead of his beloved master, he kept stopping to look up at Callie. She barely avoided stepping on him as they went out the front door! After the wiggly dog finished his business, he followed Callie back into the house. She tossed him a treat and set out to see if her mother had left her a note about the report card. It could decide what kind of day Callie would have.

Callie's stomach growled. *I wonder if Grandpa made pancakes. Oh well, I won't feel like eating them if I'm in trouble,* she thought.

Grandpa was always up early. He would drink his first cup of coffee on the back porch as he read his Bible and prayed. Then, he would come inside to make breakfast. Callie rarely saw her mother in the mornings. She left very early in her old jeep to go to work, and she often worked late. Callie missed her.

She searched the kitchen for a response to her report card, or a sign that her mother had even seen it. "She's seen it, all right, Shadow. It's gone." There weren't too many places to look. The tiny kitchen had only a few surfaces for food preparation. "Great—no breakfast for me either, ole boy." Shadow listened to her with rapt attention. He tilted his head to the right and then to the left, puzzled. He jumped into her arms when she knelt, and she carried him as she continued her search around the house.

She looked everywhere—all over the kitchen, on the tables beside the worn couch, in the bathroom, and in her mother's bedroom. She even went back to her own bedroom thinking that her mother might have left a note in there. She dreaded the thought of waiting all day to find out what kind of trouble she was in. While she was looking for a note, she picked up the Bible again, searching through all the clippings and papers for a hint of who "T" could be. She chewed her lip and looked off into nowhere as she studied the mystery of NOH. *What could it mean?*

While trying to think of a plan, her stomach growled. She rolled her eyes. *Maybe my punishment is no- breakfast-from-Grandpa-for-the-rest-of-my-life.* She sighed. *Surely not.*

"Grandpa!" she yelled as she went out the back door and headed for his workshop in the barn. The insects were still "breep-breep-breeping" and "wee-ah, wee-ahing" from last night's shift. Callie smiled. She wondered how many people noticed things like the bug sounds.

Shadow wriggled excitedly as she trotted toward the barn. "Okay, okay, you can get down." The little dog jumped out of her arms as eagerly as he had jumped into them and followed closely as she skimmed the flower-lined path.

The distinct smell of cedar rushed over her when she opened the door. Carvings of bears, fish, deer, eagles, and other animals lined the tables and shelves in various stages of completion. Callie made sure her little skunk that Grandpa had been helping her with was still there. She had named it Huckleberry. The heavy door slowly slammed shut behind her with a **SMACK**.

"Ouch!" Grandpa said, slightly nicking his finger with a tool. "Callie, honey, don't sneak up on me," he said slowly. His hands didn't always cooperate since his stroke the year before. Even regular activities were difficult at times.

Although his speech was almost normal again, he spoke more slowly than before. He had to concentrate harder to make the things that he sold.

"I'm sorry, Grandpa." She hugged him around the neck. She loved everything about him—she even ignored his bad habit of chewing tobacco. He was a funny, wise, and gentle companion for her. She missed the times they had shared fishing and walking through the woods. Every day she worried that he would get sick again.

"Lookin' for pancakes?" he asked knowingly.

"I can't start my summer without them," she replied, kissing him on the cheek.

He put down his tools and wiped his hands on his apron. Callie followed him as he walked slowly toward the house, carefully disguising his occasional limp with short pauses "to look at the flowers." Once inside, he made the fluffiest pancakes ever. She cut the golden circles into tiny pieces and savored every bite. They melted in her mouth, mingled with delicious butter and syrup.

Grandpa poured himself some coffee and sat down at the table across from her. "You know, I get up before your mother does," he said, wiping a drip from his coffee cup.

Callie nodded in agreement, only mildly interested. Then she stopped, understanding his meaning. *He saw the report card first!* "Oh." The pancake she was chewing suddenly felt like a big wad of gummy flour in her mouth. "I'm in trouble, right?"

"Well, it depends on how you look at it," he said. "Your mother will talk to you later about that."

"I was afraid you'd say that" she said, struggling to swallow her last bite. She wondered whether to ask him about the mysterious note.

"I'm worried about you, Callie. You're unhappy." Grandpa could always see right through her.

"I'm happy with *you*," she teased, hoping to change the subject.

"You know, my relationship with Jesus helps me through a lot of tough times, and I enjoy His love every day," Grandpa continued. "One of these days, you may be ready to trust Him as your personal Lord and Savior. Jesus loves you just as you are, Callie. In fact, His love is so deep that He died to pay the price for every bad thing you've ever done or ever will do. Jesus wants to be your friend, but the choice is yours." He spoke to her gently.

Callie heard her mouth say, "I know." From out of nowhere, a tear ran down her cheek. *How does he always know what's going on with me?* After a long pause, she whispered, "I might be ready, Grandpa."

"God has a purpose for your life, Callie." Grandpa said simply. "He made you. He wants to be there for you always—just like He is there for me. Oh, your problems won't magically disappear, but He'll help you know what to do and give you joy."

Grandpa told her how to ask Jesus to be the Lord of her life, and for the first time, it all made sense. Something just clicked inside. And Callie made the choice. No pressure. No fear. It was time. And she was ready. Right there at the kitchen table, over a plate of syrup, Callie talked to God and asked Jesus into her heart.

Afterward, she felt...relieved. There was a joy inside of her she had never—ever—felt before. And peace. It was the right thing for her to do and the right time for her to do it. She had a new, true Friend. Someone who loved her more than any human ever could. Her problems didn't seem as big anymore. She felt free, and it was good.

She hugged Grandpa tightly. He was beaming from ear to ear. "You've got something now you've never had before, Callie," he said with her arms still around his neck.

"What's that, Grandpa?"

He pulled back and looked deep into her golden eyes. "Everything you'll ever need."

His answer came as a surprise to Callie. She hadn't thought about Jesus that way before.

"Callie, where is Jesus in relationship to you right now?"

"He's in my heart, Grandpa," she answered with another hug.

Grandpa smiled. He left her with that thought for a moment, taking her plate to the sink. She thought she saw him wipe away a tear just before he cleared his throat.

"Well, are you ready for your special mission?" he asked as he started toward his shop. Grandpa had a way of making even normal tasks feel special.

"Ready," she replied.

She ran to retrieve her heavy backpack from the hook on the back of the door, dashed up the creaky stairs, and dumped a mess of school papers onto her bed. *Good riddance! Maybe I'll build a bonfire and burn all of it.* She stuffed the mysterious NOH note in her pocket, then ran down the steps, empty backpack in tow.

As soon as she found Grandpa in his shop again, he said, "These eagles go to Betty at the Eagle's Nest Tea Room in town. She sold everything I gave her last time. Jake will be here soon to pick you up."

Callie wrapped five beautifully carved eagles with old newspaper and carefully packed them into her backpack. Grandpa continued, "Betty will give you two hundred dollars in cash. You can use five of the dollars to get yourself a little something at the drugstore." It was very exciting. Those eagles were the first finished carvings he had completed since his stroke.

"Thanks, Grandpa. I'm going to go wait for Jake."

"Callie!" Grandpa called to her, "Keep your eyes open around the Eagle's Nest. Mrs. Longfellow's house next door to it was robbed a few days ago and..." but Callie was already out the door. She didn't hear the rest of his statement: "whoever did it is still on the loose."

What she did hear was Jake's truck heading up the long driveway. Shadow had heard it too and was circling Callie's legs in excitement. He loved Jake. Callie jumped off the porch and ran right over the bouncy dog, knocking his front legs out from under him.

"Shadow," she pleaded, "I can't help but run into you when you are between my ankles!" He looked at her with big, forlorn eyes and allowed her to check his legs for soreness. When she was satisfied that he was okay, she cradled his head in her hands, kissed him between the eyes, picked him up, and placed him inside the house. In a flash, he was wagging his tail at her from his perch in the front window.

Jake's dark green truck screeched to a stop, and Callie ran to jump inside.

"Guess what!" she exclaimed as she shed the backpack and placed it beside her. "I asked Jesus into my heart today."

Jake's smile lit up his whole face. "Way to go, Cal! You're my real sister now!" His green eyes always sparkled when he talked about anything related to God. "We have a lot to talk about."

Callie liked the sound of that. She loved spending time with Jake—just the two of them. She didn't even want to think about sharing him with anyone else.

The two friends chatted easily as the sun blinked through the wispy fog. The ancient Smokies seemed to stretch out and yawn to welcome the day. Callie felt the NOH note in her pocket a couple of times, but never found the chance to ask about it. *I'll ask him on the way back from town*, she decided.

"Speaking of you being a sister," Jake said, returning to the original subject, "I have a surprise for you."

"Great! I like surprises." Her eyes brightened in anticipation.

"Well, I hope so," he said hesitantly. "My little sister is coming today…to spend the summer with me."

Chapter 3
STRANGERS

At first, Callie thought he was kidding. She looked across the seat to see if he was smiling at all, but he wasn't. Jake absent-mindedly ran his fingers through his thick auburn hair. He was definitely not kidding.

"Did you forget that I have a younger sister in Asheville?" he asked softly.

"No, well, yes," Callie couldn't think of anything to say. Her thoughts raced through her head. She heard herself say, "Why is she coming here? Does she know how busy you are?" She wanted to say: *Well, you can just tell your sister that you are my brother, and we don't need her to mess it up.* It was starting to look like Jesus was going to be the only person she could talk to at all.

"She's writing a story for a contest. Haven't I told you about her?"

"Not really." *A story? Why can't she stay home and write her little story?*

"Maybe you two can hang out together. She's thirteen." Jake said a little sheepishly, uncertain of his own suggestion.

He's trying to sell me on this. Great. This is going to be miserable. "I'm not much into writing," Callie mumbled.

"Actually, I think she wants to write about our culture," he offered.

Callie could feel anger rising in her. "Our culture?! Is she from Mars or something?"

"No, Cal. She's from Asheville. She's just supposed to write about folks who live in the same geographic region but live differently." Jake said, visibly flustered.

"If you hadn't noticed, Jake, I'm already different in my own culture. This has been the worst year of my life because of it. I don't need someone else to come in here and make me feel bad. You'll have to find someone else to help her with her little report." Callie had never spoken to Jake that way before. She felt cornered.

The growling of the engine when Jake shifted gears was the only sound for the next fifteen minutes. Finally, Jake pulled up to Eagle's Nest Tea Room so Callie could get out. "I'll meet you here in about an hour," he said simply as he pulled away.

Callie was so angry that she didn't see the tall, skinny man in the dirty clothes passing in front of her. "Excuse me," she muttered when she bumped into him. He smelled like he hadn't bathed in a month. He grunted in reply and crossed the street, ducking into Al's Auto Supply.

The Eagle's Nest Tea Room was in a powder blue house with white trim on the windows and doors. Lace curtains hung on every window in the large home—a testimony to Ms. Betty's decorating style. Patriotic sashes and flags adorned the windows and porch railings from Memorial Day through July. Flowerpots bursting with geraniums, roses, impatiens, and pansies accented the porch. The outdoorsy name "Eagles Nest" never seemed to fit the Victorian house in Callie's opinion. Even though it was much larger than Callie's house, however, Mrs. Longfellow's gigantic home next door made the Eagle's Nest look small in comparison.

"Mornin' Honey," Ms. Betty called out in her southern drawl as Callie opened the door. Callie's mouth watered when she smelled Ms. Betty's famous apple pie baking. She passed the counter and went into Betty's office where she carefully unpacked the five eagles and lined them out on a nearby table.

"Be right there, Callie!"

Callie heard the high **JING** of the cash register, followed by Ms. Betty's ever-elegant entrance. Callie watched as the older woman counted out ten twenty-dollar bills and placed them on the table. Her bright red fingernails clicked between each twenty, and her rings bumped into each other. She had white hair, perfectly styled, and wore lots of makeup. Her uniform—if you could call it that—consisted of ironed blue jeans and a frilly blouse. Callie guessed that she wore her bright red lipstick even when she slept. Her perfume was light and pleasant.

"These are beautiful," Ms. Betty purred as she unwrapped the eagles. "No wonder everyone likes them!" Callie suspected that Ms. Betty would have liked anything Grandpa made. Grandpa's eyes sparkled when he talked about Ms. Betty, too, but Callie couldn't get him to admit that he liked her.

"Thanks, Ms. Betty." Callie folded up the money and placed it in her pocket.

"You best be careful with that, Honey," Ms. Betty cautioned. "Someone robbed Mrs. Longfellow's house just a couple of days ago. The police are still trying to figure out who did it." Callie followed as Ms. Betty gathered up the eagles and took them back into the main dining area where she displayed them on a special shelf. "I don't know what's becomin' of this town."

"Yes, ma'am," Callie replied with little concern. She opened the jingling door to the street, still agitated about her conversation with Jake. *If someone tries to mess with me, I'll haul off and hit 'em!*

The morning sun warmed the air. Callie felt a light fog dissolve across her face as she stepped onto the sidewalk and surveyed her hometown. Downtown Halo Notch pulsed with the slow, easy rhythm of a small mountain village. Homes and buildings from the late 1800's snuggled alongside those from every decade thereafter—evidence of the town's history and growth.

Out of all the buildings in the quaint town, however, the Longfellow house was easily the focal point. The house and yard took up a whole block. A stone retaining wall stretched all the way around the property, seeming to lift the whole thing up four feet off the street. A plush carpet of green grass covered the yard, tempting Callie to kick off her shoes and sink her toes into it. Huge trees with tractor-wheel sized trunks provided a shady canopy that covered the roof of the three-story house. She counted at least ten sets of green shutters and three fireplaces.

I wonder what the crook got away with? Maybe he was lucky enough to catch a glimpse of Mrs. Longfellow. She thought about that a bit. It seemed like no one had ever seen the old woman before—she just stayed hidden in her fortress all the time. Ghost stories floated around town about this mysterious person that no one seemed to know. Only her live-in housekeeper, Ms. Hogg, ever appeared from the mansion. No one knew much about her either. *For all I know, Hogg could have killed the old woman and buried her in the basement. No one would miss her.* She longed to go in and look around.

The short beep of a horn shook her from her daydreaming. A silver truck with the words, "Halo Notch Vineyard" painted on its side crossed in front of her.

"Hi, Callie!" Emma called as she drove down the street toward the vineyard.

Emma was one of Callie's favorite people. Jake seemed to like her a lot. They were around the same age and liked the same things. Callie thought she had seen a spark between the two of them. *Who could blame him for liking her?* She was fun to be with, and all the young people from church loved to hang out with her. Callie loved having her as a Sunday School teacher. Callie waved back, reminding herself to tell Emma that she had become a Christian.

Callie walked over to the corner drugstore and meandered up and down the aisles trying to think of something to buy with the five dollars Grandpa gave her. She rarely had money at her disposal, so it was a dilemma to decide what to buy. She had a tradition: buy one thing that would last a while and one thing just for fun. She picked up a candy bar near the checkout and set out to find something that wouldn't be gone in five minutes. She looked at a box of BBs and a sketchpad. She glanced around to see if anyone was watching as she examined a squirt gun, thinking it was maybe too childish. Finding nothing that she really wanted, she paid for the candy and went outside to the coke machine to buy a drink.

After she pressed the cola button, she retrieved the frosty drink and opened the top with the bottle opener attached to the machine. She liked the fizzy sound it made when the lid popped off.

When she turned toward the street, she noticed two police cars stopping at the Longfellow house. She crossed the street just as the officers climbed out of the cars. They paused to talk to each other for a moment, but Callie couldn't make out what they were saying. She was very curious when one officer climbed the steps to the front of the house while the other one sneaked around to the back door.

She wasn't the only one who noticed them. Other townspeople also lingered while the police officers disappeared out of sight. Moments passed. After a while, most of the small crowd dispersed, called away by busy schedules. The ones who could wait around found shady places to sit comfortably for the imagined drama to take place. The Longfellow robbery was the most exciting thing the town had experienced in a long time.

Callie settled onto the porch at the Eagle's Nest, eager for some action. *If they drag Hogg out screaming or carry out Mrs. Longfellow's dead body, I don't want to miss it.* She listened for gunshots while she munched on the fast-disappearing candy bar. She fidgeted, hoping that Jake wouldn't come before she heard or saw something. If it hadn't been time for him to pick her up, she would have crept over to look in one of the windows.

Deciding to organize the money in her pocket to fill up the time, she stretched the cash out on her lap. The twenties were still together. She glanced up at the police cars to see if any new excitement had developed, but the empty cruisers sat alone, waiting for their drivers to return. She smoothed out the bills from the drugstore so she could separate her money from Grandpa's.

Suddenly, she felt like someone was watching her. She cast a glance toward the entrance of the Tea Room, but no one was there. She peered through the windows behind her. No one. *Callie, you're getting paranoid*, she thought. She couldn't shake the sickening feeling that someone was studying her every move. She looked across the street as casually as she could and saw him—the nasty man she had bumped into earlier! He was staring at her from a phone booth across the street! She tried to act as if she didn't see him while quickly shoving the money into her pocket.

"Now's a good time for you to come, Jake," she whispered under her breath. She totally forgot about being mad at him. Now she had the NOH note and the weird man to tell him about.

To Callie's relief, Jake pulled up right on cue. She swung open the door and threw her backpack inside. Then, she took hold of the doorframe and hoisted herself onto the seat. "Jake, there's some creepy man..." she started... but stopped mid-sentence.

She was face to face with a total stranger.

Chapter 4
TWO WORDS

"Callie, this is my sister, Becca. Becca—Callie." Jake said.
Callie nodded at the intruder, silent.

"Hi, Callie. Jake's told me a lot about you," Becca said in her most refined voice.

Callie didn't even smile. *That's funny. He never told me anything about you,* she thought.

Jake cleared his throat. "What were you saying about a creepy man?"

"Nothing. Just some old man was staring at me. Never saw him before." Callie said quickly, wanting to drop the subject. *There goes asking him about the NOH note.*

"Did you tell the police? They were right there. It looked like Bob and Randy's cruisers," Jake questioned.

"Nope." Callie wasn't in the mood to talk.

Jake changed the subject. "Becca's staying until after your birthday. Maybe you guys can hang out together."

Oh, great. She looked out her window, full of dread. "Great. That'll be nice," she mumbled, sounding more sarcastic than she intended.

Sensing Callie's discomfort, Becca ventured, "You can show me around."

"Sure. Maybe," Callie said, sizing her up. She shot a sideways glance at Becca's manicured hands and expensive clothes. The perfume she was wearing was the same kind that the mean girls at school wore. She was physically more mature than Callie was, and she wore makeup and carried a purse. Callie wondered how many hours the girl had spent on her perfectly styled, red, curly hair.

"Actually, I'm kinda busy this summer," Callie said at last, resuming her stare out the window.

Jake's mouth dropped wide open just before he rolled his eyes at her. "Maybe you can work something into your busy schedule," he said, shaking his head in disbelief. "There's a youth get-together at the vineyard this Friday. I'll drive you and Becca, and you can introduce her to everyone."

"That sounds fun," Becca said, unsure.

"Okay," Callie said reluctantly. Her only hope was that Becca would leave her alone and find someone else to do a report on.

Becca glanced over at Callie's cut-off blue jean shorts and old T-shirt. *I wonder if I've made a mistake by coming,* she thought. She imagined her best friend, Kimi, having fun at cheerleading camp and on a cruise. Becca planned to call her as soon as they got to Jake's house. She missed Kimi already! Becca imagined the conversation...

"*Hi, Kimi. You were right about one thing. I'm stuck with a cranky hillbilly. I'm amazed she has shoes. She looks like a boy except for her braided hair. Yes, yes, well she seems clean at least. Yes, okay, I'll watch out for lice. But Kimi? You were wrong about the rest of it. I'm still getting my story. I'll get through to her somehow and she'll give me everything I need to prove to Mom and Dad that I can make it as a writer. You'll see when I get back. Have a great summer. I'll see you in August if I survive. Bye.*"

The awkward silence in the truck was miserable. Jake started to turn up Callie's driveway, but she stopped him.

"Let me out here. I'll walk," she said, not wanting Becca to see her small cabin. *It's probably smaller than a vacation home to Miss Better-Than-Me,* she thought.

"I'd like to see where you live," Becca said, curious.

Callie ignored her.

Jake didn't argue. He stopped the truck so Callie could get out. She picked up her backpack and headed up the driveway. "Thanks for the ride, Jake," she mumbled. "One thing—do you know what NOH means?"

"Sorry, never heard of it. Where did you see it?" He asked.

Callie reached into her pocket to get the note, but then decided against sharing it with Becca. "Never mind."

He watched her walk away. "That didn't go well," he said sadly to his sister.

"Is she always this rude?" Becca asked.

"I've never seen her this way," Jake replied.

"Do you think she'll give me my story?"

"Listen, Becca," Jake said, "I'm not sure exactly what you want from Callie, but I know she's not going to take kindly to you treating her like just a subject for a story. She's a great person—strong, determined, fun. If you want her to help you at all, you must earn her trust."

"Oh, I'm good at that," Becca replied. "Kimi and I found a stray dog that didn't trust anybody, but we kept working with it until now it comes right to me."

"That's well and good, Becca, but Callie is a person, not a dog. If you look down on her in any way, she won't even speak to you, and I won't blame her." He shifted the truck to a lower gear for a steep incline and added, "And I won't be happy with you either."

"Oh, she'll talk to me. I'm good at interviewing people."

"Becca, Callie lives in a whole different world than you do. Don't expect to come in here and interview her and think she'll open up and just fill you with information. If you want her to help you, you'll need to put yourself in her shoes a little and find something in common."

Jake was usually a man of few words, so when he did speak most people listened. He was obviously perturbed.

Becca was reflective. It was strange feeling like an outsider with her own brother. She had longed for him to move back home to his upscale neighborhood so he would be part of her life. Suddenly he seemed more like the mountain people than a member of her own family.

She produced a tape recorder from her expensive purse and spoke into it: "Make a list of things about Callie and things about yourself. Find things in common." She looked over at Jake, expecting him to be impressed with her professionalism. Instead, he shot a quick look at the recorder, then looked straight ahead without comment.

"What's wrong?" she asked. *Why's he acting so weird?*

"I wouldn't use that thing around Callie. She won't be impressed."

"Jake, I'm a writer. I need all my tools to do my job," Becca said tersely.

"Becca. You're a teenager. If you want to truly be a writer, you'll have to learn how to relate to people." His statement was simple and direct.

She held her peace despite the urge to remind him that her work had been in the newspaper twice and that she had won several awards. She really didn't want a fight. *At least he acknowledged I'm a teenager. A lot of people can't seem to remember that I've already turned thirteen.* Deep down, though, she knew he was right about gaining the trust of her sources.

She looked out the window at the lush forest surrounding her. The beauty of the Great Smoky Mountains seduced her senses and drew her in. It was hard to be upset when there were so many amazing things to see.

The trees opened to reveal layer after layer of rolling mountains in every shade of green. Becca could see a fragment of a road far across the valley. She spotted a car that was miles away when the sunshine bounced off its chrome with a flash of light. White clouds hunkered down against the mountains, creating the famous smoky appearance that the Smokies are known for.

Jake seemed to read her mind. "Halo Notch," he said quietly.

Becca looked at Jake, unsure of what he had said.

"Halo Notch means a little tucked away place that is sacred." His eyes were tender and expressive. A peaceful smile warmed his face.

Becca marveled. *Maybe there's more to this place than I thought.*

MEANWHILE, CALLIE'S bad mood made her driveway feel longer and steeper than ever before. It would've been a lot easier if Jake had driven, but she couldn't stand to be in his truck for one more second.

"I can't believe him," she mumbled. "If he thinks I'm spending one more minute with his stupid sister, he has another thing coming." Her shuffling gait tripped her. She lunged forward and fell to the ground, scraping her palms.

"Shoot," Callie said angrily. She threw her backpack off and sat there, ill-tempered. Both of her hands stung sharply, dirty and raw from the fall.

Nobody's gonna understand how I feel, she thought. *Mom and Grandpa will think it's just great that I have someone to hang out with. Jake's made his feelings clear. No one knows what a year I've had. No one.* She was hurt, mad, and lonely to the very core of her being.

"I'm here." The voice seemed so real that Callie turned to see if anyone was there. "I know all about you." Then it dawned on her. The momentary confusion melted into relief. It was Jesus speaking to her heart. She was amazed.

The words He spoke inside of her were so clear to her at that moment that they seemed audible.

"Yeah, but what can you do? No offense, Jesus, but this is pretty complicated. I guess I should say I'm sorry for being all mad and rude, but I'm really not sorry at all."

She was surprised that she didn't feel guilty for talking with Him that way. She felt comfortable in His presence. *I guess he has seen it all,* she thought. Then, it was as if all the frustration and sadness from her whole last school year washed over her. She felt smothered by keeping it inside, so she let it all pour out.

She recounted every struggle, every hurtful exchange of words—everything that bothered her. Her words rushed out from every secret place in her heart. She stood and paced. She threw rocks at trees. She ranted. She cried. She held nothing back. She told Him things that no human being knew except her.

She never felt like Jesus was judging her for anything. She called people "dumb" and "stuck-up" and said exactly what she felt. He listened. Minutes turned into at least an hour, but the sense of His presence remained.

Finally, peace came like the quenching of a deep thirst with cool, refreshing water. It was so good to talk to someone about it. Someone who had been there and understood. "That's why I don't want anything to do with Becca, or whatever her name is. I've had enough of people like her," she concluded.

Callie halfway expected Jesus to lecture her or give her a bunch of words of wisdom. But He didn't. It was strange. His response was two simple words that came in a clear thought: "Trust Me."

She didn't like His two little words at first. *Two words? What kind of help is that?* She waited to see if He would tell her anything else. She even closed her eyes so she could concentrate. Nothing. His words echoed in her head. *Trust Me...Trust Me...Trust Me.*

"Jesus, I'm new at this Christian stuff—I don't know how to trust You."

The strong sense of His presence was gone then. It was as if He left her with her thoughts. Callie couldn't quit thinking about His Two Words. They energized her curiosity. She was determined to find out more about trusting Jesus as a Christian.

She felt lighter and more hopeful as she gathered her backpack and headed to her house. The sunshine looked brighter than before. The trees were greener, and her world seemed more alive than before. The dark, towering wave that had threatened to drown her was gone.

The Two Words played over and over in her mind like a song stuck in her head. *What exactly do they mean?*

Chapter 5

GRANDPA'S BLESSING

Shadow wagged his whole body when Callie opened the front door.

"Hi, Shadow. You act like you haven't seen me in years!" She knelt to pat him with her fingertips, and he could hardly get enough. After a few moments of intense greeting, he was happy. Callie headed to the kitchen sink and gingerly washed her scraped hands with soap. Meanwhile, Shadow ran off to get his little stuffed bear, prancing back to present it to Callie. "Wow—a bear!" She feigned excitement over the tattered, old thing as she patted her hands dry on a clean towel. Satisfied that he had impressed his girl, Shadow trotted over to the couch and flopped down for a chew-fest on the toy's thread-bare ear.

"Grandpa! I have your money!" Callie yelled.

"Out here!" Grandpa hollered from the back porch. "Anything going on in town?"

"Not really." Her mind replayed her fight with Jake, the arrival of his awful sister, the police at the Longfellow House, and the strange man. A lot had happened in just a few hours, but she didn't want to talk about it. She plopped down beside Grandpa and counted his money back to him. He tucked it in his shirt pocket and wiped a bead of sweat from his brow.

"Did you know about Jake's sister?" she said at last.

"What about her?"

"That she was coming for the summer." Callie's anger at Jake welled up in her once again. Almost at once, she felt a nagging sensation inside. The Two Words were back again.

"Nope. Can't say that I did. Did you meet her?"

"You could say that" she answered in a low voice. "Grandpa, Jesus wants us to trust Him, right?"

"Sure does."

"What does it mean, exactly, to, you know, trust Him?" she asked, feeling awkward.

"It means that you believe His Word—the Bible—and that you count on Him to work things out." He pulled a small wire-bound notebook and a stubby pencil from his shirt pocket and wrote something on one of its pages. "You have to know what the Bible says before you can believe its words, don't you?" He smiled and handed her the roughly scrawled note. "This is from the book of Romans."

She read the note to herself: "Romans 8:28: We know that all things work together for the good of those who love God: those who are called according to His purpose."

"If you love God and are trying to follow Him the best you know how, everything will work out the way it's supposed to." Grandpa said. Then, he took the little pad and slowly wrote "John" in big letters. "Why don't you start out by reading the Book of John? It's filled with information and is easy to read."

Callie sighed. "Does it say anything about making me be nice to a stuck-up city girl?"

"Read it and see," Grandpa said with a wink.

"Grandpa, do you know what this note might mean?" she asked, producing the NOH note.

Grandpa's hands trembled as he took the old note.

Is he upset or just shaking from his stroke? Callie couldn't tell.

"Where did you get this?"

"I knocked the old Bible over and papers went everywhere. The note was in there," she replied.

Grandpa sighed, looking distressed.

"What does it mean, Grandpa?"

"NOH means Necklace of Honor." He paused before continuing. The 'T' is for Travis, my son—your mother's brother."

"I've never heard of either of those things." Callie said, perplexed.

Grandpa rubbed the whiskers on his chin, then looked away, remembering. Finally, he spoke. "The Necklace of Honor was a tradition that was passed down through several generations of young women in our family. The tradition consisted of a necklace with places for seven charms that were given by family members or close friends. Each charm was to remind the woman of something—about a word of wisdom or special thought. We started your mother's necklace when she was twelve, and it was completed by her thirteenth birthday. Because of the bad experience with Travis, I guess we simply put it out of our minds."

"Why did Travis take the charms?" she asked.

"I hate to say it about my own son, but it's true. Travis was mean." Grandpa sighed. "He would do anything he could think of to hurt others no matter who they were. He stole the charms because he wanted to hurt her. I don't know what happened to them, and I don't have any idea why he left the empty necklace."

"Where is Travis now?"

"He ran away when he was sixteen and we haven't seen him since," Grandpa replied sadly. "My heart still aches for him."

"Does Mom still have the necklace?"

"I think so. She used to keep it on a nail behind her bedroom door. Let's go see if it's still there." Grandpa rose with effort, and Callie followed him upstairs to her mother's room.

The necklace was right where he had said. It was gold-colored and had seven loops, all empty of charms.

"Do you think Mom would let me do it?"

"What's that?" Grandpa said.

"Do the Necklace of Honor. I'm twelve, almost thirteen," Callie said hopefully.

"Maybe." Grandpa thought for a minute. "It'd be a good way to replace some of those bad memories with good ones."

They left the necklace on the nail and started back downstairs. He stopped mid-way and said, "You know, we can find you a necklace if she's not comfortable using hers. I'll ask her about it. If she says yes, then let's do it. All seven charms. We don't have much time before your birthday...but maybe it'll work out. I'll pray about that."

LATER THAT DAY, CALLIE found Grandpa resting on the porch.

"Wait here. I've got something to show you," he said as he went inside.

Callie retreated to a shady bench swing under a tree in the yard.

CREAK, CREAK, CREAK The swing's rhythmic movement drafted a breeze off the cold mountain river and cooled her skin. She peered up through the leafy limbs to the clear blue sky above her, wondering what surprise Grandpa had in store.

When the screen door slammed shut, she scooted over so Grandpa could sit down.

"As I said before, our family has a tradition that goes back several generations. It's called the "Necklace of Honor." He spoke with the quiet passion of a great storyteller, and Callie sat with rapt attention. "You are a believer now, so I think it's a good time to learn the lessons and values this necklace stands for. I called your mother today, and she agreed."

Callie was excited. She didn't know what to say.

"Some of your charms will be given to you in private before your birthday. You must keep them in a special place until your ceremony. If the giver gives you words or scripture to go along with the gift, you are to memorize it and be ready to say it at your ceremony." Grandpa delivered the instructions as if she were about to become a princess of a vast country.

Callie felt important and valued but was still uncertain about the ceremony part.

"Do you understand?" he asked.

"I think so," she replied cautiously.

"Good" he said, eyes sparkling. "The giving of gifts begins now."

Callie wiggled her feet, too excited to sit still.

"My gift to you is Craftsmanship. The Bible teaches in Ephesians 2:10 that 'we are God's creation, created in Christ Jesus for good works.' That word 'creation' means that we are God's poem, His masterpiece. You really are a masterpiece, Callie—and it's not just me who thinks so!"

Callie soaked up his words. She certainly didn't feel like a masterpiece, but she wanted to believe it so badly.

He pulled a little white box from his pants pocket and handed it to her.

"Did you know that God is a craftsman?" he asked proudly.

The thought had never occurred to her before, but she nodded.

She carefully opened the box and lifted a thin rectangle of cotton. "Grandpa!" she exclaimed. She looked with wonder as she pulled out an intricately carved cedar charm. Grandpa's patient polishing had made it shiny.

"Did you make this?" she asked.

"I did indeed. In fact, I started it a while back but thought I'd wait until your birthday to give it to you. Now we can use it for your Necklace of Honor."

There were three delicate dogwood blossoms protruding from the background. "It's beautiful!"

"Turn it over, Callie—it's a two-sided deal," he said.

She turned it over, still admiring the beauty of the first side. The second side featured the same three dogwood blossoms, but this time they were stamped into the wood. The blossoms looked like an exact imprint of the first side.

Grandpa explained. "Dogwood blooms have four petals, that resemble the cross of Jesus. The blooms carved into the wood represent the imprint of God in your heart. The raised blossoms on the other side stand for God's craftsmanship through you to the world."

She examined both sides again and again, astounded at his work. "You made this after your stroke?"

"Sure did," he said proudly. "I started over several times until I finally got it right."

"I love it, Grandpa," she said simply, touched by the thoughtful gift.

"God put a lot of thought and care into creating you. You can put a lot of thought and care into everything you do. This includes how you treat your body."

Callie pondered his words as she fingered the well-planned charm. "I'll bet it took you a long time to make this," she said at last.

"Long enough," he replied. Callie expected his typical kiss on the forehead but received something very different. Grandpa reached for her hand and respectfully kissed the back of it.

She laid the charm gently in the box. "I love you, Grandpa."

"I love you, too, Callie."

"Where should I put it?"

"Let's put a nail behind your door like your mom's" he whispered. "You can use a little bag to store the charms in while you gather the others. We'll pull the charms back out on your ceremony day."

"What are my words for the ceremony?"

"You don't have to say anything for my charm. Just think on this: I am a masterpiece, created by Jesus the Master Craftsman."

"Who all's gonna to be at the ceremony? It's not the whole church or anything is it?" She dreaded the thought of speaking in front of an audience.

"Just a few very close people, don't worry. The ceremony's not about your speaking. It's about honoring you." Grandpa smiled and winked as he headed back to his workshop, leaving Callie alone with her thoughts. She lay down in the swing and gazed up through the branches, thankful for its shade. She had a lot to think about.

She was startled when Shadow came from out of nowhere and pounced on her, licking her arms. "Good grief, Shadow! You 'bout scared the wits out of me!" She nudged him gently, and he jumped to the ground. "Let's go find a bag for the Craftsmanship charm!" she said, scratching him behind the ears. Shadow circled around her feet in excitement, even though he couldn't understand what she'd said. She opened the box for one more peek, then hurried to the kitchen to look for a bag.

Chapter 6

SHOTGUN WINDOWS

"When will the air conditioner come on?" Becca yelled down the stairs to Jake.

She had been arranging her temporary residence and was getting warm. Becca wrinkled her nose as her eyes scanned her ultra-frilly little room. Crocheted doilies were on everything—the wooden rocking chair, the old dresser and chest, the nightstand. Even the ornate wrought-iron bed had crochet work on the pillowcases. Gray and cream-colored photos of ancestors hung on the wallpapered walls. She had never seen frames like this—they were large and oval with convex glass. The wallpapered ceiling followed the sharp roofline of the cabin, coming to a point high above her head. A lace-curtained window adorned each end of the room. She likened the windows to bookends, holding the room between them. The wooden floor was well worn, shiny and clean. In fact, Becca saw that the room was spotless, even though the old-timey style was off-putting to her. She strongly preferred her dramatic room in Asheville. She already missed her entertainment center, her Broadway poster-covered violet walls, her king-sized bed, and her plush seating area.

"Oh, well, I guess this is part of my summer experience," she said aloud.

"Don't have one," Jake hollered back. "I'll bring a fan up there."

Don't have one? "Thanks," she said dejectedly. She sighed. *There goes my hair.* Becca's hair had bothered her for as long as she could remember. Just last year, some boys at school asked her if she had stuck her finger in a light socket. It was always big and frizzy at the slightest hint of humidity, which the South seemed to have in abundance. She looked in the mirror above her grandmother's antique dresser.

"Okay, hair, you win for now." She pulled a hair band out of her pocket and forced her rebellious curly locks into a tight ponytail. Yuck. She dug her glittery

30

"Broadway" ball cap out of her suitcase, threaded her ponytail through the hole in the back and pressed it down on her head. *Better.*

She heard Jake's hiking boots thumping up the wooden stairs and met him at the door. "Do you wear anything besides those worn-out boots?" she said, only half-kidding.

"Hey, these shoes are made of the finest leather," he replied, pretending to model them. His joking stopped as quickly as it had started. "Besides, they're comfortable, waterproof, sturdy, and practical. I guess the answer is basically, 'Nope. I wear these just about every day.'"

He walked over to the window nearest her bed and opened it. "You might want to open the other window a little. We mountain folks call these shotgun windows," he said with a comical smile. "You could fire your shotgun from the outside and it would go straight through one window and out the other." Becca liked that word image better than her own bookends idea. She smiled.

Jake turned the fan on to draw in the air through the open window. Taking his cue, Becca climbed onto her grandmother's plump, quilted bed and opened the second window. Refreshing, fragrant air filled the room.

Maybe this won't be so bad, she thought as she hopped to the floor onto the blue and white braided rug.

"There's no maid service here, Sis, so we'll need to work together to keep the house clean. You're in charge of your room and your bathroom. We'll take turns in the kitchen and the other rooms."

Jake started to walk out, then stopped and over-exaggerated a tiptoe out the door. "See, my shoes are very quiet," he whispered as he started down the stairs. Becca laughed and threw a pillow at him, missing.

It had never crossed Becca's mind that she might have to clean up after herself. And a bathroom? Surely Jake was kidding. She wouldn't even know where to start. *There is no way I'm cleaning anything in this house. I've never been asked to do that before. Surely, he can afford a housekeeper.*

Before dismissing the thought of cleaning entirely, she wondered what would happen if she refused. *Would he send me home?* For a moment she felt doubtful. She realized that she knew very little about how to do anything for herself. The thought had haunted her before. What would she be without her parents and all that their money provided?

Determined not to think too much about unpleasant things, she resumed her thinking about her plans. *First things first—finish putting clothes away, then notes about Callie, then exploring. After all, I have to keep my priorities straight if I'm going to write that prize-winning essay and prove I can be a writer.*

She found a place for her many clothes in the dresser drawers and small closet and shoved her suitcases underneath the bed. The nightstand was a perfect place for her notebook. The bedside lamp caught her eye. It looked like it was straight out of an old movie. It had a round glass bottom in the shape of a fishbowl with a painted country scene featuring an elegant Victorian lady. The top of the lamp had a bulbous glass chimney that was milky white. The little switch turned on the Victorian lady bulb, then the upper bulb only, then both. Becca admired it for a moment, then turned on the upper bulb only and pulled out her notebook and pen. She kicked off her shoes and sat cross-legged on the bed so she could write down everything she knew about Callie.

Becca opened her new notebook and began to write on the purple paper (her favorite color). She wrote "CALLIE" in big letters on the top of the page and began her list:

Hair: long, braided

Hair color: medium brown

Eyes: gold (?)

Clothes: tan shorts, "Halo Notch Vineyard" t-shirt, old tennis shoes

Skin: tan

Personality: not friendly (is she dumb or just a cranky mountain person that doesn't trust anybody?)

Age: 12 (I think)

Becca chewed on her pen, thinking. *That's all I really know for now. Exploring the rest of the house is next.* She put the notebook and pen in the drawer and headed downstairs. She'd been so focused on seeing her room and worrying about cleaning that she hadn't even noticed anything about the rest of the house. *Does Jake even have a TV?* Concerned, she determined to find the living room first. It was strange—she only lived a couple of hours away, but she couldn't remember ever being in the cabin before. *I must have been here when I was too young to remember.* Her parents rarely even talked about Jake or their grandparents' cabin that he was living in. They just complained about the path he had chosen for his life. Their father was especially vocal about hating Halo Notch.

The downstairs was not so feminine looking. In fact, everything about it was different from Becca's frilly guest room. An imposing rock fireplace took up an entire wall that reached to the top of the cathedral ceiling in the main room. The matching leather chairs corralled a chunky coffee table and a large television in front of the big hearth.

"A TV!" Becca said aloud, relieved. She wandered past the dining room into the kitchen and was pleased to see that it had all modern appliances. "Yes! Civilization!"

"Dad bought all new furniture and appliances for Granna and Gramps for their fiftieth anniversary," Jake said as he walked in from the back porch.

"He never said anything about it. He never said much about them at all," Becca replied.

"Only Gramps is gone. Remember, Granna is in the nursing home. We'll go see her soon. Dad hated it here, but he still did a few things for them, although I'm not sure why." And then with a quick change of mood that Becca would soon learn to expect from her brother, he said, "Come check out the view!" Becca didn't care much for looking at landscapes but followed him anyway.

"Why did Dad hate it here?"

"I'm not sure. I don't think he really hated Gramps and Granna—just the whole Halo Notch thing," Jake replied. "Sometimes I wonder..."

"Wonder what?" Becca asked.

"Never mind. It's not anything I can put my finger on. Something happened a long time ago I figure...I don't know."

"Maybe." Becca was slightly curious, but having no answers, she dropped it. She didn't feel close to their parents at all. Jake apparently didn't either. *Maybe Dad was just bored out of his mind in this backwards place,* Becca thought.

She had to step over Jake's old dog to get out onto the enormous back deck.

"Watch out for Biscuit," Jake cautioned.

Becca expected him to say that the dog would bite. Instead, he said, "He's easy to trip over." He bent down and scratched the golden retriever behind the ears. "He used to help me with rescues but just lies around now."

Becca squatted down to stroke the gentle dog on the head. She was in no hurry to look over the side of some porch and listen to Jake try to convince her of the beauty of the mountains. However, when she lifted her eyes, the majestic beauty captured her. She slowly strolled to the porch railing as if in a trance at the jaw-dropping expanse of rolling mountains in front of her.

"Whoa," was all she could say.

"Nice, huh. I'm out here every chance I get," Jake said, admiring her speechless response. He plopped down in one of two Adirondack chairs and propped up his feet, closing his eyes.

Becca had never seen anything like it. She thumbed through the travel memories in her mind to decide if she had ever seen anything prettier. Grand Canyon? Nope. Niagra? Nope. The Caribbean? Nope. Pictures of all the natural scenes she could remember flashed through her mind as she compared each one to the delicious vista before her. Nothing. Nothing she had ever seen was as captivating as the rich layers of mountains and gorgeous sky in front of her.

Why haven't I noticed the mountains before? She thought. *We've been to the Smokies—how could I have missed seeing something so beautiful?* She became woozy when she looked down at the massive posts holding up the deck and her stomach gave a roller-coaster lurch. She virtually ran to seek shelter in the chair beside Jake.

He chuckled. "Don't worry, only a few people have fallen to their gruesome deaths from here," he looked over at her with a wink and grinned.

Chapter 7
HOGG ON THE LOOSE

Callie loved going to Emma's Halo Notch Vineyard. Its long, lush rows reminded her of the Italian vineyards she had seen on TV. She loved to wander through the fields, grazing on the sun-dappled muscadines. Avoiding the wide lanes between the rows, she preferred to duck under the bushy trellises as she cut across the endless fields. Visitors weren't permitted to leave the designated paths. The rosy-golden muscadines were her favorites—each as big as a large marble.

Popping them in her mouth one at a time, she would bite the tart skins, catch the seeds between her teeth, and suck every drop of flavor from each one. Just thinking about it made her mouth water.

The five varieties of muscadines made this vineyard quite a novelty. Tourists and winemakers from all over the world visited every year to admire and buy world-class fruit. Every September when the bountiful harvest was ready, Callie weighed the muscadines the customers picked. Last year, she was even allowed to ring up the purchases on the portable cash register. Emma's parents had just promoted Emma to manager of the vineyard, and she gave Callie a "Staff" shirt to make her feel a part of the team. It was one of Callie's favorites.

"Callie?" The voice broke off the wonderful daydream, returning her to home and chores. Callie dropped the plate she was washing, splashing herself with soapy water.

"You'd better speed it up, Callie. Jake will be here soon," her mother said, handing her a dishtowel. Kate wrapped up the restaurant's leftover chicken-n-dumplin's and put them in the refrigerator. "You okay?"

"Fine. I just wish Jake's sister wasn't coming to ruin everything tonight," Callie sulked.

Her mother was quiet for a moment. "Yes, about that..."

Callie felt a change in her mother's voice. She stiffened, not sure what to expect from the serious tone.

"You had quite a year at school," Kate said at last.

Oh no! Not the report card conversation! The dreaded time had finally come. "Mom, I promise I'll do better this year. I don't know what happened..." Callie's voice trailed off. She had forgotten all her good excuses.

"Callie, I know things have been hard on you because of Grandpa's stroke and my working all the time." Callie started to speak, but her mother halted her with a gentle motion of her hand. "You had a horrible time with a bully—yes, a bully. That girl and her gang really messed with you. I'm just sorry I didn't know about it sooner. You never told me."

Callie hung her head. *Maybe I could have stopped her if I had tried hard enough*, she thought miserably. She felt a knot growing in her stomach.

"I haven't talked with you about your grades because I couldn't decide what to do. I know you've been unhappy with school and with all the extra work around the house."

"It's okay, Mom. I'm fine," Callie said, hoping that the conversation would end. *Just tell me my punishment.*

"I've decided not to punish you," Mother said. Callie just about jumped up and down, but her mother stopped her once more. "I'm putting you on probation. That means that you are not being punished right now, but I'm watching to see how you handle a certain situation. I want you to spend time with Becca and really try to be her friend. Not every rich person is mean, you know."

Callie moaned. "No, no, no!" Callie pleaded. "Mom, anything else."

"Give her a chance," Kate said, hugging Callie's shoulders. "You might be surprised."

Callie folded her arms defiantly.

Her mother continued, "If you handle this situation well, we won't even talk about a punishment. If not, I'll be very disappointed in you, and we'll have to look at some stiff options."

"I'll be surprised if I don't hit her," Callie said firmly.

"Take it easy, Callie," Grandpa chimed in. "Becca's not been around church folks—she needs a good Christian friend."

"Great. Maybe she'll find one," Callie snapped, harsher than she meant to. She hated the thought of Becca tagging along.

Grandpa and Kate glanced at each other but said nothing. Callie stomped off to the bathroom for a shower, then put on her "Staff" shirt, jeans, and tennis shoes. Jake's truck pulled up just as she spit out her toothpaste. She towel-dried and re-braided her thick hair as she thought about what her mother had said. *I'd rather be punished and get it over with than spend one minute with this stuck-up girl.* But Callie loved her mother and didn't want to disappoint her. *Oh well, here goes nothing.*

Shadow barked wildly, jumping at the front door to greet Jake. *Oh no!* Callie panicked as she realized that Becca would be seeing her simple cabin for the first time. It made her stomach quiver a little. *Now she'll really look down on me.* She held her breath, listening for any comments Becca made.

The front door closed, Shadow stopped barking, and people greeted one another. Callie heard voices but couldn't make out the words.

"Callie!" Jake called at last. She felt a sharp pain shoot through her ear and realized she had been clenching her teeth.

"Just a minute!" Callie squeaked. "I'm getting ready." She looked around desperately to find something else to do to get ready but could only think of taking her hair down and braiding it very slowly once more. She cracked the door open ever so slightly so she could hear the conversation better.

"We're a little late. I hope she hurries," Jake said. "I heard a call on my radio about Mrs. Longfellow."

"Longfellow?" Callie heard her mother say. "Is anything wrong?"

"Some woman got hurt falling into her curio cabinet," Becca answered, thinking it was all very uninteresting.

She's so stupid. If she doesn't know about something, she should keep her mouth shut, Callie fumed.

"Well, she is getting on up in years," Grandpa said, "What is she, ninety?"

"At least," Kate answered.

"She didn't just fall—she was pushed, Becca. She caught her housekeeper, Valerie Hogg, stealing money from her purse and accused her of the big robbery that happened earlier this summer. Ms. Hogg pushed Ms. Longfellow hard enough to make her crash into the cabinet. Hogg ran out the door, and the police are looking for her now," Jake said, setting the story straight.

"So, you got to see Mrs. Longfellow?" Grandpa asked excitedly.

What's the big deal, thought Becca, a little bored. *Some old lady had a little money stolen and everyone gets up in arms.*

"No, I was called, but..." Jake started.

Becca interrupted, "I wonder if Callie is ready yet. You said we were late."

Grandpa answered gently, "You can tell us about it later, Jake, although I was hoping you would have caught a glimpse of her."

Callie knew that every resident in her world longed to get a look at the reclusive Mrs. Longfellow. She yearned to hear more about it, too. *Maybe Jake can make Becca go sit in the truck so we can hear all about it now.* But, knowing they were already late, she decided to call herself ready and get on with the evening. She left her little bathroom and joined the others, quickly noticing that Becca was wearing a sundress and sandals. And had manicured feet. And a toe ring. *Is she thirty or thirteen?*

"Yes, Jake, please tell us about all those priceless jewels that were stolen from the extremely wealthy, mysterious Mrs. Longfellow as soon as you get a chance," Callie said loudly. She shot a quick look of disgust at Becca.

"Yeah. Pretty exciting stuff in a little town, right?" Becca said sarcastically.

Both girls paused a split second to ponder the stolen jewels: Becca was just a little enticed by getting a great scoop on a story (no matter how small) and Callie loved a good adventure.

The "little town" comment jolted Callie from her thoughts. "Pretty exciting in any town, I'd say. Sandals and a dress? You know we are going to be outside, Becca."

Jake intercepted, "Becca has some jeans in the truck in case she needs them."

Callie just rolled her eyes. "Did you tell her we will be watching a movie on the side of a barn and going on a hayride?!" she whispered loudly to Jake so that Becca could hear.

"Callie!" Kate exclaimed, clearly shocked at her daughter's bad manners. "I'm sure that everything will be fine. Becca, you look very nice." Kate's intense stare and raised eyebrows told Callie to remember their conversation.

"If you think I should change..." Becca offered tensely. *Good grief. This is going to be harder than I thought. Oh well, maybe Jake and I can have some fun tonight.*

"No, you're fine." Callie's impatience was obvious. *Being nice is going to be even harder than I thought.* Even Callie couldn't explain her own contrariness. She marched to Jake's truck and jumped up on the seat, making sure that she would be the one sitting closest to him.

Becca looked to Jake for guidance, but he just shrugged his shoulders and shook his head.

Saying his goodbyes, he headed out the door.

Becca addressed Kate and Grandpa with the loftiness of a superior to an inferior, as she had seen her parents do so many times: "Nice to meet you." She nodded toward each one, then turned and followed Jake to the truck.

Chapter 8

FURIOUS

Callie brooded all the way to the vineyard. Jake and Becca had some kind of chit-chatty small talk, but Callie didn't know or care what it was. She hopped out of the truck as soon as Jake pulled onto Emma's makeshift parking lot in the grass.

While Jake introduced Becca to everyone, Callie busied herself with anything that would keep her away from her unwanted guest.

Becca stayed close to Jake at first but ended up with Emma for the weenie roast and hayride. Callie overheard Becca talking about the vineyards she had seen in California and Italy. Emma seemed charmed and interested in the lively discussion. Although Callie wanted to stay away from Becca, she couldn't seem to pull herself from within earshot of everything Becca said.

Huge brushstrokes of purple and peach covered the expanse of sky as the sun retreated into a gorgeous sunset. Onlookers admired its beauty, and those who were believers praised God for creation. After a while, the sun dropped over the barn and disappeared, absorbing the last traces of light with its dramatic exit. It was time for the movie to begin.

Vehicle owners backed up in two rows facing the sheet-covered wall of the barn. Jake started the projector while Emma handed out hot, fresh brownies. People of all ages gathered in the backs of pickup trucks, in lawn chairs, and in open car trunks to watch the movie.

Callie roamed around for a while, trying to find anywhere to sit but with Jake and Becca.

"Callie—over here!" Jake said, opening a lawn chair for her in the back of his truck. His voice was friendly but firm. Reluctantly, she joined them, thinking that her mother might hear a report from Jake at the end of the evening.

"Oooh, the stars are so bright and pretty!" Becca gushed to no one in particular as the movie previews were playing. "Don't you think so, Callie?" *Maybe this will break the ice. It is actually pretty out here.*

"Sure. It's always pretty out here away from the city," Callie answered.

"The last time I saw stars this close was on our cruise to St. Thomas," Becca continued, not able to keep her resolve to be nice.

Callie wanted to push Becca's chair over, but Jake blocked her before she could do it.

"Yeah, no matter what I've got here—you've got something better," Callie mumbled.

Becca was very quiet.

Callie wondered if she had heard her. She knew Jake had heard because of the warning look he gave her.

Just as the movie was starting, Becca said in a low, slow voice, "I was just trying to make conversation."

"You were just being your stuck-up self." Callie said plainly.

Silence.

I am anything but stuck-up, Becca thought resentfully, but said, "I'm not stuck-up."

"Yeah, right. Admit it. You think you're better than me."

The people on either side of their truck looked over with the "Shhhh" look.

"We're just different, Callie." Becca said, trying to make Callie understand her viewpoint. *Gain her trust, like Jake said,* she reminded herself.

"Oh, yes...how did you say it? We're from different cultures. You're from the rich people culture and I'm from the poor hillbilly culture. Forget it, Becca. I'm not buying it." Callie trembled with anger, trying hard to keep her composure.

Silence.

"I think you are just mean and stubborn." Becca said at last. An unwelcome tear of frustration rolled down her cheek which she quickly brushed away. *Why isn't this working?*

It sounded like a challenge to Callie. She stood and got right in Becca's face. The words hissed from her tight lips: "You haven't begun to see mean and stubborn yet." *I'd rather be punished than be around this girl.*

Jake grabbed Callie's shoulders and pulled her away.

"Don't worry, I'm leaving," Callie said. She escaped Jake's grasp and jumped down from the truck.

Becca was stunned. Callie was starting to sound less like a dumb country bumpkin and more like an equal. She was surprised that Callie's words stung so much.

A boy in the crowd yelled "cat fight"—and a few people laughed.

Becca was embarrassed and sank down as low as she could in her chair. *Do all these people think I'm just a stuck-up city girl?* She looked at Jake, hoping he would respond with a reassuring smile, but he didn't look back at her.

Callie was furious as she felt the eyes of every person on her. She marched through the dark field to the house. Determined, she pushed aside her growing embarrassment and resolved to hang on to her anger for as long as she could. Entering the dark, cool living room, she slammed the door behind her. Her hot emotions were already bubbling over when she flopped down on the couch. Only a pillow-muffled scream brought relief, followed by a flood of annoying tears. Callie hated to cry. It made her feel out of control and weak. But she couldn't help it. It was just like when she felt so sick that she had to throw up to feel better. This big cry was the same way. She had to do it in order to feel better.

Callie was startled when the door opened and closed quietly. Whoever it was had left the lights off, and Callie felt like hiding. She remained breathless and quiet when the person slipped an arm around her and held her close. Her body tensed up in defense, thinking suddenly it might have been Becca.

"It's me, Callie," Emma reassured.

Although still on guard, Callie managed to accept Emma's embrace.

Chapter 9
DESERTED

Callie was blowing her nose when the glare of overhead lights startled her. Jake stood at the door, hand still on the light switch. Emma and Callie both stared at him, blinking as their eyes adjusted to the brightness. His timing was terrible. Becca stood beside him, looking at the floor.

"She needs to change clothes," Jake explained awkwardly, nodding toward his sister. "Becca, the bathroom's just off the kitchen." Becca left the room without comment, carrying her jeans.

"We need to talk," Emma said to Jake. When he hesitated, she pulled him by the shirt onto the porch.

In the nearby bathroom, Becca slipped out of her sundress, leaving her tank top on. She hit her elbow hard on the sink as she struggled to pull her jeans on in the small space. Her funny bone stung terribly—it was anything but funny. She tried to be quiet. She didn't want to draw any more heated attention from Callie.

Her thoughts raced. *It was definitely a mistake coming here. This mountain girl is not only poor, but she's also hateful. I just want to go to Jake's and stay away from Callie. I've seen enough about this culture to write about it.* Her only consolation was thinking about how she would describe Callie in the worst possible way.

Callie didn't want to talk about the confrontation either. In fact, she just wanted to be alone. She could hear Emma and Jake talking on the porch but couldn't tell what they were saying. Preferring to avoid a stern talking-to, she crept quietly out the front door and around the side of the house, not certain what to do with herself.

I'll act like nothing happened, she thought. She squared her shoulders and walked with feigned confidence toward the crowd. She soon found herself passing around brownies and being especially friendly and helpful. She didn't want people to think that the conflict had been her fault. After all, these were folks from her church family. The determination to put on a good front energized her. But in the back of her mind, she wondered what her punishment would be. She had obviously blown her chance with Becca in just a few short hours.

Her act was going well until the boy who had said "cat fight" yelled out—"Hey, Callie! I thought you were a Christian! Guess you were wrong about that!" He walked away laughing, not seeing the shock that slid across Callie's face. She wanted to knock his block off. Instead, she quickly handed off the brownie pan to a passerby and retreated to the dark side of the barn to think.

He's right. I guess I'm not a Christian after all. A Christian wouldn't be having the feelings I have or acting the way I did.

She found a secluded spot in the corner of the barn. *No one will find me here. Except a snake or something.* It occurred to her that she couldn't even see what she was sitting on. *Uh, maybe somewhere else.* She carefully ascended the ladder and tiptoed to the movie side of the barn. She was so close to one of the movie-screen sheets that she could have touched it through a knothole in the boards. The film was one she hadn't seen. She listened to the dialogue and sound effects and tried to imagine what was happening but couldn't really figure it out. When she stood to stretch, she peered out from her perch to see what the crowd was doing. Becca and Jake were back on his truck, watching the movie and sharing popcorn as if nothing had happened. Emma sat cross-legged in her overalls, right in the middle of some teenagers, her golden hair in a ball cap. She was wearing Jake's jacket. Everyone seemed to be having a great time. Callie watched, feeling lonely and ridiculous.

After what seemed like years, the movie ended, and the crowd left.

"We'll get the sheets tomorrow," Callie heard Emma say. Becca and Jake put the blankets and lawn chairs in his truck and drove them back to Emma's house. Callie could no longer see Emma anywhere.

"Callie?" Emma whispered from the top of the ladder.

"How'd you know I was here?" Callie answered, surprised.

"It's where I would have come."

"I was a jerk tonight," Callie said matter-of-factly. "I must not be a Christian after all."

Emma waited awhile before answering. "Being a Christian doesn't mean you are perfect. It means you're forgiven. We're all a work in progress."

Callie tried to understand. She had always admired Emma—this businesswoman who was as comfortable on a tractor as she was in a boardroom.

"I've never seen you act anything like you did tonight. What's going on?" Emma implored.

"I know I'm not supposed to hate people, but I hate her." Callie felt wrong inside, knowing that hate was the opposite of what God wanted her to feel.

"I don't think you do. I think she reminds you of the bully at school. You hate that you have to share Jake with her. I think there are a lot of things about her you hate, but you can't possibly hate her 'cause you don't know her," Emma said wisely.

"I know enough about her to want her to go home," Callie said angrily, knowing in her heart that Emma's words were true.

"Jake should've told you she was coming."

"She wants to make me some English project."

"That's what I heard," Emma rose and offered her hand to help Callie to her feet. Callie unenthusiastically followed her to the house.

Jake met them at the door with steaming hot chocolate. "Sit," he said warmly, but firmly. He handed her the hot chocolate and sat beside Becca. All eyes were on Emma.

Becca nervously fingered her cup, dreading the conflict. She had no idea what to expect from this Emma person. She didn't even know what to expect from her brother—she'd been away from him for so long. She felt alone and miserable, her determination to be a writer dampened by her frustration over her antagonistic subject.

Callie was defensive. Even though she knew she was partially to blame, she didn't want to admit it.

It surprised everyone when Emma said, "You both are staying here until you can work something out. During the daytime, you'll be non-paid workers, starting with cleaning out the old barn on the back of the property. At night, you'll have time to negotiate. No television. No phone privileges. You'll just have to figure it out. We've already talked with your parents, and they support this."

Callie's eyes widened. She had only heard Emma speak like that one other time before, and it was to straighten up two rowdy boys when the youth group went camping. It was obvious that she meant business. Jake's eyes widened, too, but he looked away quickly, not challenging her.

Becca spoke up hesitantly, "What about clean clothes and toothbrushes and stuff?"

"You can borrow my pajamas while your clothes are washing. I have a few extra toothbrushes." Emma said matter-of-factly.

Jake stood, "Well, I'd better be going." He nodded to Emma. "Call me when I need to come pick 'em up." And out the door he went, not even looking back.

Both girls were shocked.

"What just happened?" Becca asked her enemy.

"I have no idea," Callie replied, shaking her head.

Chapter 10

HIDDEN HAZARDS

Becca and Callie didn't have time to object before Emma said, "Time to clean the kitchen." She handed Callie the dish brush and soap, handed Becca the drying towel, and began preparing the leftover food for storage.

Callie, still in a daze about Emma's strange behavior, mechanically filled the sink with soapy water and started washing everything that Emma handed her way. Becca dried in silence and placed the dishes somewhat clumsily on the counter next to the sink. Emma finished her part and sped away without a word, leaving the two strangers alone to do their work.

"Don't you have a maid to do this?" Callie mumbled.

"The maid comes once a week," Becca answered truthfully. "She doesn't say a lot, but she's nice enough to cook meals in advance so I'll have something to eat." *Talking to Callie is better than talking to nobody, I guess.*

"She cooks and cleans?" Callie said, trying to imagine what that would be like.

"She cooks for me. My parents work all the time or go out with their friends and clients. I'm usually alone." Becca answered sadly.

Callie thought about the warm fellowship that she had with her family and suddenly felt sorry for Becca.

When the task was completed, they put the dishes away. Turning around, they noticed the evidence that Emma had been in the room with them—towels, bed linens, two sets of pajamas, and new toothbrushes were stacked neatly on the kitchen table.

"Did you see her come in?" Becca asked.

"No. This is strange. Emma's usually really nice," Callie replied.

They divided everything without quarreling and set out to find Emma so they would know where to sleep. Walking softly down the hallway, they found their hostess already asleep in her own bed.

"Well, where do you want to sleep?" Callie asked. *Maybe she'll go to sleep soon so I'll have some time to think.*

"There's a bed in here. I'm taking it," Becca said as she opened the door to Emma's office/guest room. She was struck by the tidiness of Callie's and Emma's homes, even though her own home was much larger and more elaborate.

"You can have it. I'll take the couch."

It was the most talking that the two had done. They went to their separate corners for the night, both realizing that they would need their sleep for a potential Round Two of their fight the next day.

Callie turned off lights in the little farmhouse as she made her way back to the bathroom to change clothes. She thought about Becca's response to the house cleaner question. *How strange it must be to eat alone night after night in a huge house!* When she opened the bathroom door, she jumped. A makeup-less Becca was standing there—blanket, sheets, and pillow in hand.

"What is it?" Callie asked.

"I don't want to be in there alone," Becca replied frankly. "It's too dark out here. I'll sleep on the floor in the living room with you." She looked much younger without her makeup. Her skin was blemish-free and freckly. Callie stared without meaning to.

"Now you know why I wear makeup," Becca said, embarrassed. "My mother thinks my freckles are ugly. My father makes fun of them all the time."

"I think they make you look like Jake," Callie said simply. "They're nice." She led the way into the window-lined living room and threw her bedding on the couch. Then, she pulled one overstuffed chair over to face the other one, creating a bed for Becca. *At least we don't have to sleep together,* Callie thought. Then she prayed, *Lord, please forgive me for how I acted before. Help me through this night. I really—really—don't want to be with her, but You said to trust you, so I'm trying to do it.*

"Thanks for the bed, Callie," Becca said as she settled into the chair-bed and pulled the covers over her.

"It's okay. Better than sleeping on the floor."

"Callie?" Becca asked hesitantly. "Jake said you like to work in the vineyard. You're gonna want to stay here, aren't you." She dreaded the answer. She just couldn't imagine staying at the vineyard all week (or month!) with a bullheaded Callie.

"I love working in the vineyard."

"I thought so." Becca wondered how far Callie's stubbornness would go.

"Emma says we're working in the barn, not the vineyard. It's a dusty old barn. They don't even use it for the vineyard."

Becca thought for a long time. "You hate me, don't you." It was more of a statement than a question. She had to know where she stood with Callie or miss the opportunity of proving to her parents that she could be a writer.

Callie thought for a moment. *Do I hate her? Really?* "I hate people like you."

"Like what?"

"Rich, stuck up, prissy, show-offie. Admit it: you think you're better than me."

Becca hesitated, knowing the truth.

"Admit it," Callie challenged again.

"I think I get better grades than you. And have more money than you. And have better clothes than you. And have better stuff than you." Becca couldn't believe her own candor. The darkness of the room made it easier somehow.

"I think your writing thing is stupid. I won't do it," Callie said.

"I think your refusal to help is stupid. I don't see what the big deal is." Becca kept her voice steady even as her rarely provoked temper rose.

"How would you feel if a stinking-rich princess came to your town and looked down on you? What's worse...what if she wanted to find all the differences between your pitiful little world and her fabulous jet-setting world so she could write about it for everyone to read? How would you feel about that?" Callie sat up, peering across the dark room at the black lump in the chair.

Becca was silent, not sure how to answer. She hadn't considered how it might feel to be on the other side.

"You just don't get it. We're gonna be in that stinking barn for the whole summer!" Callie spoke loudly, unable to control her volume in the heat of the moment.

Becca rolled over away from Callie so she could think. "I came here to write. I want to prove once and for all...oh, forget it." Her mind raced through scenes of her father making fun of her dreams of being a writer. He and her mother were determined for her to be a doctor or lawyer. She was miserable at the thought of going back home empty handed. *I'd rather work in a barn all summer long than go home and listen to my parents laugh at me.*

Callie was deep in thought as well. She prayed, *Jesus, why did you stick me with someone like her? Don't you remember how hard my year was? Don't you remember how I was made fun of for being a poor tomboy?*

Slowly they drifted off to sleep, too weary to think about it anymore.

EMMA WOKE THEM UP ONLY five hours later. After a eggs-and-toast breakfast, she drove them to their barn. "There are gloves, rakes—everything you need—just inside the barn door. The water hose is fine for drinking water. Here's a walkie talkie in case you need me. I'll bring your lunch by noon. Watch out for snakes." She left them to their work and disappeared into the fields.

Callie shook her head, amazed at Emma's seeming hardness.

Becca sighed heavily, dreading the work, wanting to leave. *If only Callie would give in...*

Callie was angry at the whole situation. *If only Becca would give in...* "Last year, Emma told Jake that she was going to tear this junky barn down." She tossed a dirty pair of gloves to Becca who put them on straightaway.

Callie shook her own gloves out several times before sticking her fingers inside. "Spiders love these," she said, not minding if she scared Becca. "I'm starting in the loft and raking stuff down. You can start where you want." She shimmied up the ladder easily, toting the pitchfork as she went.

Becca waited until Callie turned away before jerking her gloves off and shaking them out. *Just in case.* Then she followed Callie up the ladder, clumsily struggling with a rusty old rake under her arm.

Particles of stubble and dust floated gracefully in the sunrays that invaded the musty loft. Ancient hay covered the wooden boards, ground to a fine powder in many places. Becca rubbed her itchy eyes with her sleeve, thankful that it was still clean. The heavy, choking air was hard to ignore, but Becca was intent to do her very best. She wanted to prove to Callie that she could work as hard as any obstinate mountain girl.

Callie was used to barns and hard work, but she hated the thought of doing useless busy-work. The only thing that kept her working full speed was the vision of Becca failing. It energized her every time she started to tire. She peered through the slats in the rickety wall, but the barn was too far away from the orderly rows of vines for her to see anything. She could only barely see the rooftop of the working barn where they had viewed the movie.

The barn became stuffier and sweltering as noon approached, and grimy dirt collected on their sweaty faces. Callie and Becca worked silently, pushing the old hay down onto the ground below. Becca coughed uncontrollably at times, her eyes dripping in the virtual blender of debris. Callie felt a little sorry for her. She gave Becca her bandana to use to cover her nose and mouth like a cowboy.

Emma brought sandwiches, chips and lemonade at noon. They ate and drank hungrily. Refreshed by the break, they washed off their faces with the water hose and went back to work. Becca found brooms and handed them up to Callie so they could sweep the last bit of hay to the ground below.

"At least there aren't snakes on the top floor," Becca said, hoping Callie would talk to her a little.

"I wouldn't count on it," Callie replied, going back to where she had left off. It wasn't long before Callie yelled out "Snake!"

Becca thought Callie was kidding until she saw Callie toss the long, twisting snake out the baling door with her pitchfork. Determined not to show fear, Becca merely shuddered; she watched where she stepped after that.

They had only worked another hour or two when Callie yelled out. "Ouch! You stupid thing!" Becca saw bees swarming around Callie's head.

"Are you okay?" Becca asked with real concern. *I'm not even sure which way to run for help, and the walkie talkies are down the ladder where the snake is now.*

"It's just a bee sting, but it hurts like the dickens!" Callie said, grasping her swelling hand. Becca dashed over to her, forgetting the possibility of snakes, and saw Callie's hand becoming puffier by the second.

"Let's take a break," Becca said, taking charge. "Maybe if you rinse it with the water hose, it will help." She took both brooms and tossed them down the ladder, following after.

Callie climbed down slowly, still protecting her misshapen hand. They were relieved to see a worker in a farm truck waiting for them at the barn door. Becca expected Callie to start yelling at her or blaming her for everything, but she never did.

Becca put the tools away and gathered up the walkie talkies while Callie climbed onto the front seat and showed her stung hand to the driver. Becca couldn't believe her eyes when she saw one of the nastiest things she had ever seen: the man spit out a slimy, brown wad of chewing tobacco and placed it, dripping, on Callie's hand.

"Drawz out the stingin'" he drawled out between chews. Becca noticed that Callie kept the tobacco in place but didn't look at it.

THAT NIGHT, JUST AFTER their showers, sticky humidity morphed into a needed summer rain. Fierce streaks of lightning illuminated heavy thunderheads above the drenching downpour. Emma looked over with concern in her eyes at her two guests across the table. Callie's bee-stung hand was red and swollen.

Becca's allergies were obvious, even though she hadn't complained. Her stuffy, dripping nose and red puffy eyes seemed to be getting worse by the minute.

If the girls hadn't been so miserable with their newly acquired ailments, the supper would have been splendid. Emma was the gracious hostess, serving scrumptious mashed potatoes and gravy, roast beef, fresh green beans, slaw, and a sliced yellow tomato. Yet, the girls sat silently, too tired for lively conversation.

After supper, they cleaned their plates and helped with the dishes. Emma gathered flashlights and candles for their imminent power outage and made popcorn for them.

"The electricity always goes out when it's like this outside," she informed the girls. She laid out blankets on the living room floor, so they could watch the storm through the windows.

It wasn't long before the lights went out. The two weary girls retrieved the candles and flashlights and joined their hostess for the storm party. No one said anything about "working things out."

"I love the storms," Emma said at last. "What doesn't destroy the vines makes them stronger."

The girls nodded, wondering if she was talking about something more than just vines. Becca rubbed her puffy eyes.

"How bad are these allergies?" Emma asked finally.

"It's no big deal." Becca brushed off Emma's question, keeping her resolve to be strong.

"Becca, really," Emma pressed.

"Hay, dust, mold—everything outside it seems," Becca admitted with some embarrassment.

"That barn is full of all three!" Emma exclaimed. "Why didn't you tell me?"

Becca just looked away.

"Honestly, you're both stubborn." Emma left the room with a small flashlight and returned with a cold, damp washcloth for Becca and a plastic bag full of ice cubes for Callie's hand. "Maybe this will help. I don't have any allergy medicine around here."

After a while, the storm's drama faded, leaving a steady rain. Only a few moments of silence went by before Emma sighed and stood up, smiling. "I'm worn out. I sure hope you work something out soon. We could have a lot of fun, you know." She looked from one unsociable girl to the other, then shrugged her shoulders. "I'm going to bed," she said, and she disappeared down the hallway, vanilla-scented candle in hand.

The girls didn't speak a word. The only sound was that of distant thunder and rain pattering on the roof. Callie counted only one bolt of lightning far away.

All Becca wanted to do was to go back to Jake's and to get away from Callie. *I'll get my story from somewhere else. Besides, I didn't do anything to deserve her treating me this way. If she would say, "I'm sorry," we could leave this place.* She was incensed at the injustice, not feeling any responsibility for the conflict. "I'm bored," she said finally.

"I like storms," Callie said, truthful about her fascination of storms—even though this one wasn't particularly interesting. She relished the thought that Becca was unhappy but felt a little guilty about it. Then, something stirred deep inside of her. It was like a voice but wasn't audible. *"Make it right, Callie, for My sake."* She pushed the Voice away stubbornly, not wanting to give in. *"It's up to you, Callie, to take the first step."* Callie knew it was Jesus talking to her, inside her mind. She knew it had to be Him because it certainly wasn't her idea to make things right.

"Well, I'm going to bed," Callie said to Becca. She went to her couch and lay down. Trying to cover up her head to get away from the Voice didn't work. It was on the inside.

"Oh, okay," Becca replied, unhappy to be alone in a strange place. She lay down slowly and closed her sticky, stinging eyes, not knowing that the worst was still to come.

Chapter 11
THE BIG DEAL

The urgency Callie felt to apologize to Becca grew stronger every moment. She fought it for all she was worth—it was so hard to give up being mad. She hadn't realized that her hands were tightly fisted until a surging pain in her bee-stung hand brought it to her attention. Her brain kept practicing words of apology so strongly that Callie had to stop herself from blurting it out.

"Becca?" she whispered. "Are you awake?" She crept over to Becca's side and found her sleeping.

"Well, Lord, she's asleep. I guess I'll have to tell her tomorrow," she whispered to Jesus. The decision to do the right thing gave her some relief. She curled up on the couch and dozed off.

Moments later, Callie awoke to the sound of talking. Noticing Becca's empty bed, she went to see what was happening. She found Emma and Becca in the kitchen. Becca had the washcloth over her eyes and was breathing strangely.

"Her eyes are much worse and she's having a little trouble breathing," Emma said. "I've called Jake and he's coming to get her."

Becca turned to face Callie, and she was alarmed that Becca's eyes were swollen shut.

Callie wasn't sure what to do. She didn't want Becca to leave before she'd had a chance to apologize.

"Callie, will you get her things?" Emma asked.

"Sure." Callie looked at the clock—3:30 a.m. She was worried. "Has...has this happened before?" she asked Becca.

"Two times—but it was a long time ago," Becca said between breaths. "I thought I'd grown out of it." Becca was surprised yet again at her own honesty with Callie. *I mustn't let my guard down,* she reminded herself.

Callie backed up a few steps and then hurried to get Becca's things. She wanted to ask, "Is she going to be okay?" but Emma was turning on lights and heading back to her room. Callie was afraid to ask Becca. She didn't know if she should. She had heard about a second-grade girl at school who had died because of a severe allergic reaction. At the time, she had wished that the mean girl had died instead of the sweet little girl—but wishing that on anyone seemed twisted and sick now.

"Callie?" Emma called from down the hall, "Will you sit with her while I get dressed? Jake'll be here in a few minutes."

"Sure." Callie sat down at the table and tried to think of something to say but couldn't. She prayed. *Lord, what do I do? Please help her to be okay.* His answer in her heart was unmistakable: *"Make it right, Callie."*

So, Callie opened her mouth and the words poured out: "Becca, I'm sorry for how I've acted. I'm a Christian, but I sure haven't acted like one." The words kept tumbling out as if on their own: "I just...I just didn't know you were coming, and you remind me of the girl who made my life horrible this whole past school year, and I don't want to be part of some research project, and I'm mad at Jake for not telling me about you, and you obviously have a lot of money, and I don't and... and ...I don't think I should be made to spend my summer with somebody I don't like." She took her first breath. "I guess... I mean I know I've been a jerk. Will you forgive me?"

Becca was silent for a moment while she thought about what Callie had said. She daubed her puffy eyes with the washcloth and wheezed a shaky breath.

At that moment, Emma rounded the corner with a questioning look on her face. "Everything okay in here?"

"Everything's fine," Becca said at last. "Yes, Callie, I forgive you. I haven't been so great myself. I'm sorry." *Maybe Callie's not so bad after all.*

Emma pulled out some homemade chocolate chip cookies from the cookie jar and put them on a frilly piece of china. She poured three glasses of milk and brought them to the table. "Callie, will you move those contracts from the table and put them by the phone? Hopefully, I can finish those up tomorrow." Callie did.

The wheels started turning in Becca's mind. Her whole face showed it, even with her eyes closed. She smiled. "Emma, what's a contract?"

"It's a written agreement between two people or groups of people that lists everything they agree on. These are from my customers who want to have first choice from my harvest for the next three years." Emma handed the practically sightless Becca a cookie and slid the glass of milk closer to her.

"Maybe we could make a contract," Callie said, catching the idea. "That way, everything will be spelled out, and we can both get some of what we want."

"I'd like to—not only for my paper—but because I'll die of boredom if I don't," Becca said honestly.

"Good idea, girls," Emma said, pulling paper and a pen from the drawer. "I'll write everything down."

"Okay," the girls agreed.

"Okay. I'll be nicer to Becca," Callie offered, feeling much better about the situation.

Emma wrote it down.

"Exactly what will you do to be nicer?" Emma prodded.

"I'll do some activities with Becca...maybe swimming, horseback riding, teaching her to shoot, going tubing with the youth group. Stuff like that," Callie said.

Emma wrote it all down.

"I want one really big activity like a sleepover or something," Becca said. Her mind snapped to attention. *I'll have to get her alone so that she'll talk to me. If I'm going to prove to Mother and Dad that I'm a writer, I've got to get Callie to tell me about herself.*

"Or a long hike!" Callie said, excitedly. "Emma, do you think Mom would let me take her alone?" *Hiking is much better than sleepovers—what would we do the whole night?*

"Possibly. You can ask," Emma said, writing "sleepover or hike" on the paper.

"There's a cave not far from here and Mrs. Jennie's abandoned house...oh, I hope they'll let me take her...it'll be a blast!" Callie said. This animated side of Callie was something Becca had never seen. The room was electric with ideas.

"Agreed." Becca smiled at their progress.

Callie continued, "I want you to agree not to interview me. Ever. Nor take my picture. Ever. Nor talk about your writing thing to me. Ever." She was adamant. She thought Becca might resist, but Becca said nothing.

Emma stopped writing and rolled her eyes a little at Callie's demands. But she wrote it all down.

Becca thought for a minute. "Fair enough."

"Deal." Callie liked this contract business. "What will you do and what do you want?" Callie took her first bite of a delicious cookie and sat back in her chair.

"I will live this month like you. No offense, but we are different. I'll only watch as much TV as you do, I won't stay on the phone, and I'll wear more comfortable clothes—no fingernail stuff and whatever else."

"No makeup," Callie said.

"I hate my freckles."

"Doesn't matter. I don't wear makeup." *I'm not budging on this one,* Callie thought stubbornly.

After a brief pause, Becca agreed. "Okay. No makeup." *At least Callie thinks I look like Jake.*

"You will answer questions about things like facts about animals, the cave, and such—general information things. If you do this and help me learn about mountain life, I will give you half of the prize money if I win." Her shallow breaths whistled softly when she exhaled. Becca felt around on the table for her milk, and Callie helped her to grasp the glass. Both girls were pleasantly surprised at the act of kindness. Becca thanked Callie and took a long drink while Emma wrote as fast as she could to keep up.

"Agreed. Especially the prize money part." Callie reached for another irresistible cookie and watched Emma make two lines at the bottom of the page for signatures.

Emma looked at both girls, amazed at how fast the contract had shaped up. "You guys just proved you can work together when you really try. I wish my contracts worked out this easily. Maybe I should send everyone to the old barn to work. Sign here." She passed the pen to Callie and she signed. "Becca, do you want to sign later?"

"I can sign now. Get me started." She took the pen, and Emma aimed it at the signature line for her.

"Knock knock," Jake said as he stuck his head through the front door. "Don't you guys know it's the middle of the night?" He threw his backpack on the counter and pulled out his stethoscope and an allergy shot.

"Hey, we're cutting deals in here. The girls have made a contract for the rest of the summer," Emma said proudly.

"A little stick," he said to Becca and gave her the shot. "I knew the barn torture would break you two," he teased. He listened to Becca's breathing for a long time and then checked her eyes. "Let's give the shot a few minutes to start working. I need to take you to the hospital to get something for your eyes. I think you need to get away from these fields for a while."

Callie's concern for Becca returned. "I want to go," she said.

"There's no need..." he started.

Emma interrupted him, "Actually, the girls are finished here. They've worked it out, so they're free to go."

"I guess it's okay...but only if I get a cookie, too," Jake said as he plunged his hand into the cookie jar for a handful of cookies.

Despite her discomfort, Becca couldn't help thinking about all the things she wanted to write in her purple notebook.

Chapter 12
RADIANCE

The sky was coal black a few nights later. Thousands of tiny lights blinked on and off as light'nin' bugs danced in the moonless night. Callie peered intently from her rooftop perch, trying to guess where the next lights would appear. Just then, a sound from behind her caught her attention, and she saw her mother climbing awkwardly through the window to join her. Callie chuckled at the struggle. She was glad for her company.

"You just got home?" Callie asked.

"Yes, I thought the wedding party at the restaurant would never end. They made a big mess," Kate said with a weary smile. "How've you been since movie night at Emma's?"

"Good. Becca's feeling better."

"I'm glad you two came to an understanding. I've got something for you," Kate said, reaching into her pocket. "I was gonna to wait until the full moon to give it to you, but I want to go ahead." She looked at the sky where the moon hung just a few nights earlier. "You'll just have to use your imagination." She pulled a small, black velvet bag out of her pocket and cradled it in her hands. "This is for your Necklace of Honor."

Callie's eyes shone. She couldn't imagine her mother buying something in such an expensive-looking velvet.

"Callie, it was very hard on me when your father died. It was even harder once I found out I was pregnant just a week later—harder still when I miscarried. One night when I was on the porch that your daddy built, sitting in the chair your daddy built, I just prayed that God would help me somehow. That He would show me something to give me hope. It was a night when the sky was clear, and the moon was full. And I noticed the moon. It was beautiful, yet it was strong at the same time. Do you know why it was beautiful?"

"Because of the sun shining on it?" Callie replied, remembering the science behind it.

"That's right. Without the sun on it, we can't even see it. It's just like a dark, hard rock in the sky. And God spoke to my heart and told me that when He shines on me—and you, Callie—we're beautiful and radiant, too."

Instead of handing the bag to Callie, Kate pulled out the charm herself and held it up just so the light from Callie's bedroom revealed its basic appearance.

"What is it? A white rock?" Callie asked. It looked like a blob of dried glue. She didn't want to disappoint her mother, but it was not very spectacular.

"It's a called a moonstone, Callie. My mother gave it to me a long time ago. Looks like a plain white rock, doesn't it?" She reached in her back pocket for a small flashlight and handed it to Callie. "Shine the light on it," she said eagerly.

Callie flicked on the light and held it close to the moonstone. As soon as the light hit its surface, she saw blue and purple twisting around a ribbon of milky white. "It's beautiful!" She exclaimed.

Her mother gazed at it, too. The transformation was astonishing!

"That's how we are when God shines on us...we're breathtaking," Kate said, making a point. "Your beauty comes from Him. The Bible says in Psalm 34:5, "Those who look to the Lord are radiant with joy." You can be strong and beautiful at the same time—just like the moon and this moonstone. Your beauty doesn't rely on how you feel or on what other people say. It relies on whether you are looking to God."

Callie lifted her eyes from the moonstone to her mother's radiant face. It was true. She was beautiful. A warm peaceful feeling flooded Callie's heart, and she sat up a little taller. She felt beautiful for the first time in her life. It felt good. She never wanted it to end. *Thank you, Jesus,* she prayed.

Her mother kissed her on the cheek and hugged her close. "This is my gift to you for the Necklace of Honor. I love you, Callie."

Callie snuggled into the embrace, not minding that she felt like a little girl for just a moment. "I love you too, Mom. What do I have to say for the ceremony?" she asked, hoping that it wouldn't be too embarrassing. *Surely Mom doesn't expect me to tell everybody that I'm beautiful!*

"Nothing. Just think about what we talked about tonight and smile," her mother said as she wriggled back through the window. "By the way, I talked with Grandpa and Jake about the hike, and they felt good about you going. I do, too, if you follow their instructions."

"I will. I promise," Callie said, her eyes sparkling with excitement.

Chapter 13

THE PERFECT PLAN

Callie rose early on the day of the big hike. She was way too excited to sleep in!

Shadow seemed to sense the importance of the day, too. He was already licking Callie's hand and wagging his tail before her feet hit the floor. Instead of waiting for Callie to join him, he flew down the stairs and jumped at the front door, wanting to get on with his day. Callie dressed quickly in well-worn hiking boots, blue jean shorts, two T-shirts, and a light jacket.

"I'm coming, Shadow!" she yelled down to the prancing dog at the front door. When he "bouffed," she said, "Hang on a second, buddy!" She trotted downstairs and opened the door, following him outside into the cool, foggy morning.

While Shadow sniffed at the bushes for the perfect spot, Callie thought about the glaring differences between her own life and Becca's. Jake and Becca grew up rich and privileged. Even without Becca's housekeeper, makeup, perfect nails, and clothes, Callie was constantly reminded that they were from different worlds just by her mere presence. It was true that their cultures were different. Callie had a hard time thinking of Jake as being wealthy. He seemed to have totally walked away from that life. *Maybe I don't know him as well as I thought. It's weird.* A twinge of anger shot through her. *How could he have kept all this from me?* Not wanting it to ruin her day, though, she decided to figure out what to do about him later.

Jake and Becca were already on their way to Callie's house before the sun's glow peeked around the mountain. He knew this day was very important—not just because of the time the girls would spend together—but also because it was the first long hike Callie would take on her own. Becca had mixed emotions—she was nervous about keeping up with Callie but excited about the adventure. The day was full of unknowns to her, and she would have to wait for everything to unfold. It could be great fun or a complete disaster.

Callie helped Grandpa clean up after breakfast and then thought about the day's possibilities. She hoped they would see a black bear. It was likely they would see deer in the early morning fog. She knew from experience that there were also beavers, snakes, and bats in the mountains. The more she thought about it, the six-hour hike seemed hardly long enough to do everything she had planned. As she gathered items for the day's hike, she made sure to include a quart of water for each of them. She also had a bandana and her knife (*just in case*), and two flashlights (*thank you, Grandpa*). Jake was bringing lunch.

One other item would also be going with her: a mysterious cream-colored box tied with lace. She had found it on the kitchen table that morning with a note attached from her mother: "For Your Necklace of Honor. Open at Mrs. Jennie's house." Wanting to protect the box from the water bottles, she found a grocery bag and tenderly placed the gift inside, placing it into her backpack. *I wonder what it could be. And who could it be from?* She had noticed that the lace looked old, not new. It was a mystery for sure.

Callie's heart was full of anticipation for the day. It was her chance to be the expert, and this was her territory. Becca would have to rely on her. The rich city girl could not buy Callie' life knowledge of these mountains, no matter how much she was willing to pay. Becca had never experienced the first-hand excitement of a day full of adventure...and potential danger.

Callie had already planned the path they would take. They would follow the trail east through the woods to the top of the ridge and walk carefully over the narrow walkway across the top, called The Bridge. On the other side, the wooded mountain descended steeply for hundreds of feet to the bottom. They would hike about halfway down where they would come to a fork in the trail. The path to the right led to a hidden cave—the path to the left, to a waterfall.

She was especially excited about going to the cave, the first stop. Callie loved its dark shroud of unknowns. It seemed like another world. Ancient rock formations lined its ceiling and floor. *I hope I can remember to tell Becca that the Smoky Mountains are some of the oldest mountains in the Western Hemisphere.* She looked forward to seeing the odd-looking bats that huddled on the cave's ceiling. Some species of bats there were almost extinct. Callie hoped that Becca wouldn't freak out. Jake had been all the way from one end of the cave to the exit, two miles away. He said it was easy to become lost in the maze of tunnels, though, and made Callie promise she would never go beyond a certain point. She was fine with that. Getting lost in a dark cave and leaving behind only a skeleton and a flashlight was not her idea of a good time.

Lunch at the falls would be next. Then, the hideout behind the falls. Their final stop would be an old house in a clearing. A woman named Jennie Townsend had lived there for many years, but she had died about eight years ago, leaving the house deserted. She had been a good friend to Callie's family. Mrs. Jennie knew all about herbs and mountain medicine. She was even a midwife. When Callie was sick as a baby, her mom and dad had taken her to the wise woman who knew which herbal concoction would bring healing to her. Callie was sad that she couldn't remember more about Mrs. Jennie. *If Becca's interested, I'll tell her about the old remedies Grandpa has told me about. I must remember to tell her that every part of a dandelion is edible.*

Callie loved Mrs. Jennie's house. It was the perfect playhouse for a pioneer girl. Of course, she would never ever tell Jake or Becca (or anyone else!) that she had fantasized about living alone there—a strong and independent mountain woman.

What if Becca thinks all this is stupid? A nervous quiver shot through her stomach. *If Becca laughs at me, I'll never speak to her again.*

Despite the contract and her growing trust for Becca, she still imagined her former enemy showing up in little flip-flops, perfect nails, and a ton of makeup. *Why, that better-than-me girl probably won't make it ten minutes on those mountain trails! That's it,* she decided, *I'm not taking any chances. We just won't go. Jake and Becca probably haven't left yet anyway.* Trying to think of some excuse to cancel the hike, Callie moved toward the phone.

But before she could pick up the receiver, she felt an attention-hungry, bright-eyed Shadow rubbing against her leg. He followed her everywhere; sometimes she forgot to stop and enjoy his companionship. She bent down and scratched him behind the ears, causing him to freeze mid-wag to absorb the joy of her love.

Callie knelt, knees on the floor and patted her lap. In a flash, Shadow hopped up and pressed against her. She wondered whether she should take him on the hike as she had done when she hiked with Jake a couple of summers ago.

But, remembering that his little legs were too short to climb over the rocks, and that she had carried him much of the way, she decided he should stay home.

Suddenly, Shadow's ears perked, and he tilted his head in attention to a sound Callie could not yet hear. He bounded to the door. Yep—Jake's truck was coming up the long, winding driveway to her house. She opened the door and sat on the steps with Shadow on her lap, waiting. She wasn't sure if she felt excitement or dread at spending a whole day alone with her tentative friend. She liked her new word "tentative." Jake had just introduced it to her recently. It meant that she wasn't sure yet how their friendship would turn out. If she made a list of friends, she would write Becca's name in pencil. If they became real friends, Callie would go over it in ink or marker. If the day was a disaster, she would erase Becca's name and try to forget they'd met. The hike would decide the fate of the *tentative* friendship.

Callie stood up and released Shadow when she saw that familiar truck easing to a halt. As Jake hopped out, smiling as usual, a tiny cloud of dirt lingered in the air for a couple of seconds. Then the passenger door opened. Callie expected Becca to be wearing fashionable clothes with mosquito-attracting perfume. But as the door opened, Callie froze. There stood Becca in hiking boots, faded jeans, and two ordinary t-shirts layered with a worn-looking jacket around her waist. Her wild, curly hair was French braided much like Callie's. Her face was make-up free. She was child-like and attractive, despite her many freckles. The only jewelry she had was her watch, and her fingernails were unpainted and short. She looked exactly like a younger "girl" version of Jake.

Becca also watched Callie's response to the way she was dressed. Becca was used to wearing makeup and painting her fingernails in very creative ways. She had been developing her own special image this past school year and enjoyed having a signature style. This day, however, comfy blue jeans replaced her Bohemian skirts. Plain sunscreen replaced carefully applied makeup, and hiking boots replaced her embellished flip-flops. Her wild, curly red hair was awkwardly braided. She had fought with her hair all morning. It was certainly going to rain. Her hair could gauge the humidity better than a meteorologist's barometer could. She needed about two cans of hairspray, but she used sunscreen in her hair instead. *Mosquitoes love anything perfumy-smelling!* Becca's "new look" was not new to her. There was always a side of her that loved nature, but she just didn't choose to show that side very often. Being with Jake, and now with Callie, brought out the adventurer in her.

Becca's radiologist mother and real estate developer father rarely had time to take her hiking. She had wanted to go many times but never did—and she was determined to surprise Callie with her strength today. She chuckled to herself as she retrieved her daypack from the back of the truck. *Wouldn't it be funny if Callie had trouble keeping up with me?* She doubted it, but it was fun to think about anyway. Becca had left her notebook at Jake's house. She smiled to herself and patted her pocket that held a half-size pen. *I'll write on my hand if I have to.*

She even left her camera at home so she could concentrate on the experience itself. She didn't want Callie to think she would break their contract by taking a picture of her. She was determined to memorize the words and images of the day so she could record everything later. She did bring a mirror, however. Her hair made her very self-conscious. She didn't want to come back after a day of hiking to find out that her hair had been poofing out all day! She slid it secretly into her pocket, quite sure that Callie would think it was stupid to bring it.

Callie and Becca entered the house after quick hellos, cautiously excited about the day. Really, it was just a day—they weren't even staying the night. Still, each girl had a nagging sense that the simple hike through the mountains could turn into something bigger than they had planned.

Jake and Grandpa discussed the latest batch of cedar that Grandpa would be carving, the coming rain, and the garden.

Callie picked up her pack and started to leave, but Jake held up his hand for the girls to wait. Both girls could tell that he wanted to talk to them before they left.

Callie dealt with her pent-up energy by organizing the backpack and counting her supplies. She must have petted Shadow on five different occasions. She even walked absent-mindedly to his food bowl two extra times. Yes, she had fed him, and he had gone out to the bathroom. She didn't really want to talk to Becca just now, so she kept busy. *Hurry, Jake. We gotta go.* She yearned to get started.

Becca, on the other hand, became quiet and still when she was nervous. She sat beside Jake on the couch, content to be beside him. Secretly she wished that he would go on the hike, too. She rolled a stray wispy curl around her finger, releasing it gently to become a delicate spiral. She had no idea how gorgeous her hair looked to other people. The other arm she kept folded in front of her.

At last, Jake turned to help the girls on their way. He stopped and smiled. Becca was sitting on the couch in a virtual trance, stroking the delighted Shadow on the ear. Callie was unpacking the daypacks again, trying to take inventory and organize for the umpteenth time.

Becca wondered if they would come back as best friends or bitter enemies. At this point, it could go either way. They had gotten off to such a bad start; it was hard to believe they could be friends at all. *Jake should've told Callie about me.* The girls were practically opposites. Callie was usually reserved and practical while Becca was usually expressive and creative (unless she was nervous). Both were strong in their own ways.

Jake turned his attention to Callie. He went over to her and pulled her aside, out of Becca's hearing. He asked her about the route she planned to take to the little house and back, knowing that she would not be using a well-marked trail. Fortunately, they had hiked many times in this region and knew the same landmarks. She knew the potential dangers, so he kept most of his safety lecture to himself.

"The cave's out for today, Cal. A hostile bear is on the loose, and you don't need to corner him in a tight cave," Jake said.

"He's only hostile because people made him that way," Callie replied angrily. She hated how campers fed the bears, making them aggressive. "I'll be careful, you know I will," she said, trying to convince him.

"Sorry, Cal. It's out of the question. They'll catch him soon. You can go to the cave another time. Promise me you won't go there today." He was gentle but firm.

She looked straight in his eyes. "I promise." Callie told him what he wanted to hear, but there was no way she would miss taking Becca to the cave. It was the first time she had ever lied to him.

"Good. Now I won't worry. This means that you should be back sooner than originally planned," He hugged her shoulders loosely.

Callie hesitated for a second. "Right," she replied finally, wondering how much faster they'd have to move between points in order to make up the time spent in the now-forbidden cave.

Becca watched Jake playfully punch Callie in the arm and secretly envied their closeness. He had left home to live with their grandparents when Becca was little. She fought back her feelings of jealousy—it would only make things worse between Callie and her.

She smiled as he came toward her.

"Ready to spend a whole day with your mortal enemy?" he said.

She rolled her eyes at him and gave him a big hug. "Very funny," she said softly. She knew in her heart that her attitude had changed a little toward Callie, but she wasn't ready for Jake to know that yet.

As he walked toward the truck, he called out, "Callie, you're in charge. Have a good day, girls!" He whipped the truck around and headed to work at the rescue center.

The girls stood awkwardly, not knowing what to say next, but the slamming of the screen door broke the silence. Grandpa had come back inside from retrieving his coffee cup from the back porch. The two adventurers gathered their packs and prepared to take off while Shadow zigzagged between their feet.

"Sorry, buddy, you can't go with us today." Callie picked him up and passed him to Grandpa. "Shadow tries to pick a fight with every bear he sees," she explained to Becca.

Becca moved closer to Grandpa. "Do you really think we'll see a bear?" she whispered nervously.

"Possible. They do live in these woods," he replied. "Just follow Callie. She knows what to do."

They walked out the back door, gear in tow.

"Does Jake know where you are going?" Grandpa called to Callie.

"Jake always knows where I am even when I don't want him to!" she said teasingly. She felt a twinge of guilt about the cave. *Except today.*

"When will you be back?"

Callie looked at her watch—8:00 a.m.—and quickly calculated what she should say. "If you don't see us by supper time, you have permission to start worrying. The hike will take about three hours both ways, and we will probably explore and stuff for a couple more hours."

"Explorers need protein," Grandpa said, handing her his can of peanuts. Callie started to object, but Grandpa held up his hand. "You don't want this old man to worry about you the whole day, do you?"

She kissed him and hugged him around the neck.

"Okay, peanuts. But if a bear eats me, you'll know he's had extra protein today," she said.

Becca jumped a little at the "bear" comment. She dashed a quick look at Callie to see just how serious she was about it.

"Don't worry, Becca, bears don't eat girls—too salty," Grandpa said with a twinkle in his eye.

Chapter 14

THE OMINOUS BRIDGE

Fog hung like a bridal veil over the mountain river. Surging water lunged over rocks with unusual force—the result of a snowy winter and rainy spring. The sun, a glowing yellow crystal, was beginning to warm the air. Though harmless-looking rain clouds gathered in the distance, the girls were too busy thinking about the possibilities of the day to even notice them.

Becca thought about how she would describe the various rocks. Some were as large as a car, while others were smaller than a pea. Her senses were on special alert. After all, she had a winning essay to write. She hoped she would remember enough to do her writing that evening. *I wish I had my camera.*

Callie inhaled the fragrant air deeply into her lungs and felt herself relax. This was her element. She felt like a goldfish coming home to its bowl after accidentally flopping out. The fog felt like a spray bottle gently misting her skin. She admired the majestic outline of the largest mountain upstream as she walked in silence.

Both girls wondered what the day would bring. Becca hoped that she could keep up with Callie and wondered if Callie would try to make it harder on purpose. She noticed that Callie had athletic, tan legs and glanced at her own white ones. Truthfully, she avoided physical activity, preferring her books, writing, and television. She did like to go bowling, but it wasn't the same. Callie had well-worn hiking shoes. Becca's shoes were new and stiff.

Callie led the way to the trailhead further up the creek. She hoped that Becca wouldn't whine or fall behind. *Lord, help me to be nice today. You know if she gets annoying, I'll have to leave her out here.* She smiled. *Just kidding, Lord.* She hoped that Becca wouldn't chatter all day long. Callie didn't think she could stomach eight hours of endless noise. *Oh, well,* she thought, *maybe I can enjoy this in spite of Becca.*

The girls hop-scotched across the thundering mountain stream and headed for the darker woods. Becca hoped that a wider trail would open up—the narrow path was hard to make out at times. When she saw a large, dark object back in the woods, she wondered if it was a bear. But Callie marched briskly forward, so she didn't ask.

To Callie, the woods were a warm and friendly place with familiar landmarks guiding her way. She especially loved it in the morning. The birds sang cheerfully as the squirrels chattered, chasing each other from branch to branch.

The mountain river's frigid water lowered the temperature of the surrounding area. Becca could feel her hair becoming frizzy in the damp air. When she reached up to tuck her curls back into her braids, she saw the goose bumps on her arms. She hoped that the sun would warm the air soon. Still, she followed Callie with resolve, determined to remain tough. She quietly untied her jacket from around her waist and put it on—not caring what it might look like draped over her backpack.

Callie broke the silence to warn her companion to look out for loose rocks and slippery roots as they ascended a steep incline. At the top, they both looked down to admire the river's beauty, and Callie pointed out a swimming hole that they could visit another day.

Some of the rocks were difficult to conquer. Becca lost her footing and slipped. Her left leg slid into a hole between two big rocks. She was embarrassed and hurt a little but said nothing. Though it was difficult to move, she pulled and wriggled until she was finally free. Callie yelled back to see if she was okay. Becca thought, *no, what do you think? I fell in a hole, and I'm hurt!* But she said, "Sure, I'm coming" as she trotted off after Callie, no worse for wear.

Callie was surprised and happy that Becca didn't complain. She took Becca to a special clearing just off the trail. They were just in time to see the early sun over a nearby ridge. After a moment, they moved on. They were too excited about their adventure to slow down so close to the beginning of their journey. Callie caught a glimpse of Becca's face. It was just like looking at Jake. It was amazing how much this brother and sister favored each other.

"What is it?" Becca asked.

"Nothing. You just look like Jake." Callie replied.

Becca liked that answer. She loved her brother.

The sun squeezed between the tree branches to light the way, and the trail gently sloped in front of them. A soft padding of dirt and fallen leaves replaced the sharp rocks as they walked among the laurel bushes; they marveled at the number of purple and white clusters. Because this area was flat and uncluttered by underbrush, Callie thought they might see a deer in the shadows. She even thought that one could be watching them from the woods at that very moment.

Becca seems more relaxed than I've ever seen her, Callie thought. *She's not talking constantly like I thought she would.*

Becca was enjoying the experience as she admired the sun's gentle glow in the cozy forest. It was magical. From out of nowhere, she sneezed, startling a deer nearby. Callie turned slowly and looked at Becca with raised eyebrows and Becca smiled sheepishly and shrugged. Callie chuckled and shook her head, half-rolling her eyes at her allergy-plagued companion.

It wasn't long before the easy walkway became steeper and rockier once again. Becca tried to keep up, but her stiff, uncomfortable shoes made it difficult. Callie was surprised at her own patience as she waited for her along the way. *Maybe this friendship thing could work out.*

They resorted to using their arms and legs to scramble from rock to rock as the climb became more challenging. Higher and higher they went until the sound of the river faded into the forest. When they reached a little plateau, they stopped for water. Callie told Becca to conserve it as Jake had taught her. "Take three small sips," she said, "You'll need some for later."

The parched Becca reluctantly rationed her water and sipped obediently, surveying her surroundings. She tried to see what was ahead, but trees blocked her view.

"It's beautiful up here," Becca said as she wiped the sweat from her brow. Her thick, curly hair felt like an itchy rug on the back of her neck. She quickly took down her braid in favor of a ponytail and felt a breeze blow across her neck. She wondered why she hadn't pulled her hair up before. She noticed that Callie was barely sweating.

Callie put her water away. "Are you afraid of heights?"

"I don't want to dangle over a 1,000-foot canyon by a little vine, if that's what you mean," Becca replied.

"Don't worry, it's not that bad. Almost. But not quite." Callie said teasingly.

"Oh, wonderful," Becca replied with just a little sarcasm, hoping that she was up for the next challenge.

Callie led Becca around the corner to a bright, rocky pathway. Becca had wondered why Callie had asked if she was afraid of heights, and now she was beginning to worry.

Callie halted at the edge of the woods and turned to Becca. "This is breathtaking. It's called The Bridge. Take your time and don't be afraid."

Becca nodded her head, wide-eyed. She cautiously inched forward, heeding Callie's warning. The treeless path before her led across the top of a very high ridge. It was only about as wide as a single-lane road. The grassless trail was very rocky in some places. A sharp, menacing drop bordered the trail, flanked by tree-covered slopes. Becca's hands began to feel clammy. She held on to a little tree—the last tree until the other side of The Bridge. She was unable to scan the gorgeous expanse on either side because she was busy trying to calm down. She hadn't really considered herself afraid of heights until that moment. A sickening panic grew inside of her. *If one of us falls,* she thought, *it's over.* She peeked over the side carefully, still clutching the tree. Endless mountains and valleys stretched out before her, but sheer terror prevented her from enjoying it. A nearby pebble bounced down the side of the mountain and out of sight.

"Whoa—that's a long way down," she whispered. "Did...did... Jake know we were coming this way?" She meant to yell loudly enough for Callie to hear, but the words barely squeaked out of her throat. Her sweating hands tingled, and her rubbery legs began to quake. An eagle above her caught her eye. To her dismay, she found that looking up made her even dizzier. She felt the sensation of the rapid, downward lunge of a roller coaster. Still, she was determined to be brave in front of Callie. She summoned her courage and looked across the path to estimate the distance, noticing that Callie had already reached the other side. She guessed that the scary part of the trail was about 50 yards long—about half the length of a football field. She weakly told herself she could do it, even though she couldn't imagine taking even one step further.

Callie waited. She remembered how nervous she was the first time she walked across The Bridge. She knew that fear was the real danger. The actual probability of falling was small. *Unless you get too close to the edge.* Crossing over, or even thinking about it, was terrifying for some people. She hoped Becca could handle it. Callie dreaded the thought of having to drag Becca off The Bridge if she freaked out. She watched anxiously. *I hope this doesn't take too long.*

Becca took a slow, deep breath and eased forward, feeling as if a big wind could pick her up and drop her over the edge. *Just do it. Don't think. Just walk.* She tried to fool herself into believing it was just a regular path. No problem. As she watched her feet moving mechanically over the rocky terrain, it seemed like a dream. *This isn't so bad,* she thought, pleased at her progress to the halfway point. *Callie will never know how afraid I am.*

Everything was just fine until she lost her footing and fell forward onto the ground. Nothing she landed on was soft. She was face down, scratched, and dirty. Her wrists hurt from trying to stop the fall; she closed her eyes tightly to regain control over her rising panic. A stiff wind from the valley suddenly slapped her on the face and distracted her from her self-composure. Everything started spinning. Sadly, she lost her concentration in her battle against fear.

"What am I going to do now?" She lamented. "I hate this." She was paralyzed with terror. She knew she couldn't stay on the trail the rest of her life, but she didn't want to get up. She was in the middle of the open ridge, frozen between moving forward and going back. *It's the same as this summer,* she thought somewhat bitterly. *I can't go back to the way I was before I met Callie but moving forward in this friendship is just as scary.* Deep in her heart, she knew she'd never be the same. She fought back the tears. *I can just hear Callie making fun of me for this.*

Instead, Callie was worried. "Are you okay?" She yelled across the open expanse.

"I'm sorry, Callie. I can't do this," Becca moaned.

"Are you hurt?" Callie yelled again.

Becca did a quick mental assessment of her condition. "Just my pride."

"What?"

"Just my pride," Becca yelled as loudly as she could.

Callie took a few steps toward Becca and then hesitated. Becca was very tense, and Callie knew that they both could tumble if they tried to hold on to each other. She wasn't quite sure how to handle the situation. The only reason they came this way was so that they would be able to make it to Mrs. Jennie's house and back in a reasonable time. The Bridge was unsettling to her, too, but Becca didn't need to know that. *Maybe this whole day was a bad idea.* She observed Becca's struggle while she waited for an idea to arrive and wondered how rescue workers would retrieve a hysterical person.

Finally, Callie noticed a steady, warm wind blowing; it swept gently across Becca's shoulders, rustling her shirt. *That's it,* Callie smiled, inspired.

"Becca?" Callie called. "Wind blows—tree grows."

"Callie, is that some sort of a joke?" Becca yelled.

"Just wait a minute. I have to tell you something. Wind blows—tree grows. Can you hear me?" Callie said. She knew she had to yell loudly so that Becca could hear; the winds around The Bridge were famous for snatching words right out of a person's mouth and plunging them into the valley below.

"Yes." Becca didn't know where this was going, and she surely didn't see the point. *Maybe I can crawl back to the side and go home...*

For some reason, Callie had thought about a twisted wooden cross that Granny had given her. She imagined herself sitting on the porch, listening to the old woman's words.

"Just relax for a minute, Becca. Listen to what I'm saying. Granny has really bad arthritis. She's suffered from it since she was twenty-five."

Hands numb with fear, Becca tried to raise herself a little, but found that she couldn't even do that. Nausea crept up her throat. She wasn't in the mood to hear about some old lady.

Callie cupped her hands around her mouth for a makeshift megaphone and continued yelling, "One day, Granny told me a story about her big, old tree on the hill above her house. She said, 'Callie, do you know why this tree has been here so long?' I said that it had good soil, sun, and rain. 'Yes,' she said, 'but we mustn't forget the wind.'" Callie spoke slowly, emphasizing every word.

"Granny said, 'Callie, what if I gave you a sapling to plant, and you promised to take care of it? You made sure it had water, sun, and good soil. You decided to protect it from the wind, and you built a wall around it to keep it safe. Supposing one day, you thought it was big enough to survive on its own, and you tore the wall down. Do you know what would happen to the tree when the first strong wind blew on it, Callie?'"

It annoyed Becca that Callie was telling a story at that moment, but she couldn't do anything but listen.

"I said, 'No, Granny, what would happen?' She said, 'Child, it would snap right in two because it had never had to stand against the wind before. I tell you this because it is a story of strength. If you never face danger and trouble, you will snap when you are finally let out to face the world on your own.' Granny said that the winds of hardship can make us strong."

It sort of made sense to Becca, but the fear remained.

"Becca, that's what she told me when she gave me a little wooden cross that I have in my room. It is supposed to remind me of Granny and the strength she shared with me."

Becca thought about the story from the ground, wondering why Callie hadn't come to help her up. Someone had always been there to help her—her parents, her parents' money, all the friends she had because of her parents' money, all the people who were hired to help her... Becca stopped, suddenly aware that everyone she had always relied on wouldn't be there to help her in her greatest time of need. Her inherited wealth was always a safety bubble, shielding her from disappointments, failures, and harm. Where was it now? *I'm on my own*, she sighed, angry at herself for just now realizing it. Her thoughts of being independent were just that. Thoughts. It occurred to her at that very moment that she had been completely dependent on others. The realization incensed her. *If I'm going to be the strong, independent person I thought I was, I might as well start now.*

Her focus changed as she considered Callie's story again. It was sort of easy to understand, but it didn't have the effect on her that it obviously had on Callie.

"Callie, that story means more to you than to me because it's your story," Becca yelled. "Your Granny told it to you."

"Becca, I think this story means more to you than you know, and I believe you will have the strength to stand up and walk the rest of the way over here," Callie answered with assurance.

"Thanks for the vote of confidence, but what makes you think so? It's a story from your Granny, a woman I never knew," Becca said, growing impatient.

There was a dramatic pause.

"Because the lady I called Granny is your Granna. I've known her all my life."

Becca was silent.

Callie loved how this was working out. She felt like she had just said "Check mate." Callie walked to the far side of The Bridge and sat on a rock, folding her arms. Becca would be coming soon. She knew it.

Becca was shocked. Her own grandmother? *Unbelievable!* She didn't know about her grandmother's arthritis, and she was a little jealous that Callie had such a close relationship with her! Thinking about her brave and loving Granna gave her courage to rise above her fear. Just then, she felt a gentle breeze caress her face. It made her feel...*ready*. Fear was her hardship at that moment, and she decided she would stand against it. Granna's story had strengthened her. She carefully stood and began to walk. Her strength snowballed with every step. The path felt wider than before. She overcame her fear and was ready to get on with her day. She was also ready to take a closer look at her grandmother's wooden cross of strength.

"Glad you could make it," Callie said with a smile.

"Thanks, Callie," Becca replied smugly, knowing that she had conquered more than just The Bridge.

Chapter 15

PITCH BLACK

Beyond The Bridge, the path sloped again. The two girls filed down the winding trail through a section of tall, naked tree trunks. At one spot, Becca caught a glimpse of the roaring river through a grove of thick laurel trees. She could hardly wait to see the waterfall! From the sound of things, it had to be close.

The girls walked happily along without talking. It wasn't long before they came to the fork in the trail.

Callie paused, contemplating her decision about which way to go. Jake's words blared loudly in her head: 'The cave's out for today, Cal...Sorry, Cal, it's out of the question... promise me you won't go there today...' His deep, green eyes seemed to pierce her very soul. Still, she was determined to show Becca the cave.

She heard her own words next: 'I promise... I promise... I promise... I promise... I promise...' *Stop! I'm going and that's final. Jake will never know. Besides, it's not like I'm doing anything bad. There's no stupid bear in there. Jake was just trying to scare me.* She pushed the guilty thoughts out of her mind and marched down the trail toward the cave.

Becca had no idea about the inner battle Callie had just fought.

The looming rock formation before them fascinated Becca. It looked like a school bus that had driven off the side of the hill frontward onto the ground. She had never seen such an interesting rock before. She didn't even notice that Callie had disappeared behind it. She cautiously approached the side of the rock, thinking that Callie was going to jump out and scare her. Even when she made it all the way to the other side, she saw only a large rhododendron tree tucked in front of a rock cliff.

"Okay, Callie. I know you're here somewhere!" Becca called, scanning the area for any hint of her guide.

Then, suddenly, Becca heard Callie call her name like a moaning ghost, "Behhhhhhcahhhhh." Becca wheeled around, shocked to see a smiling Callie leaning up against the tree. She seemed to have appeared out of nowhere! Callie motioned Becca to follow her.

Becca made her way around the rocks and over the tree's exposed roots. As she neared Callie, she saw the haunting entrance to a cave. A muddy, earthy smell wafted from the darkness. Becca heard the echoes of water dripping in the depths of the underworld.

Callie watched Becca's reaction with satisfaction; she loved introducing people to natural wonders. Though the morning sun lit up the entrance to the cave, everything beyond just a few feet was completely dark.

Becca tried to think of words to describe the cave's blackness. The name that suited it best was fresh asphalt. "Do bears live in here?" Becca asked weakly, unaware of Jake's warning.

"We've seen some evidence of bears sheltering here," answered Callie, "but they don't live in caves. Bears don't like to live in places where they might be cornered." *See, Jake? Another reason why this is safe.* "They'd rather sleep in other places, like in the holes left by uprooted trees." Callie poked around in her backpack and pulled out two flashlights, handing one to Becca. "Bears in and around the Smokies don't even officially hibernate through the winter, they just get slow and sleep a lot," she added as a point of information.

Callie's heart beat little faster. This was her first time here without an adult. Even with flashlights, the cave's darkness could really be spooky. She was glad they had new batteries. Becca looked ready; they both turned on their flashlights and stepped through the invisible curtain leading into the cool blackness.

It was alluring to Becca. She had seen many caves on television, but it was very different to experience it firsthand. The sights, sounds, and smells were unlike anything she had ever known. The scared part of her wanted to get out of there as soon as possible—but the curious part of her pushed her onward. Questions filled her head. She had to trust Callie completely.

"What if we get lost?" she asked nervously.

"We won't go beyond what's familiar," Callie replied. There was no way that she would venture beyond what Jake had shown her. Thinking of Jake made her feel bad again. She tried to push it out of her mind.

There was something new and interesting everywhere Becca looked. She thought maybe she could write an article just about this. She touched the rough walls of the cave and wondered how old they were. Seeing a part that was broken off, she knelt to pick it up. It was grayish tan on the rough side and white with deep orange ripples on the smooth side.

"Look at this, Callie!" she said. "I wonder what this is made of."

"Grandpa says the orange part is iron. He says that iron is like blood—one drop will spread through a rock. The white part is Caltrate. Stalactites and stalagmites are made of the same thing," Callie said.

"Cool," Becca said, impressed. She admired the odd shapes hanging from the ceiling and jutting up from the floor. "I can never remember which ones are on the floor and which ones are on the ceiling."

"Stalactites are on the ceiling. They hold on *tight*. There are a few big ones in the room down here," Callie said as she led the way to a huge round cavern. "Hey!" Callie said loudly. Three distinct "heys" bounced around the room.

"Oooh!" Becca tried it. "Ooh...ooh...ooh," came the echo.

The ceiling must have been more than two stories high. They scanned the walls with their lights and Becca stepped into the room. She noticed that Callie didn't follow, so she stopped and looked at her.

"Jake said it's easy to get turned around in here and not be able to find the way back out. There are other tunnels, and they all look the same once you get inside." Then, she had an idea. "Let's turn off the flashlights for 30 seconds."

Becca really didn't want to, but also didn't want to seem scared.

"On three: one...two...three." **CLICK**

Darkness. The only thing they heard was the water dripping in the background and the sound of their own breathing. Callie opened her eyes as wide as they would go to take in any hint of light. Nothing.

Becca thought of the old saying about not being able to see your hand in front of your face. She tried it and couldn't see anything at all. She fought off the growing feeling that something was about to grab her. "You know what you said about bears not living in caves because they don't like to be cornered?" she asked Callie timidly.

"Yeah, what about it?"

"Well, you did say that they shelter in caves—like maybe rest or something?"

"Yes."

"So, how do you know that we wouldn't accidentally corner one that is resting in here?"

Callie couldn't answer that question. Her mouth became dry all the sudden and butterflies filled her stomach.

"Callie, you aren't gonna sneak up and scare the living daylights out of me, are you? 'Cause if you do, I will hate you forever and probably hurt you somehow with my own bare hands," Becca said, almost panicking.

"I'm plastered to this spot until the lights are back on," was Callie's shaky reply.

"Please tell me it's been thirty seconds," Becca said.

"It's been thirty hours," Callie said quickly, as she turned her light back on.

Becca was only a half second behind her. "Well, we can have something to tell our grandchildren. I'm glad we got to..."

Becca chattered on, but Callie didn't hear her. Something else caught her attention. It sounded like a low growl coming from behind her. *Good grief! Now you're hearing things.* She pushed past Becca quickly. "Hurry—we're running out of time," she said, leading the way. She hoped Becca would take her cue and hustle.

Becca heard the change in Callie's voice and practically ran to catch up. She was finished with that eye-straining darkness anyway.

The unusual grumbling sound would nag Callie for the rest of the day.

The light from outside looked like a dull train light at first but quickly brightened and overcame the darkness. Callie often looked behind them to make sure there was nothing following. Becca looked back, too, to see what Callie was looking at. Neither of them said a word about it. In many ways, it was scarier coming out than going in. They stopped briefly at the mouth of the cave and took a sip of water before continuing their hike.

"That was great, but I wouldn't want to camp here. Too spooky. I don't think I could sleep," Becca said.

"I know exactly what you mean," Callie replied with her eyes glued to the dark tunnel. "Especially with the bats..." the thought distracted her from the growling sound. "Oh! I forgot! Come see!" The ceiling near the cave's entrance had a deep crevice that went straight up. Callie tiptoed carefully underneath the area and shined her flashlight on a rock about halfway up.

"I don't see anything," whispered Becca.

"Look above the light," Callie said softly. Dozens of small, dark brown bats huddled together on the cave walls. Becca inhaled quickly, alarmed. "They eat bugs, Becca, they won't hurt people. They have only enough energy to do what they need to live. If we scare them and they fly around, it could literally make them die."

Callie remembered one of Jake's bragging friends who freaked out when seeing real live bats and started hitting them with a rock. It always made Callie mad when animals suffered because of the mean things people did.

Becca was a little nervous but not afraid. They were the most hideous things she had ever seen. Without thinking, she said, "Rabies"—except that it sounded like a frog's "ribbet." She chuckled. Her dad always said that about skunks, bats, raccoons, or almost any wild animal. He didn't even know how much he sounded like a big frog croaking when he said it. It was funny, but he didn't know it. Her dad never thought anything was funny except for when he made fun of people. She explained it to Callie, and the girls had a good—but quiet—laugh.

Callie tried it a few times and Becca laughed. Becca added her father's stern facial expression he used when he said it, and it became even more hilarious.

The bats didn't seem to appreciate the laughter and became jumpy and restless, flapping their wings and repositioning on the ceiling. The girls looked at each other with wide eyes. "Rabies," they croaked quietly in unison. They almost burst out laughing and ran out of the cave, sides hurting and tears streaming from trying to hold it in. When they were safely outside, they laughed so hard that Becca fell on the ground, holding her side. Every time they stopped laughing, they'd look at each other and start again. The day was really turning out to be much better than they had ever imagined.

The sun had evaporated the morning mist by the time the girls exited the cave, replacing the cool humidity with sticky steaminess.

"Might rain," Becca said simply, feeling her hair respond to the moisture in the air.

"We won't melt," Callie replied simply, unconcerned.

When they reached the fork in the trail, they both heard water swooshing over the falls below them. With a shared smile, they marched down the rocky path, glad they were on their own.

Chapter 16

THE STAND-OFF

An endless wall of water thundered over the rock cliff, just out of their view. It was one of Callie's favorite places, and she couldn't wait to show it to Becca. They rounded a corner and caught a perfect postcard view of the gorgeous waterfall. Both girls stood absolutely still, as they drank in the sight: the hazy spray near the impact point at the bottom, the huge boulders lining a rounded swimming area, the clear veil of water about halfway up, and the playful splashes hitting the rocks at the very top. The falls were about two stories high and as wide as a double garage door. They gazed at it a little while without speaking and then took off down the path.

"We're almost there," shouted Callie. "We'll have a picnic at the bottom."

"Great! I'm starved!" Becca replied, close at her heels.

The steep path was narrow, and smooth tree roots bulged up from underground. Hiking boots skidded and rocks wobbled under their feet as they scampered to the bottom.

When they reached the falls, they saw an explorer's dream: a huge, natural water park. The water's loud rumble muffled every other sound. Callie yelled out some of the highlights—the swimming hole, the path that wildlife use to get to the water, the direction to Mrs. Jennie's house—but Becca just nodded and smiled. She was too captivated by the sights and sounds to pay attention. She didn't even listen to Callie telling her about how rescuers save people near waterfalls or about the 3-foot Hellbender salamander found only in the Appalachian region.

They felt the cool, misty updraft from the falls, and Becca stopped and closed her eyes. She wished she could stay here all day. The water-generated breeze around the falls had a fresh, mossy fragrance she hadn't smelled anywhere else. She loved how the air felt on her skin. She wished she had an inner tube to bob in the calm water and thought that it would be a wonderful place to snorkel. These secluded falls were the prettiest she had ever seen. It was love at first sight.

Callie had walked on a few steps before she noticed that Becca was off in a dreamy world of her own. "This way," Callie said, as hunger poked her in the stomach. She led the way downstream to a big flat rock. "Your table, madam," she said to Becca.

"Mahvelahs," the sweaty, "elegant" lady replied.

The girls ate quickly, too hungry to stop for conversation. They feasted on peanut butter and jelly sandwiches, chips, and lemonade until they were full. They saved Grandpa's peanuts and some apples for later.

Finished with their lunches, they repacked their snacks and their garbage and took off their shoes so they could play in the water.

Becca rolled up her jeans and plunged her toes in the stream. "Cold-cold-cold-cold-cold," she inhaled in a quick whisper, eyes wide. Still, the water felt good on her hot feet. It was perfectly clear. She could see tiny minnows darting around the pebbles on the bottom. "Callie, come see the fish!"

Barefooted Callie came over, her expert eyes scanning the riverbed for crawdads, salamanders, and pretty rocks. Every once in a while, she assumed the stance of a hunter, poised and ready to pounce on unsuspecting prey. She would lean over the water, watching motionlessly for a crawdad to leave the safety of his rocky hideout. Then quickly, she would lunge her hand into the freezing water and grab one by the tail. All in all, she caught only a few but found the thrill of the hunt extremely entertaining.

Becca didn't even notice Callie. She was busy narrating her experience as if it were a documentary film. Not a rock nor butterfly escaped this writer's vivid descriptions.

Callie jumped up suddenly as if she had heard an alarm clock ring. She quickly dried off her feet, donned her hiking boots, and began rattling off orders to Becca. "Come on. Put your shoes on. I have something to show you closer to the falls."

Becca was puzzled—and a little annoyed. She really wanted to stay at the water longer, but she obediently tried to clean and dry her feet enough to put her shoes back on.

"We just got here!" Becca mumbled under her breath. "I didn't come all the way down here to be dragged all over the place without getting to enjoy anything. Besides, I may never get to come back here again—this afternoon she'll have us practically running up and down these hills..." She was fuming and fussing so much she didn't notice that Callie was halfway back to the falls without her.

Becca hurriedly unrolled her jeans and ran after Callie, hating the icky feeling of her wet socks. She was glad her boots were waterproof, but it didn't help when her feet were wet inside them. It also didn't help that a small pebble had invaded one of her shoes. She hoped Callie would give her a chance to remove it since it was hopeless to reposition it with her toes as she ran.

Callie had heard some of Becca's grumbling about having to leave but hurried along anyway, knowing they were pressed for time. She shuddered as she relived the moment, *yet again*, when she looked right into Jake's beautiful green eyes and lied to him. It was fun at the cave, but not fun enough to erase her feelings of guilt. Now she had new guilt for rushing Becca.

The two girls made their way along the busy water in silence, careful not to lose their footing or twist an ankle. Gray and brown rocks of all sizes packed every inch of the path—many were either the size of a lunch box or the size of a beanbag chair.

Becca couldn't figure out where they were going. The path ended at the falls.

Callie's destiny was right in front of her: the pointed rock with the long vines hanging down. She turned to make sure Becca was behind her and stopped to let her catch up. Callie leaned against a rock and admired the falls while she waited.

Finally catching up, Becca shouted, "Wow—pretty!"

Callie nodded and smiled. "This way," she said as she disappeared behind the rock through the curtain of green vines. Becca followed her to find a small hiding place behind the vines. It had a pebble-covered beach the size of a trampoline with part of the circle in the water. Strangely, the water's roar seemed muffled from the inside of this unusual space. The girls stretched to touch the forceful curtain of water on the back of the waterfall, impressed by its power.

Damp air hovered all around like a continuous fog—the perfect climate for several varieties of moss and rock-loving plants. It was a wonderful hideout. While Callie looked in the water for anything interesting, Becca took off her shoe. She dug and wiped in her boot several times before finding the annoying pebble and dumping it on the ground. Wrinkling her nose disgustedly, she struggled to put the wet, limp sock and her hiking boot back on.

After only a few minutes, the little hideout began to feel too damp and cool. So, since the pebbly ground was too rough for comfortable seating anyway, they decided to move on.

"Will we have time to swim when we come back?" Becca asked as she stood up and brushed off her jeans.

Callie stopped and looked at Becca, not sure how to respond. "Aw, we can swim down by my house," she said, doubting that it would satisfy Becca. She wasn't ready yet to tell her about the cave detour.

"It's not the same," Becca said quietly, disappointed.

Callie wanted to drop the conversation, so she said, "Watch your step" as she maneuvered around the rocks at the exit of the hideout. The way out the other side was harder to manage than the way they came in. Only a few foot-sized stones made up the path from the falls to the other side of the river, and Becca was so busy watching where she was going that she had to catch her balance to keep from running into Callie.

Callie had seen something that brought her to a complete halt, and her balance faltered as she strained to be still. Becca traced Callie's line of vision to a shoulder-high ledge on the wall. There—within a foot of Callie—was a snake, poised and ready to strike Callie in the head.

Callie recognized immediately that it was poisonous. The diamond-shaped head and tell-tale rattle gave its identity away. The tightly coiled serpent, with his tan body and cream-outlined black diamonds, was easily within striking distance. Its long tongue lapped the air as it flexed its muscles, daring her to challenge its strength. Callie knew enough about the Eastern Diamondback Rattlesnake to know that its bite was definitely worse than its threatening stance—but she had never seen one in person. *I must have roused it from sunbathing when I reached for the ledge,* she thought gingerly. She estimated him to be at least 5 feet long and as big around as one of her legs near its middle.

Her head swooned at the grave danger she faced. She reached out in slow motion and took Becca's hand, squeezing it with a "get back" motion as a warning to stay still.

Unfortunately, Becca was stuck with her right foot on a stable rock and her left one on a shaky one. She could feel her left foot giving way, and she was sure she was going to fall. An annoying itch sprang up on her nose, but she was afraid to move.

Callie felt Becca swaying and whispered angrily, "Freeze."

Becca barely moved her lips as she replied, "Falling."

The snake, with its menacing, unblinking eyes, fortified his position by tightening his coils even more.

"Fix it," Callie shot back, light-headed from holding her breath.

Becca grasped Callie's hand for support and was able to move her left foot so she could stand with both feet on the stable rock.

All four eyes focused on the hypnotic rattler. Minutes felt like hours. Callie's leg muscles trembled their protest from straining for so long.

A bee teased around Callie's head and landed on her shoulder. Becca squeezed her hand again as a warning of the bee's presence.

"Leave it," Callie whispered.

The bee left as quickly as it had arrived, and the girls saw the snake's body begin to relax. Soon, he slithered away, allowing free passage to the other side.

"I hate snakes," Becca said after they reached solid ground.

"I don't," Callie replied to Becca's amazement as they continued their journey.

"Well, if something bad had to happen today, at least we got it over with."

"Surely," Callie responded, hoping she was right.

Chapter 17

THE HONEST TRUTH

The girls were quiet for a while as they resumed their journey. Callie knew that a bite from the unfriendly snake would have been deadly—they could never have gotten help in time. She was glad it was over, and glad that Grandpa had thoroughly educated her about all the snakes in the region. She already felt the pressure to provide a good time for Becca. Now she felt responsible for their very lives.

Her personal thoughts transitioned smoothly into prayer. *Thanks, Jesus, for keeping us safe. Please be with us the rest of the day. Mom says You already know what's gonna to happen before it does—that You are already with us. You're in charge today. You know better than us, anyway.* While praying, her thoughts drifted back to her Big Lie. Just because God was in charge didn't mean that everything would be easy. She still wasn't sure if she should tell Becca. Without realizing it, she hastened her speed.

Becca noticed the change of pace and felt sure that Callie was hiding something. Eventually she asked, "What's wrong? Is there something you aren't telling me? Are you upset about the snake?"

"Don't worry about it. Just concentrate on having a good time," Callie said, as she took a deep breath and slowed down a bit. Her silent prayer continued...*Lord, I messed up. I know I shouldn't have gone to the cave. If we don't get back in time, they'll all be worried, and I'll be grounded. I just wanted to go so bad. Now I'll never get a chance to come out here again without an adult. Please forgive me for disobeying. I was hoping to tell Becca about how You changed my life. If she finds out that I lied and disobeyed, she won't even listen to me.*

A hot tear ran down Callie's cheek as she recalled the day that she stood in front of the congregation and told them she had become a Christian. Since then, she had been a hothead on movie night and a liar today. *I feel like a fake,*

Lord, but I want to do right. Jake said You forgave everything when I decided to follow you—past, present, and future. I don't know how You do that, but thanks. She took a deep breath and wiped away two more escaping tears, feeling some better.

"Don't worry, the next time we are near the water, Becca, I'll be happy to push you in," Callie said with a smile, hoping to relieve the tension in the air.

Becca stopped and looked into the face of her new friend, assured by the lighthearted challenge. "You have to catch me first" she said as she ran ahead, tagging Callie as she passed.

Callie looked at her watch: 11:30 a.m. She tried to calculate the time it would take to do everything they planned but it was difficult—she was distracted by the vision of her lying to Jake playing repeatedly in her mind. She plodded forward, feeling like a rental horse stringing along behind the tail of the horse in front of it. Her emotions bounced around in her heart between feeling hopeful, feeling guilty, and feeling anxious about the unfamiliar shortcut she was ready to use if needed. She wanted to tell Becca but didn't want to start an argument and ruin the day. Their friendship was just beginning to become comfortable. Now it could unravel.

Becca stopped to look at something interesting, so Callie went around her for a few steps and then paused absentmindedly to wait. Soon, Becca looked up from a beautiful group of vivid black and royal blue butterflies on the path, still aware that Callie was acting strange. "Are you mad at me or something?"

"What? No—it's nothing." Callie said, not convincing Becca. Callie sighed. She was tired of holding it in. "Actually, it is something, but I'm not mad at you. At all. The truth is that Jake told me not to take you to the cave today. I promised I wouldn't."

"But wasn't the cave part of the original plan?" Becca said, not sure whether to be mad at Callie or at Jake. *What's the big deal about the cave? We were careful.*

"It was—until word got out about a bear that's been bothering people in a campground a few miles from here. Jake said he didn't think there would be a problem, but he didn't want us to accidentally corner an aggressive bear in the back of the cave. He told me this morning not to go. So, I lied. I promised we wouldn't, but I'd already decided that nothing was going to stop me. Now we don't have as much time to goof around. I'm sorry." Telling Becca the truth brought Callie some relief, but she still dreaded Becca's response.

Becca was quiet.

"I wouldn't have taken you there if I'd seen tracks or scat on the trail," Callie continued, "I just wanted you to see it. That bear is probably far from here." Still, the sound of the growling in the back of the cave lingered in her mind.

Becca didn't know what to think. She felt angry with Callie for lying to her brother, happy that she went to the cave, and nervous about meeting a bear. Finally, she spoke in a low voice, pausing between each statement while her mind sorted out the situation. "I did like the cave. And nothing happened. It explains why you're in a hurry. It's okay. We'll get back in time somehow. It just won't be as fun." She was frowning a little, not sounding very happy.

"Are we okay, then?" Callie asked.

Becca hesitated, "I guess I just didn't know you were a liar."

The words thumped hard against Callie's chest. She was miserable. Speechless. She turned to walk on, avoiding Becca's gaze.

Becca had wanted to believe that Callie was different from her friends back home. She was tired of the lying, cussing and gossiping she heard at her school. She just didn't expect a Christian to act this way. *Oh well, nobody's perfect,* she decided, disheartened. She wanted to go home.

The path ahead was more level than at the falls. Becca could see that they were entering a shady hollow and wondered how much further the house was but didn't ask. She wasn't as excited as she had been.

Finally, Callie stopped. "Look, I know you are disappointed. I shouldn't have lied. I've already prayed this morning and asked God to forgive me and to guide me the rest of the day. Even if we get back in time, I will tell Jake that I lied."

Becca was looking down at the ground, relieved to hear that Callie was going to do the right thing. It took courage for Callie to admit she was wrong and to face up to it. She smiled softly and waited to see if Callie was going to say anything else.

"Will you forgive me?" Callie asked, looking full into Becca's face.

Becca couldn't think of any of her other friends who would have asked for forgiveness that way. A fast "sorry" was all she had ever gotten in the way of an apology, and even that was rare.

"Of course," Becca said with a nod, ready to give this day—and this friendship—another try. She extended her arm with a dramatic, "after you" motion and said, "Lead on, O Captain." It was Becca's turn to feel bad about the things that she had thought about Callie when she first arrived.

Callie's mind couldn't change gears quite as fast as her expressive friend. She was puzzled until she realized that Becca had forgiven her. She passed by Becca who was still posed with arm extended.

"Thanks," Callie said, feeling a growing appreciation for Becca's companionship.

They both had a little skip in their step as they headed for the hollow ahead. "The house isn't much farther," Callie said, having fun again. *Thank you, God. I'm glad the adventure is back on track!*

Chapter 18

INTRUDER

They followed a dry creek bed into the darkened world of the shady hollow. They could see nothing of the horizon in this dense wooded scene other than an occasional glimpse of the gray sky peeping through the canopy. The air hung heavy, attracting annoying little gnats that hovered around their eyes, feasting on the carbon dioxide the girls exhaled. The adventurers pushed through the humid air, crunching last fall's leaves underfoot. Though the climate was far from refreshing, they tried to soak in every detail of their rich surroundings.

Callie, thoughtful and logical, quietly enjoyed the familiarity of the woods and the order in creation—while keeping careful track of the time. Becca, open and artistic, described every color, every shape, and every fragrance for her never-ending narrative. Fussing squirrels, random bird noises, and the marching of four booted feet were the only other sounds in the hollow.

Suddenly Becca noticed something dark moving just off the trail in front of them and pointed it out to Callie. "Uh...Callie?" She froze and stared at the shape, wondering if it was a bear. Callie saw it too. Cautiously, they tiptoed closer to each other.

"You know the thing I said about the snake being the worst thing that would happen today?" Becca whispered.

"Shhh. Stay still and we'll see if it goes away. If it looks over, don't act scared. Just back away and hope it doesn't charge." *Could we be in danger again? It doesn't seem possible. What a crazy day.*

The shape swayed back and forth, but they couldn't see for sure what it was. Callie sidestepped over to a rock and drew herself up slowly to get a better look.

Becca watched nervously, hoping that Callie knew what she was doing. She felt a cramp in her calf muscle. *What's the deal with my legs today? These new boots are horrible.* She tried to shift her weight enough to stop the sharp pain. It didn't help. She slowly reached down to rub her leg and to try to stretch it out but suddenly felt dizzy and remembered that she was still holding her breath. She told herself to calm down, to forget the leg cramp. She relaxed her breathing and looked back in the direction of the swaying shape, still massaging her leg. It hadn't moved from its original spot.

Then she heard Callie scream. Startled, Becca lost her balance, fell to the ground, and then jumped straight back up to run away. But she twisted her leg into worse pain than before.

Callie started laughing. "It's just a big old squirrel's nest that has fallen and is swinging back and forth above the ground." She knelt, expertly removed her friend's boot, and pushed Becca's toes back toward her knee. The muscle released its spasm, and Becca's leg cramp was gone. "Grandpa gets these charley horses all the time and I have to fix him," Callie said. "I was just joking around—I'm sorry you fell."

Becca put her boot back on and rubbed her leg for a little while longer just for good measure. She had to get Callie back for this. "Callie! A big spider's on your shoulder!" she yelled, jumping back quickly and pointing.

Callie brushed off both shoulders at the same time. "Did I get it?" she said as she jumped around.

It was Becca's turn to laugh, "Yep. It was as big as the bear." Now they were even. When their journey continued, Becca asked Callie, "Tell me about this house we're going to."

"Mrs. Jennie lived there for years, but it's deserted now. My mom and dad really loved her. She was very old and knew everything about Appalachian remedies with herbs and stuff. I stayed with her for a few days after my dad died. Did you know that every part of a dandelion is edible?"

"No, I didn't. Why would anybody eat a dandelion?" Becca said with a grimace.

"They used to roast the roots for coffee, cook the greens—stuff like that," Callie replied. She remembered tasting the flowers before, but they weren't that good.

"Do you remember her?" Becca asked as they walked.

"Mrs. Jennie? Not really. I just sorta remember a few little scenes of sitting on her lap, drinking milk at her table, and splashing in her old washtub. She talked to me about my dad being in heaven, and she told me stories. I must have gone there a few times, but I'm not sure. I wish she were still alive. I'd love to know her now."

Callie stopped and removed her backpack, pulling out a small grocery bag. Opening it carefully, she withdrew the little gift. She admired it, her curiosity threatening to overtake her.

Becca caught up and looked over her shoulder at the little box. "What is it? One of your birthday presents?"

Callie nodded. "Mom gave it to me this morning to open at Mrs. Jennie's house. I guess I should wait, but I don't really want to."

"How far away are we?" Becca asked.

"It's not much farther—just over the hill and around the bend," Callie replied.

Becca was as excited as a child on Christmas morning. She was very different from the "Big Journalist" she had been at the first of the summer. "Okay, take the ribbon off now. Take the tape off at the top of the hill. Take the paper off at the bend and open the box at the house," she said, eyes dancing with pleasure at the thought of Callie's mystery gift.

"How old are you?" Callie teased, amused. She stuck the gift back in the backpack and took a few steps. *Okay, it's going to drive us both crazy. I can't wait after all.* Only five seconds later, the box was back out, and the ribbon was off.

"I'm five. Like you." Becca chuckled. She knew in her heart that being a Christian didn't mean a person was perfect, and she was sorry she had thought Callie was a fake. Becca always thought of herself as a Christian. She believed in God. She thought she did, anyway. *Why not?* It seemed better than being an atheist or something. Her family took her to church sometimes, especially Christmas and Easter programs. Dad had told her that it was good business to go to church. She even went to church camp when she was in the fourth grade. She'd heard all the stories, knew the Bible characters' names, and knew a few songs. Believing in God was just something you did—like being a good American. Yet, it never affected her decisions. She wouldn't really say that she was best friends with Jesus or anything. She thought of Jake and marveled at his excitement about God. His eyes always lit up when he talked about the Bible or what a good job God did on creation. If anyone was a Christian, Jake was. He had something extra, beyond just saying he believed in God. She was beginning to see the same thing about Callie. She was proud of Callie for deciding to be honest to the grown-ups about going to the cave. Callie seemed concerned about what God would think of her; she was ready to tell the truth and face her punishment. *That's different.* She was so deep in thought that she literally bumped into Callie who had stopped at the top of the hill to remove the tape from the little present.

Callie took off the tape ceremoniously, trying to conceal her excitement. Still, her hands were a little shaky with eagerness to go ahead and rip off the paper. But she had promised to wait until they got to the house. She sighed, handed it to Becca for safekeeping (she knew she couldn't resist opening it) and looked to see how far it was to the big curve in the trail. She walked faster than she had all day. It was just a silly waiting game, of course, but it was fun.

Soon they stopped in the curve and Becca handed over the package, smiling. Callie removed the paper and squeezed her eyes shut and handed the box quickly to Becca, who laughed at this side of Callie she had never seen. It wasn't long before the sky opened up in front of them, and they entered a clearing. They saw the old home straight ahead.

First, the gift. Callie turned around to face Becca, lifted the lid, and started to look in, but then froze. Something was wrong. She reeled around to look at the house again. Someone had been there and had trashed the place. She stuffed the box in her backpack and ran ahead. Becca thought she had lost her mind.

"What about the present?" she yelled. *All that suspense and now she doesn't care?*

Callie shushed her with a wave of her hand and darted behind a tree. Becca joined her, wondering what was wrong. She watched Callie and copied her every move. *Is Callie trying to trick me again?* But Callie's face showed real concern this time.

Becca loved the thought of adventure. Things that were ordinary to other people were fodder for Becca's active mind. She didn't know whether to be scared or to be excited. Maybe she was a little of both. She never knew whether to run away or to jump right in when faced with a scary situation.

Callie moved slowly to the next tree, eyes fixed on the little house. *Is someone there? It's supposed to be empty. Supposed to be.* In the woods nearby, she saw an old, beat-up red truck, jacked up with a tire beside it on the ground. She stormed toward the house with a confused and frightened Becca following close behind. Even though she hadn't said a word to Becca, it was clear that Callie planned to march up to the door and throw everyone out.

This is getting way too weird! Becca thought, panic rising in her chest. "Wait, Callie—let's think about this."

Callie stopped, but it wasn't because of what Becca had said. A man in a dirty shirt and jeans walked down the old driveway toward the main road. He turned briefly and looked in their direction, and Callie grabbed Becca's arm and pulled her down low, hoping he had not seen them. He was tall and lanky with a scraggly beard and long, filthy hair. *It's that weird, nasty, skinny man from town!* She still remembered how odd she felt when she caught him staring at her. *What's he doing up here?* Callie wondered.

"Who's there?" he yelled. They waited silently to see what he would do. He craned his neck and listened, still looking in their direction. He slowly reached behind him for something that he had tucked in the back of his belt.

He had a gun!

Chapter 19

DISCOVERY

The man squinted his eyes and scanned the area. With the pistol in his hand, he looked like a gunfighter from the old west. The girls crouched low and waited. They tried to breathe as softly as possible, inhaling shallow breaths and pushing the air back out slowly, afraid to move. Callie prayed once again for help and protection. Becca was on the verge of panic.

They could barely make out the man's face in the distance. It was drawn and wrinkled, evidence of hard living and bitterness. His too-large jeans were worn and crumpled, held onto his skinny body by a dull, brown belt.

Becca wondered how long it had been since his last bath. Although it was impossible to detect body odor from such a distance, Becca imagined the smell of stale, sweaty clothes.

The standoff seemed to last forever—evil villain versus the unseen girls. After only a few minutes, he scratched his greasy head and shuffled down the overgrown dirt driveway. The girls waited until he was well out of sight before they stood and backed away.

"Let's go, Callie. This guy is dangerous and creepy," Becca said as she began to walk back the way they had come. Callie never responded. After about twenty-five steps, Becca looked around to find that Callie was on the side porch! Becca ran to her with short, tip-toey steps.

"What are you doing?" She whispered loudly. "Do you want to get us killed? There might be someone else in there!"

Callie ignored her. She peered through a dark window. Seeing nothing, she ducked out of view and slipped around to the back side of the house. *I have to know what I'm up against before I go in.* Fearlessly and angrily, she looked at the trashy yard, the tobacco-stained porch, and the general disrepair all around her.

She wished she had brought her grandfather's pistol. She would have stormed up to the man and given him a piece of her mind.

Jake's rescue team had recently passed by on their way to help an injured rock climber. He had warned Callie that the weeds were grown up around the outside, and he cautioned her to watch her step on the old floorboards and the rickety porch. He hadn't mentioned anyone being there. Callie was convinced that whoever it was had come after Jake's team was there. The more she saw, the angrier she became. She was determined to bring the interloper—or interlopers—to justice.

Becca wanted desperately to run away but instead ran to catch up with Callie. "Please, Callie. Let's go back and tell Jake so the police can take care of this." No response. She tried to appeal to Callie's logic. "We are already short on time. If we stay here much longer, we will be late and will both be in trouble." But nothing could deter Callie from her mission.

Becca tried another approach: "Look, you can stay and play SWAT team. I'm going back. I think I can find my way. The snake's long gone by now and I'll be careful. Don't worry about me." She tramped toward the woods, watching for Callie's reaction and hoping that her bluff would lure her away.

"Becca, stop," Callie said. "Come here for just a minute." Callie braced her back against the side of the house and slid down to a squatting position. "Fifteen minutes. That's all I'll take. We can jog a little through the lower trail to make up time. I need to see what's going on here. This was Mrs. Jennie's home. I can't believe that someone would just move in and destroy it. No one should be here. This guy's up to no good. I think he's alone. Just let me check. Fifteen minutes." Callie hoped that Becca would stay.

Becca sighed heavily, dreading the next fifteen minutes. "Okay. But please, only fifteen. This place is eerie."

With a nod and a smile, Callie got to her feet and continued her investigation. They circled around to the back door and mounted the cinder block step. Callie tested the doorknob. *Locked.* "Hoist me up so I can look in the window." Becca rolled her eyes but obediently joined Callie beneath the back window, bent one knee a little, and made a step for Callie by locking her hands together. Callie put one foot in Becca's hand and pulled herself up so she could see inside. She tested the window. Stuck. The front door was clearly visible to the driveway, but it was the only way.

They hastened to the front and crept up onto the front porch. The door was open just a little. Callie grasped the locked doorknob and pushed her way in.

A musty, damp smell filled their nostrils. Dust covered every surface and floated in the air around them. Callie walked in while Becca looked in vain for a light switch. She closed the door behind her, leaving them in a scary, cramped place. The girls turned on their flashlights.

There were only two garbage-laden rooms—a scantily furnished bedroom and the main room, with a table and one chair. All the so-called furniture was abused and barely usable. The wooden plank floor was uneven and damaged in places. The fireplace held only some old ashes and a few spider webs. Stains covered the chipped—formerly white—porcelain sink. A mound of oily rags practically hid the wood stove where yummy apple pies once baked and garden-fresh produce used to simmer. *It doesn't seem possible that Mrs. Jennie lived here just eight years ago,* Callie thought sadly.

A pungent smell rose from one corner of the room where a mountain of empty tuna fish, bean, and beer cans lay in a heap. Callie kicked one of the cans in anger, and a mouse scurried out. She turned aside and saw the table where she had enjoyed meals as a little girl. An overflowing ashtray had replaced Mrs. Jennie's fresh flower centerpiece. A green lighter, an empty beer can, and some newspaper clippings replaced the dainty handmade placemats that Callie just barely remembered. The only thing that kept her from running away from the place and its senseless destruction was her determination to make the man pay for what he had done.

The girls separated to investigate, looking for more information about Mr. Creepy—his new nickname. Becca's fear subsided as her writer's curiosity took over. She began to read over the newspaper clippings—ripped out, not cut out—to see how they were connected.

"Callie, these papers are from different dates. Listen."

"June 12, 1978. ROBBERY IN HALO NOTCH HISTORIC DISTRICT."

"There's a historic district?" She read on...

"The home of Mrs. Herbert Longfellow, 118 Main Street, was robbed last night. Money, silver, and valuable heirloom jewelry, with an estimated value of over $100,000, disappeared while the resident slept. The silver and jewelry were part of a dowry brought to America from England over 100 years ago. Mrs.

Longfellow had no insurance on the stolen property. Anyone with information regarding this burglary is encouraged to contact the sheriff's office."

"Here's one from June 17, 1978..." She continued.

"ANNUAL JULY 4TH PICNIC ANNOUNCED... ROOSTER LAYS AN EGG... NEW HARDWARE STORE OPENS...Here's something else..."

"LONGFELLOW HOUSEKEEPER ARRESTED. Valerie Hogg, housekeeper to Mrs. Amelia Longfellow, is under arrest for assault and battery against Longfellow. Mrs. Longfellow said that Hogg had been threatening her ever since she caught her stealing money from the cookie jar and accused her of the burglary. At 6 p.m. on June 16th, Mrs. Longfellow said that she felt afraid that Ms. Hogg might hurt her, so she tried to call the police. Mrs. Hogg allegedly entered the room, tore the phone out of the wall and pushed Mrs. Longfellow into the glass curio cabinet. The victim sustained many injuries from the fall and was treated at her home. The housekeeper was apprehended a few blocks away from the mansion. Hogg is in police custody for additional questioning in light of this new development."

"Here's another one. June 19, 1978..."

"HOGG AT LARGE. Hogg is now the prime suspect in the June 12th robbery at the Longfellow House. She escaped from the police while enroute to the police station on June 16th. Mrs. Longfellow reported that her late husband's 0.38 caliber pistol is missing from the sugar jar in the dining room. Ms. Hogg is armed and dangerous. Contact the Sheriff's Office if you have any information about Hogg's whereabouts. Police are reminding residents to be on the lookout for the suspect and to keep their doors locked."

"That's strange. Three articles about the robbery. Why would he keep them? Maybe he knows Hogg. Maybe it's just a coincidence," Becca said.

"Or maybe because he knows she's innocent!" Callie exclaimed.

Becca continued to scan the paper, unimpressed by Callie's theory. She heard a loud noise behind her and turned to see Callie pulling up a board on the floor.

"What are you doing?" Becca yelled.

Callie ripped the board away excitedly. "I found it! It's here! He's the real thief! Look!" She pulled out a blue canvas duffle bag and unzipped it, revealing a huge collection of silverware. "Don't you see? He's saving those papers because he's keeping an eye on what's happening about the case."

"But why would he stay here? Surely, he would take it and run..." Becca said, perplexed.

"The cash. Here. In this fat envelope. Ooh...the jewelry. Look at this!" She held up an old shoebox and opened it so that Becca could see the beautiful emerald necklace, the diamond-encrusted broach, the elegant ruby earrings with matching charm, and a huge collection of various gold items inside. There was even an old, teardrop shaped hatpin, covered with sparkling gems of every color. Becca's mouth dropped open. She moved toward the box to get a closer look, then stopped suddenly and ran over to the window to make sure Mr. Creepy wasn't coming back. Seeing nothing, she ran back over to Callie to look at the treasure.

"There must be over $10,000 here. I knew old lady Longfellow was filthy rich!" Callie said while counting the cash.

"But why would he stay here?" Becca mused again. "It doesn't make sense. If I had stolen all this, I'd be several states away by now—or even in Mexico or something. It just doesn't make sense."

"If he did do this—which it's pretty obvious he did—he's been up here for quite a while. He must have gotten here just a few days after Jake's team came by. How was he able to keep from getting caught?" Callie added.

Becca nervously went back to the window to check for Mr. Creepy's return. Still nothing. Both girls racked their brains, trying to figure out why he was still in the county, only about ten miles from the crime scene. Callie put the money back in the envelope ($12,347 to be exact), stood, and began to pace. Back and forth from the back window to the hole in the floor. Back and forth. Back and forth. Then, she joined Becca at the front window, not sure what to do next.

Becca left Callie at the front window to do some pacing of her own, walking in a big pattern around the inside perimeter of the house. She looked out every window she passed—two in the front room and two in the bedroom—during each lap. "That's it!" she exclaimed from the bedroom.

Callie ran to the back room to find Becca pointing outside. "The truck! It's broken down, and he can't leave yet. If he steals a vehicle, it will cause the police to track him. If he's trying to stay out of view, he wouldn't just walk into Al's Auto Supply to get something to fix it, especially if the money could be traced somehow."

"But he did go to Al's Auto Supply," Callie corrected. "I saw him there."

"Then he must be getting desperate," Becca replied. "And desperate criminals are dangerous."

"Agreed. We've got to tell the police."

"Did you tell somebody?" Becca asked.

"Tell somebody what?"

"That you saw a strange man in town at the auto store. I mean, doesn't everybody know everybody here?"

"No, that was a...bad day. I mean, a lot happened that day," Callie replied. The memory of the day she met Becca played vividly in her mind. "I guess I forgot. Besides, he didn't do anything. He just walked by and stared at me when I was counting some money."

"I wonder how he got to town. Maybe he hitchhiked?" Becca suggested.

"Maybe." Callie searched her thoughts for any other recollection of him but couldn't think of anything except for how familiar he looked somehow. "Let's take the stuff he stole with us and turn it over to the police." She grabbed her backpack and prepared to stuff it full of loot. "I'll take the silver because it's the heaviest. You grab the rest."

"No—wait. If he does catch us, he'll kill us. Let's just take a few things...maybe the emerald necklace, a $1,000 bill, and a piece of silver. That way, he might not miss it and we can still prove to the police that we've found the real thief," Becca said, remembering for the first time to look at her watch. 1:00 p.m. They had been there for over an hour. There was no way they could get back home in time. "Let's get out of here. We are out of time."

Callie picked out the three items. She had to admit it was a great idea. While she was repacking the envelope, the shoebox, and the duffle bag back into the floor space, she heard Becca gasp in alarm.

"He's coming! Callie! Hurry!" Callie shoved the three confiscated items in her backpack and pushed the floorboard down with her foot.

"This way—the back door," Callie whispered. But the door was stuck from the inside.

"Hurry. Pull harder," Becca said desperately, all the while keeping her eyes on the front door.

"It's no use. It won't budge," Callie said, her mind grasping for options.

"He's on the porch," Becca whispered frantically.

"Come on," Callie said, grabbing Becca's hand and dragging her into the back room. Breathlessly the girls hunkered in a corner near the window facing the front of the house.

The front door swung open. The man lumbered in, heavy boots on the creaking floor. The girls heard him put something hard on the table and take a few steps toward them. They looked at each other wide-eyed. Did he know they were there? He stopped, and they heard him lift the floorboard. Callie closed her eyes, trying to remember the arrangement of the bag, the envelope, and the shoebox when she first found them. Had she put everything back the way it was?

"What the—?" the man said with a hoarse growl. There was a thud on the floor, then the unzipping of something—the duffle. The man was checking to see if everything was there!

Becca stared at the door. Callie, however, looked straight at the floor in front of her. She searched her memory, trying to recall step by step what she did when she found the stash. *Okay. I saw the duffle bag first and then pulled out the box. Was the envelope inside the box or on top of it? I saw the cash second but counted it last. That's right. Box on bottom, envelope on that, duffle on top. Oh, no.* It hit her. *I put the envelope in the box before putting it back.*

The man mumbled. "Money's gone. The envelope was right here this morning." The girls heard him shuffling and digging around in the sub-floor space. "Oh, here it is—what's it doing in the box?" After that, mumbling again. The only words they could understand were the curse words he sprinkled throughout his whole conversation with himself.

"What?" Becca shaped with her mouth, questioning Callie. Callie just shook her head, agitated at herself for being so careless.

"Later," she mouthed back, not able to explain it just then. She motioned to the window just a few feet away.

Becca nodded. Callie held up her hand for Becca to wait there while she stood slowly to her feet. Halfway to the standing position, Callie's knee popped loudly. She froze. Had he heard her? Four frightened eyes focused on the doorway, waiting for the man to burst through at any moment. They could hear him murmuring and moving again. They heard the man pull out the chair and sit down; he picked something up from the table and the girls heard a click. Callie recognized the next sound when some bullets dropped on the table. He was loading his gun! She stood completely and crept toward the window, trying not to step too hard on the creaky floors. She tugged at the sash to open it and found that it would move just a little when she jiggled it. Becca came to help, and they were able to open it together. Callie held Becca's backpack and helped her over the rough windowsill and out the window. Then, Callie passed both backpacks to Becca and hopped out the window herself. Donning the backpacks, they prepared to run.

All at once, they heard the man yell out, "Who's there!?"

He stomped into the bedroom, cursing as he went. Just as they rounded the corner to the side of the house, he stuck his head out the window and caught a glimpse of Becca's backpack. Immediately, he ran through the house and out the front door in their direction, bellowing threats. He would surely catch them if they ran out into the open area around the house.

The girls could hear Mr. Creepy barreling toward them. They had no time to lose. In a split second, Callie grabbed Becca's arm, and they dove into the spidery darkness under the house.

Chapter 20
SALTY PEANUTS

It wasn't the first time that day that the girls were in a dark, closed-in space. Just a couple hours earlier, they were exploring the mystical underworld of the cave. The ceiling in the largest space of the cave was well above their heads. The largest space of the house's coffin-like underbelly, however, was merely inches above them.

They held their breath, listening to the man's angry tirade, watching his legs run all the way around the house. He stopped and retraced his steps once or twice, apparently thinking he had heard something. Callie and Becca crawled backwards on elbows and knees toward the middle of the smothering darkness, hoping to avoid discovery if he did look underneath.

"I'll get you—don't you worry!" he sputtered. He circled once more. He took a few steps, stopped, and growled.

They began to check out their hiding place. Stacks of river rock held up the house. Clumps of weeds lined the outer edge. Cobwebs seemed to knit the boards of the foundation together in places, with grayish mold looking like a wood patch in others. Leaves and debris from earlier storms and heavy winds littered the uneven ground all around them. Stale, dusty air hung over their heads, invading their noses.

Becca felt a sneeze growing but tried not to think about it. She blew a little air out through her nostrils to try to remove the tickle. The man stepped closer. Instinctively, they backed up a little more. Becca's nose felt like it was full of pepper. She lowered her elbow and pinched her nose with her thumb and finger, holding it tightly and looking over at Callie in desperation, eyes watering.

Callie's eyes warned Becca to be quiet. Becca nodded, redoubling her effort to squelch the unwanted sneeze. They heard the scuff of the man's shoes at the same time and looked over to the place they had jumped under the house. He was standing right in front of them, facing the woods.

Callie nodded to Becca, motioning with her head to move toward the other side of the house. Becca agreed. Maybe they could ease their way out from under the house and sneak off into the shelter of the woods. They labored backwards over the rough terrain. Becca's urge to sneeze subsided, so she quit pinching her nose and put all her effort into her awkward crawl.

The man stayed planted in the same spot, mumbling to himself and cursing. Their escape progressed nicely—until a body-shaking sneeze exploded from Becca's nose. The force of the sneeze hurled her head upward against a board. "Ow!" she yelled automatically. Tears of pain welled up in her eyes as an ever-darkening cloud of sparkles threatened to overtake her consciousness. Callie caught Becca's head to protect it from hitting the ground.

When Callie checked on Mr. Creepy again, she saw what she already suspected: they had been discovered! His evil eyes met hers in a moment of suspended time. In that split second of paralyzing fear, Callie's blood ran cold. *We have to get out of here NOW!* she told herself, willing her body to move.

"You little brats!" he shrieked. "I know you've been messing with my stuff. Get out here right now or I'm coming in after you." Curse words. He tried to squeeze up under the house after them but wouldn't fit. He was a furious volcano about to explode! "Come out right now, or I'll get something that will make you get out or stay there dead forever!" In a flash, he was gone.

Becca held her head and sighed, "I'm sorry, Callie. I'm so sorry. I couldn't help it. I thought the sneeze was gone. Now we're caught, and he's going to kill us."

"Stop it. We've gotta move now before he gets back. Pull yourself together. We have to make a run for it," Callie ordered. They gained momentum as they crawled backwards. The sound of their predator running in the room above them motivated them to hustle.

"He's gone to get his gun. Move!" Callie barked. Becca doubled her effort while trying to ignore her aching head. They both heard the front door slam.

Threats of destruction billowed out of the man as he struggled to reach them under the house. He fired his pistol. The bullet whizzed between the girls just as they reached the edge of the house. They squinted in the bright light and ran blindly toward the woods, hoping not to fall over anything.

The man laughed maniacally as he rounded the house after them. "You can't get away from me! I ain't afraid to put bullets into both your pretty little heads!" He fired again at them as they entered the woods, missing them by at least 10 feet.

"At least he's a horrible shot," Callie yelled to Becca.

"I hope he stays that way," Becca replied weakly, her head pounding with every step.

The man was about a basketball court's distance from them, still in hot pursuit. They noticed that he didn't yell and cuss as much when he ran.

The girls were unable to think of an earth-shattering plan, so they ran forward, focused only on their getaway. At the first turn, Callie said, "This way," and she and Becca cut quickly to the left. They headed down a steep embankment—a shortcut to chop off the big curve from the winding main trail. She hoped that the man hadn't seen them.

"How's your head?" she called to Becca.

"Horrible, but I'm still here," Becca replied, surprised that she could keep up with Callie.

Callie's hunch was wrong. A loud **CRACK** assured her of his continued pursuit. The sound echoed through the mountains as the bullet buzzed past their heads, ricocheting off a large boulder and into the woods. The girls pushed ahead, thinking that they were covering more ground than their tracker. They didn't even look back to see where he was. When they reached the trail again, he was waiting for them.

"Now I've got you," he laughed between huffing and puffing. "Hands on your heads," he barked.

Becca and Callie looked at each other and then at his gun. "Do it!" he thundered.

They slowly raised their hands and placed them on their heads.

"Now, I don't know what you seen back there." Curse words. He scoffed, words hissing from his foul mouth. "It don't matter no how. You're too young for anyone to believe you anyway."

Their hearts were beating fast in their chests as they faced the seeming end of their young lives. They each tried to formulate a plan for escape, longing to communicate with each other.

Mr. Creepy circled them slowly. He smirked as he crossed in front of their faces, close enough for them to smell his sickening body odor and the rancid breath. He spoke again, this time low and slow, "Empty your backpacks. You first." He pointed his gun at Callie. Becca stood quietly, mentally taking inventory of her pack, thinking of anything she could use as a weapon. Callie kept defiant eye contact with the man as she slowly removed her backpack and pulled it in front of her. *Those awful, piercing hazel eyes! Did he know that she had the samples of the loot?* She wondered what to do as she unzipped the pack. What could she use to distract him? She felt around in the pack for something to throw at him.

"Hurry, girl!" he said, annoyed. "I'm losing my patience!"

Just then, Callie's fingers touched the can of salty peanuts that Grandpa insisted she bring with them. She glanced over at Becca, trying to tell her without words to watch for the cue.

The man took a threatening step toward Callie. Callie flipped off the lid of the peanut can with one hand and held it by the can's bottom. He reached to grab her, but she flung the salty peanuts into his eyes. He recoiled, yelling, trying to wipe the salt out of his eyes while still grasping the gun in one hand. Becca put her right boot on his rear end and pushed hard, causing him to tumble down the embankment. Callie thrust the mostly empty can back in her backpack and zipped it up.

"Great job! Let's get out of here!" she shouted to Becca, with growing respect for her new friend.

Becca was impressed, too—not only because of their teamwork, but also because of how smart Callie was. *Boy, was I wrong about her.*

There was no time to stand around congratulating each other. Mr. Creepy was already starting to get up, punctuating the air with his vulgar words. Off they went as fast as their legs could carry them. He shot again. Missed.

"This guy doesn't give up!" Becca yelled, trying to catch her breath. "Can't we hide somewhere?"

"Not until we get far enough ahead. Maybe over the hill," Callie huffed.

The trail grew steeper as they climbed the hill on the far side of the hollow. Mr. Creepy lagged behind.

Still not out of danger, they wondered if they were ever going to feel like they had truly lost him. "We're not too far from the falls. Do you think you can make it?" Callie called back.

"I'll try, but I'm out of shape. My mind is all for it, but my body wants to rest," Becca said, exhausted.

"Do not give up or we will be killed." Callie stressed every word.

"I'm with you," Becca replied.

They topped the hill and started down the other side. They had no idea where Mr. Creepy was. They couldn't hear him yelling anymore.

"Maybe he'll give up and go back," Becca said between breaths.

"That's what I'm praying for."

The sound of the falls grew louder. Callie stopped just long enough to hold back a limb for Becca to pass through ahead of her. All at once, Callie and Becca heard a muffled shot, but the roaring of the falls distorted the sound. It seemed miles away. Becca ran ahead, but Callie paused for a moment longer. She had a strange sensation she'd never felt before. It was as if she had received a quick shove on her right shoulder. In fact, she turned around to see if Mr. Creepy had actually pushed her, but he was nowhere to be seen. She staggered forward a little, then picked up steam and trotted clumsily ahead.

When Becca realized that Callie wasn't right behind her, she stopped, too. Suddenly she spotted the enemy and yelled to Callie, "He's up there above you climbing on the rocks! Callie, come on! It's our chance to get away!"

But Callie didn't move. She seemed dazed.

"What's wrong? Hurry. We have to go!" Becca implored. Then she saw it. A dot of dark red the size of a quarter appeared on Callie's shirt near the shoulder. Slowly, it spread, bigger and bigger. In shock, Callie didn't feel it.

"Callie, he shot you!" Becca said, running to help her friend.

She could imagine Callie falling forward in slow motion to her death with a haunting, dazed look on her face—just like in the movies.

Callie put her hand over the blood. "I don't feel anything," she said softly.

Becca jumped into action. She looked up at Mr. Creepy who had lost his footing and slipped on the steep rocks. Rattled by the fall, he was struggling to stand.

"We MUST reach the waterfall, Callie. C'mon. You can do it." Becca pulled her own jacket from around her waist. She folded it up tightly and placed it over Callie's wound. She used the backpack strap to hold the jacket in place and to apply pressure. She hoped it would work. She didn't allow herself to think beyond getting to the waterfall.

Mr. Creepy yelled something as he scooted down the rocks toward the girls. Soon, he was back on his feet, shaking his head. Becca was still looking back at him when she accidentally placed her hand on Callie's injured shoulder. Callie's shirt felt wet. Becca pulled back her hand and looked at it. Her red-tinged fingers were damp with Callie's blood.

"It's really bleeding, Callie. We've got to move," Becca urged.

Callie couldn't get her thoughts together. All she wanted was to be home. She knew she was hurt, but she didn't feel anything. The violent man who chased them, the eye contact he had with her while they were under the house, the bullet wound in her shoulder, the threatening rain clouds, and the fact that it was already time for them to be back—all these things floated in her head, disconnected. She knew that she had to rely completely on Becca until she could think again. Her knees buckled under her.

"No! C'mon Callie. You have to stand up and walk. We're almost to the falls. We can do it together. There's no time to waste." Becca coached Callie back to standing position and they began to move slowly toward their hiding place. The falls were just out of sight because of the trees, but its sustained whooshing sound assured them of its presence.

Callie leaned against Becca lightly, trying to do as much on her own as she could. The burning pain that crept into her consciousness seemed somewhere off in the distance. They limped forward in an ever-growing rhythm, fueled by the knowledge that Mr. Creepy could catch them at any moment. Becca looked back often but didn't know what she'd do if she saw him. He was a stealthy hunter, and they were his prey.

Sparse, heavy raindrops began to plop on them, making their journey to the falls even more uncomfortable.

Callie's fuzzy mind gradually began to clear. The sequence of events leading up to the last gunshot made sense. She sighed deeply, relieved to have regained her senses. But then suddenly, she felt pain. Harsh, raw agony took over the whole right side of her upper body. The fierce burning sensation made her cry out. She stopped and began to wrestle with the makeshift bandage (Becca's jacket) and the backpack with her left hand.

"Get it off!" she yelled, frantic with pain. "Hurry!" she yelled when Becca didn't respond at once.

Becca thought that the blood would gush out even more if she removed the jacket and backpack. "Leave it," she said firmly.

"Get it off NOW!" Callie ordered.

"No. LEAVE IT," she screamed at Callie for the first time ever. Tears kept Becca from seeing well as she pulled Callie's left arm away from the backpack. She wasn't mad like she sounded, but she couldn't let Callie hurt herself.

"It hurts!" Callie retorted. The pain was the only thing on her mind.

"Look. I may not be an expert, but it seems to me that we have to keep some kind of pressure on the wound. We can't stay here out in the open. We have to move on," she said sadly, wishing she could do something to ease Callie's misery. Becca removed the jacket from Callie's waist and made it into a sling. She placed it carefully over Callie's head so it could rest on her left shoulder to immobilize her right arm. Callie tried not to cry, but tears rolled continuously down her cheeks despite her efforts. She concentrated on calming herself so they could move forward. It was their only chance.

Mr. Creepy had heard Callie's cry. Focusing on the sound, he hastened his speed. However, the volume of the waterfall and the coming rainstorm made it almost impossible to locate them by sound alone.

Becca led the way, practically dragging the injured girl behind her. She felt responsible for their very lives. *I wish Jake were here. He'd know exactly what to do.* She wanted Jake beside her now more than ever. It never occurred to her to wish for her mother, the doctor. Her Prize-Winning Essay Contest even left her mind. Callie's safety was her only goal at that moment. Becca wasn't about to stop moving forward, even when Callie winced in her tense grip. *This is the second time today that I've had to do something difficult on my own.*

Callie followed blindly forward, not seeing anything but her own feet and the back of Becca. Even though she felt like she might pass out, she trudged onward. She wanted to pull her good arm away from Becca's stronghold but didn't have the strength.

It couldn't be much farther to the falls. The sound of the water seemed deafening. Raindrops smacked the leaves and collapsed onto the ground. It tickled their scalps as it fell onto their hair, dousing it more thoroughly with each drop. Suddenly, the loud shooshing downpour of a summer storm filled the woods behind them, catching up with their slow pace. It overtook them, soaking them completely and limiting their visibility. Mr. Creepy could have been right behind them, and they wouldn't have known it.

Finally, the girls reached the edge of the swimming hole at the falls. Since their feet were already wet from walking in the rain, they decided to wade through the shallows and avoid the rock path below the snake's ledge. Icy water covered their ankles as they waded clumsily over submerged rocks. It wasn't the best of circumstances. Becca helped Callie to go in front of her. Callie tried to stop and look at the snake's ledge, but Becca nudged her forward. The cold water, the rain, and the urgency of the situation helped her to keep her mind off her shoulder for the moment.

Then, Becca caught a glimpse of the soaked, perplexed criminal at the edge of the woods. Tension and fatigue marked his sallow face. He flopped back his stringy, sopping hair with one hand while tucking his gun in his belt with the other. Stepping toward the river, he scanned the falls with his cold eyes—too late to see Callie and Becca disappear behind the waterfall.

After a moment, Becca peeked out to see if she could see him. There he was, standing on the rocks beside the water! "He's by the water," she whispered to Callie.

"What's he doing?" Callie said weakly.

"He's looking at his pistol...checking the chamber for bullets...feeling his pockets..." Becca reported the play by play.

"Is the gun empty?"

"I'm not sure. Maybe he's just filling it up all the way," Becca said without taking her eyes off him.

"Shot one—under the house. Two—the hill. Three—the shortcut. Four—after the kick. Five—at me. Is that right? Did he shoot another time?" Callie's head was swimming. She couldn't remember for sure how many shots he had fired.

Becca joined Callie's line of thinking. "The pistol would hold six bullets, but we don't know if it was full when he grabbed it to follow us. Of course, it sounded like he was reloading while we were in the bedroom. If he has one or two more bullets, I guarantee he's not afraid to use them." Becca looked at Callie for only a second. When she peeked back out of their hiding place, Mr. Creepy was gone.

"What's he doing?" Callie asked.

"I don't see him," Becca said with concern. Suddenly she felt like he was watching her, so she backed away from the edge. "He could be anywhere. He could be coming toward us around the rocks right now." Becca was afraid. *We're trapped in here with no escape. I wonder how long it would take the rescuers to find our dead bodies behind a waterfall?* "What do we do?" she asked herself aloud.

"We wait," Callie said as she reached for a rock.

Chapter 21
FOOTPRINTS

The girls waited nervously in their rocky hideout. Callie sat like a statue, holding a softball-sized rock in her left hand. The look in her eyes was one of intense agony. Feverishly struggling to remain conscious, she tried to concentrate on the task at hand. Becca gathered a few softball-sized rocks too and hid along the wall next to the entrance. The plan was to pummel rocks at the man from both directions if he stepped behind the falls. It was their only defense.

They waited in silence, ready to pounce. Hoping they wouldn't have to. If only they knew where he was! Callie fought to keep her eyes open, yearning instead to squeeze them tightly shut to block out everything. It felt like a red-hot poker was stabbing her in her shoulder blade.

Becca's eyes darted from Callie to the entryway every few seconds. She knew in her heart that her brave but injured friend was virtually defenseless. *It's up to me to be strong for both of us.* She hadn't really noticed how pretty Callie was until then. She wasn't glamorous like a model, though. Her beauty was simpler and more natural. Her thick hair was shiny and healthy. Her skin was clear and tan. Full eyelashes lined her big, golden eyes. Her teeth weren't perfectly straight, but her smile was genuine and disarming.

Becca envied Callie's freedom from peer pressure to be physically perfect. It was probably in Callie's school the same as in Becca's, but it didn't seem to faze the mountain girl at all. She especially admired Callie's independence. *Callie's used to watching out for herself. I'll bet she would have known exactly what to do if I had been hurt.* She remembered what Callie's Grandpa had said when she asked him about a bear. "Just follow Callie. She knows what to do." *My parents wouldn't trust me to know anything—I've never had to take care of myself.* For a moment, she wished she could trade places with Callie for a while. *Why am I thinking about this now?*

At that very moment, however, Callie's face looked old and strained. Her eyes were red and puffy; they didn't sparkle as they had earlier in the day. She pursed her lips tightly to control their quivering. Dried blood stained the fingers that gripped the rock. She held her other hand in a limp fist, unwilling—or unable—to move her injured arm without searing agony.

Becca checked her watch. They should have been home over an hour ago. She wondered how long it would take Jake and the others to figure out that something was wrong. A pins-and-needles sensation in her feet told her that she had been squatting down too long. She looked at the ground. The pebbles beneath her feet were in a shallow bed of water. Sitting down wasn't an option, so she stood slowly and wiggled her toes until they felt normal again. She eased carefully over to the hideout's doorway to check for Mr. Creepy and felt like a secret agent as she slid stealthily along the rock face. Terror mixed with intense curiosity. It was a dangerous situation.

Soon she grew impatient. Becca peeked around the corner outside but saw no sign of the enemy. She was ready for him to grab her, but nothing happened. The suspense was horrible. She was just a little tempted to run out with her hands up so he would shoot her and just get it over with. Instead, she backed up underneath the falls to give her report to Callie.

Inside, she found Callie, hunched over with her head on her knees, rock on the ground in front of her. Becca ran to her and knelt. "Callie, are you okay?" she whispered in alarm. *Surely, she isn't dead! Maybe she's just passed out.*

"Callie, can you hear me?"

Callie raised her head. "Yes... I take it he wasn't there," she said softly.

"I didn't see him. He could still be waiting for us, though. It's still pouring rain." Becca was discouraged, overwhelmed.

Callie tried awkwardly to get up without using her right arm. She grimaced. "We can't stay here—we have to ..."

Becca reached to support Callie's arm but grabbed it too hard. Callie flinched, "Ow!"

"Sorry." Becca helped Callie to stand. "I know. We have to try to get out of here." She mentally retraced their steps from the cave to the falls and wondered if they could make it back. There were some big rocks to travel around and a hill to climb; she wasn't sure they could do it. Not only would it be difficult for Callie to do physically, but they also risked being discovered.

"I guess it's crazy to think we could make it home. Anyway, we might run right into that nasty bear while we are trying to get away from Creepy," Becca said, discouraged.

"We have to try," Callie managed to answer.

It was time for Becca to move into action. "Here goes," she said aloud. Inside her heart, though, she was angry: *Where's your God now, Jake?* She removed her own backpack and pulled out her water bottle. She found Callie's also and filled both with the flowing water from the falls. She dug a hair band out of her backpack and pulled Callie's hair out of her eyes for her. She felt as though she should retrieve her waterproof jacket from Callie's shoulder and replace it with something better. The cleanest thing she had was the inside of her outer shirt. It wasn't sweaty from her body nor dirty from exposure. She removed it and folded it in a tight bundle.

Becca looked Callie straight in the eye. "I'm going to put this over the bullet hole." Callie nodded, eyes full of fear. Becca wondered what would happen when she removed the wadded up jacket from the bloody wound. *Will the blood squirt out everywhere? Will Callie pass out? Should she be sitting down?* She proceeded slowly as if she were trying to detonate a bomb.

Becca didn't really want to look at the wound. *You can do this,* she told herself. She gently stretched the neck hole in Callie's shirt to reveal the bullet's entry point. The dime-sized hole looked like a blob of dark red gel. She wondered how Mr. Creepy could have shot the front of her shoulder while he was behind her. *Maybe Callie turned...*she thought. The wound had stopped bleeding and started juicing a little. Becca was surprised at herself for not getting sick. *It must have happened when Callie pulled back the limb for me to pass. If she hadn't stopped to help me, this bullet might have missed her.*

Callie's blood-smeared shirt was a mess. The slick jacket hadn't absorbed any of the blood but had spread it all over the place. Becca shook out the jacket and rinsed off her hands. She placed the folded-up t-shirt on the hole and told Callie to hold it in place. *If Mr. Creepy walks in now, he'll just have to wait until I'm done,* she fumed.

Callie watched, fascinated by the appearance of the wound. She was thankful for anything that would distract her from the horrible pain. Becca used Callie's backpack to make a sling by putting it on the front of Callie's chest. Tears rolled down Callie's cheeks once more as she watched Becca cinch the straps tight. But she didn't complain. It made her arm feel secure and relieved some pressure. She looked like a one-armed person in a bulletproof vest. *If only it was really bulletproof!* Callie thought helplessly.

Becca knelt and quickly placed everything else in her backpack except Callie's pocketknife, which she slipped into her own pocket. *This might come in handy.*

The two girls stepped through the hanging vines into the pouring rain on the cave side of the falls. They looked around but didn't see anyone. Becca felt as if they were walking the plank off a huge pirate ship—with ravenous sharks waiting for them. It was almost impossible to step, look, help Callie, hold on, watch for Mr. Creepy, step, look, look...

After slipping a couple times, Callie said, "Keep moving. Don't look back. We might fall." Sweat beaded on her upper lip and forehead from the effort of climbing over the rocks. She thought about the teenager who had died near a waterfall last summer because he had trusted a rock that turned out to be very slick. She didn't mention the story to Becca.

They finally reached the edge of the water and hid behind a tree. Callie leaned her head against the trunk and closed her eyes. Becca carefully scanned the area for any sign of their pursuer. Nothing. She didn't trust him at all. He had already shown them how far he was willing to go to stop them.

The pelting rain shower had moved on a little, leaving a slow, soaking rain in its wake.

I wish I could magically send her to the hospital, Becca thought helplessly as she kept an eye on the very pale Callie. She noticed that Callie was clenching her teeth tightly.

"Try to relax a little, Callie...if you can. Maybe take a deep breath," Becca suggested.

A searing pain shot through Callie's body when she tried to inhale deeply. "Ow," she exhaled. "Can't." She quickly resumed her shallow breathing.

Becca surveyed the trail that led back toward home. *It was so easy to skip down! Going back up is going to be hard for Callie. Maybe even impossible.* She noticed a weeping willow tree growing just a few feet away and remembered that Jake had told her about how people used to use its bark as a painkiller. She still thought it was funny that it was the source of aspirin.

"I'm going to the tree over there to get some willow bark," she said to Callie. "Maybe it will help the pain if you chew on it."

Callie nodded, familiar with the old remedy. "Careful. Hurry," she said between breaths.

Becca looked high and low for Mr. Creepy. There was no sign of him anywhere. She tiptoed carefully over to the willow and cut off as much bark as she could fit in her pockets.

"Here. Try this," Becca said when she returned. She brushed off a thin slice of bark and handed it to Callie. Willing to try anything to relieve the pain, Callie chewed diligently.

"What does it taste like?" Becca asked.

"Bark," Callie said, shivering at the bitter taste but keeping it in her mouth.

"Do you want to try to make it up the hill?"

"No. You go. Leave me some water." Callie tried to lower herself to the ground. She winced in pain. "I'll be fine." She sounded more confident than she felt.

Becca didn't want to leave. She started to argue but was interrupted by a loud gunshot.

"Above the falls," Callie said.

"Do you think he saw us?"

"He saw something—or thought he did," Callie whispered. They heard him yelling out curses and knew he was coming closer.

"We'll hide in the cave," Callie said.

Becca didn't even want to talk about it. Even the thought of hiding in that scary dark cave made her tremble. Besides, she couldn't imagine Callie climbing up that hill.

The curses came closer. There was no time to argue. The frightened, solemn girls began the slow journey to the cave, leaving muddy footprints behind them. Becca grabbed a leafy branch and tried to scribble the prints away as best as she could, but it was impossible to scratch over the mud-sucked imprints of their shoes.

"Walk on the side," Callie said. "We can't stop."

The walk to the fork in the trail seemed to take forever. Callie settled into a resolute march, driven by sheer adrenalin. She concentrated on the slow rhythm of her climb. Left...right...left...right. Nothing mattered except reaching that cave.

Becca's feet and legs hurt terribly from wearing the new boots. She longed to take them off. Longed to rest. Longed to look up and see Jake coming toward them. But he wasn't there. She dreaded the man behind her and dreaded the cave in front of her. It was the first time in her life that she felt totally lost. There was nothing to do except move forward.

During that one day, they chatted, shared deep thoughts, explored together, and faced a deadly enemy. Two contracted companions left Callie's house that morning hoping for fun and adventure. Now they were a team of two friends, bound together by the struggle to survive.

Finally, Callie spoke. "See him?"

Becca turned around to look for Mr. Creepy but saw nothing. "Nope. Wherever he is, I'm just glad he's as soaked and miserable as we are," she replied, breathless from the climb. "Do wet guns still work?"

Callie knew that Becca wanted her to say, "No, of course not. Wet guns don't work." The truth of the matter, however, was that Callie didn't know, so she just said, "Depends."

"I hate to mention it, Callie, but I don't think your prayers are working," Becca said at last. She wondered if saying a few words to an invisible God ever made any difference at all.

"Jesus won't leave us. He promised. He ain't a liar," Callie said between breaths.

"You have a gunshot wound, Callie. Your arm is probably broken—maybe in several places. We are running from a murderous psycho. It's raining. We have almost nothing to eat. My legs and feet are screaming for rest, and it feels like we'll never get home. Oh, yes, and with our luck, the cranky campground bear will be waiting for us at the top of the hill. Maybe I'll tell God all of that!" The words tumbled angrily out of Becca's mouth.

"You should. He can handle it." Callie's words were calm and sure. "It's not over yet. We're not dead. God's in control." She stopped briefly to catch her breath and to listen for footsteps. "Come on," she said at last. "The cave awaits." And she resumed her climb up the trail.

"Not the cave. Callie. Callie."

Callie kept walking.

"You are so stubborn," Becca said, exasperated. Deep down inside, she found comfort in her friend's confidence and hoped she was right about her faith.

Soon they came to the fork in the trail and saw School Bus rock. It was the moment of decision: should they try to stay ahead of Mr. Creepy and head toward home, or should they stop and hide in the cave? It was already 7:00 p.m. They should have been home hours ago. Although they technically had about two more hours of daylight left, the heavy cloud cover above them made it dark and dreary.

Suddenly, another gunshot rang out across the valley below, making the decision for them.

Chapter 22

HUCKLEBERRY

"This guy never quits!" Becca exclaimed. "How far away do you think he is?"

"Hard to say...sounds echo in the mountains," Callie said as she marched toward the cave. She spit out the bark and wiped her mouth. "Yuck."

"Can you make it alone? I wanna walk on the trail toward your house a little way and leave a fake trail for Mr. Creepy." Becca said.

"Hurry," Callie whispered. "I...I need your help." Callie's statement surprised them both. They paused for an awkward second before turning away.

"I'll be back. Soon," Becca reassured her. Then she disappeared around School Bus Rock.

Callie's arm throbbed hard, distracting her thoughts. She forced herself to concentrate on moving forward once again. *Check to see if the bear's been here,* she reminded herself. She investigated the area in front the cave's entrance for paw prints, scat, freshly broken limbs, or garbage. No stinky body odor smell. There was no visible evidence of the presence of a bear. She remembered the strange sound she heard in the cave earlier in the day and wondered if a bear was hiding in the darkness. She peered into the gaping blackness beyond the cave's entrance. *I wish I could flip a light switch on in there.*

Her own words came to her mind: "God can handle it. It's not over yet. We're not dead. God's in control." A twinge of doubt shot through her mind. She was tired, hurting, and hungry. Even her faith felt tired. She did what Jake had told her. She talked to Jesus. "Jesus, I don't like this one little bit. I wanna be strong and brave, but I'm not. I give up. I wanna go home. Help me through this night." Her words were few but honest. She was glad He could handle it.

Random thoughts floated through her head. A campfire would feel so good. *At least it's warm outside. Where's Becca? I need a new backpack. I'd like an ice cream, please. Chocolate with peanut butter.* She saw tiny flecks of light around her eyes and a funny little gray fog closing in on her. Then the sensation of falling. She reached for the cave wall for support, but misjudged the distance and lunged forward, collapsing on the rough stone floor. She struggled to get up but fainted.

Becca was busy making a false trail of footprints. Some people might think it odd, but Becca felt stronger than before. She liked the idea of leading their pursuer the wrong way. She hoped that Jake and the others would figure out that there was a problem and come soon. Maybe Jake would see that the path was marked with two sets of the same shoes. It occurred to her that Mr. Creepy might realize it as well, but she put that out of her mind, preferring to believe he was as stupid as he was mean. She made her fake footprints go all the way to a rocky area where the footprints would be hard to see anyway. After her second set of prints, she tiptoed along the side of the trail away from the muddy middle to the cave's entrance to join her friend.

"No bear?" she asked, rounding the corner.

Callie didn't answer. She was face down on the ground.

"Callie!" Becca shrieked. "Callie! Are you okay? Are you dead?" She ran to Callie and knelt.

Callie moaned. "Not that I can tell," she managed weakly.

"What?" Becca asked, confused. "Not that I can tell what?"

"No bear."

"But are you okay?" Becca persisted.

"Okay about what?" Callie responded foggily.

"You were lying face down when I came in here."

"No, I wasn't." Callie shook her head as if she thought Becca was crazy.

Oh, brother. She's delirious. Oh, well. I'll play along, she thought, getting worried. "I made the perfect false trail," Becca said, wanting to forget how strange Callie was acting. "Now what?"

"Settle in and wait," Callie said, while maneuvering her body awkwardly to a sitting position. *Why do I keep feeling like I'm gonna pass out?*

Becca removed both of their soaked socks and shoes, draping the socks on a nearby rock to dry. *Hopefully we won't have to run. Callie couldn't run anyway, and I'm sure not leaving her—no matter what happens tonight.* She unloaded the backpack methodically and lined everything out on the ground. "We have a lot of garbage with peanut butter and crumbs. There are a few peanuts left, not many. We have water. Waterfall water. Not sure if it's safe to drink. We have yucky bloody stuff. There are two small apples that need washing off. That's about it." She pushed the bag with the gift box aside, too busy to think about it.

"Eat the apples. Throw the rest. Far away." Callie grimaced. *This must be what having a big hot sword in your chest feels like.* "We'll be rescued tomorrow or walk out if we aren't murdered or eaten tonight." She grinned nervously at the gravity of her own words.

"Oh, great. Our last meal." Becca rolled her eyes at Callie and wiped the apples off on her shirt. She handed an apple to Callie.

"Not me. You."

"Callie, you need to keep up your strength. You must be hungry," Becca implored.

"No. Eat it or toss it," the nauseous Callie replied. "Toss everything that smells like food."

"Do you think we might attract the bear?" Becca asked timidly. She did not want to see a bear anywhere except in the zoo.

"This bear's not afraid of humans," Callie replied hoarsely.

"The garbage?"

"Throw it. Everything. Keep the water." Callie leaned her head back on the rock and tried to use her neck muscles to reposition herself. Nothing was comfortable. Her shoulder blade burned with a deep ache. It felt like someone had ripped off her arm. She wanted to scream for someone to turn down the pain so she could have some relief. She had thought that the bitter-tasting willow bark didn't work, but now she missed it. Picking a little wood fiber out of her teeth, she wished she could have tried it in hot tea but knew they couldn't risk starting a fire. There was no dry wood anyway. It was ironic—a fire might ward off the bear but attract the criminal.

She could see Becca moving around but really didn't care what she was doing. All she cared about was trying to find some relief. It seemed impossible. She didn't realize that she was sighing in her pain.

Becca polished off the last bite of her apple when she heard Callie groaning softly. *If only Jake was here. He'd know what to do.* She removed the gift box from a bag it was wrapped in and placed it gently into the backpack. Using the bag for the food-fragranced garbage, she left the shelter of the cave for a moment and launched the packet into the woods, watching to see where it landed. *If Callie needs food later, I'm going after that apple,* she thought.

Becca returned and crouched down beside Callie. "Maybe we need to take off the backpack and try something else."

"It hurts to move...hurts to breathe." Callie's face showed the stress of her misery. "I think my arm's broken."

"We have to immobilize it better." At least Becca knew that much. Her resources were very limited. She was aware that Mr. Creepy could walk around the tree at any moment, so she lowered her voice. "Hang in there, Callie. I have an idea."

Becca sat down on a rock and pulled out Callie's knife. She carefully cut the legs off her own jeans and cut the fabric into strips. *Now for something to hold the arm securely.* She smoothed the rough bark off a nearby stick and went to work on Callie's arm.

It was harder for Callie to move now; her arm was swollen and stiff. Becca gently helped Callie sit up so she could remove the backpack. Then, Becca attached the stick to Callie's arm with the fabric from her jeans as gently as she could. The fabric strips held the stick in place. The new splint wasn't perfect, but it was the best she could do.

Becca placed their few supplies and the stolen loot in Callie's backpack and set it aside. She gripped the pocketknife tightly as she thought about how she might use it as a weapon. It seemed pitifully harmless compared to a gun, but at least it was something. Quietly she crept to the rhododendron that blocked the entrance to the cave and shook the rain from its branches. After she cut and stacked the smooth, waxy leaves into a bed, she helped her injured friend to lie down. Although it wasn't a comfortable solution, it felt better than the rough cave floor.

Nightfall will be here soon, Becca thought. A foggy haze moved in behind the retreating rain. Finding nothing else to do, Becca sat down beside Callie and looked around. "Does the splint help at all?"

"Some. Thanks." Callie closed her eyes, thankful for her no longer "tentative" friend.

A small huddle of little brown bats stirred in their shrouded nook near the ceiling. It was time for their nightly quest for food. Their gentle rustling made Becca nervous. She recalled a movie in which bats swirled in waves covering and attacking people. She flattened herself against the cave wall so she would maybe seem smaller to them. She wondered what other dangers lurked in the cave's gaping black hole. A rush of uneasiness tingled through her insides. She drew her legs up to her chest and stared intently into the darkness.

As if on cue, the small cloud of bats flurried out of the cave. They bounced along in the air like little stones skipping across the water. It was nothing like she had feared. The bats were much fewer in number than she had thought, and she didn't feel threatened at all. In fact, it was a magical moment—something she knew she would probably never experience again.

"They eat bugs," Callie whispered. Bats were fascinating to her.

"Yeah," Becca replied, sharing Callie's wonder.

As the last one fluttered overhead, Callie croaked, "Rabies," like they had earlier in the day. Becca giggled, relaxing for a moment.

"This sure is a day I won't forget," Becca said. "It's the biggest adventure I've ever been on! I wish you weren't hurt."

"Me, too." Callie's words seemed normal, but her voice was strained and low.

"I wonder what else could happen to us today," Becca asked.

"Don't even go there," Callie said. *I don't even want to think about anything else bad happening. I just wanna go home.*

Becca was worried. She looked outside to see if anything was moving but saw nothing.

Callie's nerves were on edge. She needed a doctor. She really, really wanted something for the pain. Deciding not to complain, she prayed in her heart again: *Lord, I don't wanna to be a baby, but I—we—need your help. Please let us see your love in all of this.*

It was getting darker outside by the minute, and the air was heavy and humid from the rain. A soft, brief shower meandered through the woods, and water droplets trickled slowly off the leaves and rocks. Instinctively, Becca reached for the backpack and pulled it closer to her. She took out the flashlights and shone the light into the cave's darkness to make sure they worked. They did. Reluctantly she turned them off and laid them down by her side. *This is really happening. We're stuck here.*

The girls peered out from their hiding place, hoping not to see anything moving in the darkness. They would have welcomed the bright lights of Jake's team but doubted that rescuers would come during the night. Becca imagined a huge dimmer switch in the sky as the woods became darker and more mysterious. Soon the light was completely extinguished. Their eyes strained to focus on familiar shapes, but it was no use—the moonless sky covered the mountain in a dark, heavy blanket. It was like staring into binoculars with the eye piece covers still on.

For the first time since going to the house, Callie thought about snakes. Their incident at the waterfall was proof that poisonous snakes were close by. She searched her memory for any information about where snakes sleep. She shifted her position a little when she thought about the rock she was leaning against—it had a little space underneath just to her right. It was the perfect place for a snake.

Becca's thoughts darted from one fear to another. She felt pressure in her chest and realized that she was holding her breath. *Callie seems so calm.* Becca felt anxiety and fear washing all over her.

Then, something moved just beyond the tree at the cave's entrance! Without thinking, Becca grabbed Callie's arm. They listened intently, wanting to turn on the flashlights to see what it was but afraid to anger a hostile bear or to give their position away.

There was no doubt: something was there! They strained to hear anything that would provide a hint of what it could be. The wind was calm, so it couldn't be leaves blowing. Callie tried to remember whether squirrels were nocturnal—but it sounded heavier than a squirrel.

Becca tightened her grip on Callie's knife. It wasn't a great weapon, but she could open it and throw it if she had to. She found a hand-sized rock and placed it right below her knife-holding hand, thinking that she would need her left hand to help her stand. All her energies focused on the sound. *If it's Mr. Creepy, why doesn't he come and get us? Or why doesn't he hide and wait? Why would he just keep making noise? Of course, it could be the bear...* The suspense was terrible.

"I'm shining the light," Becca said in her quietest whisper.

"Point it down," Callie replied.

Becca pointed the flashlight downward on the ground in front of her. She hesitated a moment; she was as afraid to turn the light on as she was afraid not to. The sound from outside continued...whatever it was seemed to be coming closer! Becca flicked on the flashlight, aiming the light downward.

A tiny circle of light pierced the blackness. Becca held the light firmly in her hand and turned toward the faint outline of Callie's face in the shadows. Callie strained to see the unidentified intruder still cloaked in darkness. Becca raised the flashlight up about an inch from the ground, hoping that the larger circle of light would reveal something.

"There!" Callie said. "Shining eyes. It's an animal."

"The bear?" Becca asked, afraid of the answer.

"Maybe. Lift the light higher."

Becca lifted the downward pointing light about two inches above the ground. Two eyes shone like hot marbles from beneath the tree only a few feet away. Becca was poised for action, although she wasn't sure if she would run or try to fight.

Callie let out one hoarse chuckle. "Ow," she whispered sharply.

"What?" Becca whispered.

"Sh h h h," Callie said in a laugh-cry. She sounded like a leaky tire on a bumpy road. "It's a skunk."

"Oh, brother. Why am I not surprised?" Becca lamented. She eased the light up a little higher and finally saw a small skunk gazing at them from under the tree. The girls sat very still. After a moment, the skunk went back to its foraging.

Callie leaned her head back again, reminded of her pain and her tiredness. A weary smile pulled at her lips. She was too hurt and too tired to care about anything. She envisioned the little skunk project she was carving with Grandpa.

"That wuz Huckleberry," she said with an exaggerated southern mountain accent.

"Who?" Becca asked, wondering what in the world Callie was thinking.

Callie spoke in a mumbly voice as she shared the poem she was making up on the spot.

"Huckleberry's
Very wary—
Can you be his friend?
I will warn you at the start
He has a stinky end!"

Becca started giggling. She was a great audience!

Callie began again..."Huckleberry isn't scary,"

Callie stopped at the end of her creativity. She was just too uncomfortable to think anymore.

Becca joined in the poetry writing...

"Just don't make him frown,

If he sticks his hiney up

You'll soon be feeling down."

Becca tried to control her laughter, but she was tired too, and it was hard to stop. The laughing was a good release for all her built-up tension. It was even funnier since it was the first time she had seen this side of Callie.

Callie laughed, too: "Huh...huh...ow...huh." Laughing hurt, but she couldn't help it.

Between muffled laughing, Becca said, "Oh, my sides are hurting. Someone's gonna hear us. Besides, you're gonna start spewing blood everywhere." Her words made it even funnier. Callie chuckled, too. After a few minutes, they stopped abruptly. It was like trying to hold back a tickly cough.

They burst out laughing again, Becca with a deep belly laugh and Callie with "huh...huh...huh." The harder they tried to be quiet, the more they lost control. Becca's nose started running. Her eyes watered. And then, she snorted.

This time, Callie's laughter sounded more like "ow, ow, ow" than "huh huh huh." Becca wiped the tears from her eyes. Just as they were finally calm, the little skunk turned its back to them and raised its tail a little.

"The end." Callie said with one last "huh." The skunk kept its spraying pose for a moment but never sprayed them. Soon, he waddled off into the darkness.

The cave was quiet once more.

Becca was impressed. Even though she giggled through the whole thing, she liked the words. Especially the "hiney" part. She was glad they were finally able to be themselves around each other. "I think you're a writer, too, Callie." Becca said.

Callie chuckled again. "Nah, I'll leave that to you," she said, feeling good about the compliment. It was one of those you-had-to-be-there moments. She knew it probably wouldn't be funny any other time. She was grateful for the temporary distraction from her pain.

When Becca was satisfied that the skunk was gone and that nothing else was there, she turned off the light to save the batteries. A campfire would have been so nice, but it was out of the question. It was quiet. And dark. Neither one felt like sleeping.

Fear closed in, and they were stuck with their troubles once again.

Chapter 23

THE LITTLE BOX

The girls sat together in exhausted silence, chilled by the night air. There wasn't a single source of light to relieve them of the smothering darkness. Rainless clouds covered the stars.

Becca was sick of her wet clothes; she longed for a warm bubble bath and her own bed. Callie had never been so miserable in her life.

"What time is it?" Callie asked.

Becca held the flashlight about two inches from the ground and clicked on the light. She checked her watch: 10:07 p.m.

"It's gonna be a long night, Callie. It's just after 10." She rolled her eyes and let out a breath—it had felt as if they'd been there so much longer than that. She eased the ray of light toward the inside of the cave to check for anything scary. When she edged the light toward the outside, Callie stopped her.

"Creepy's out there somewhere."

"Thanks for reminding me," Becca said sarcastically. "I'm already scared out of my wits." *There.* She said it. The admission of it was a relief in one way, but made it seem worse somehow. Tired tears filled her eyes.

Callie's guilt overshadowed her fear. *Why did I have to go inside the house after seeing that someone was there? If we'd turned around without going inside, we would have been home hours ago; I wouldn't have a hole in my shoulder.*

She fell back into her new habit—silent praying. *Jesus, this is my fault. Everybody's gonna hate me and never trust me again. I'm so sorry.* "I'm sorry for all this, Becca," Callie said.

Becca said nothing.

Callie paused, then added, "I'm scared, too."

Becca reached over and squeezed Callie's hand, relieved.

"It's not your fault," Becca said. When Callie started to object, she said, "You didn't do anything today that I wouldn't have done. I could have refused to go in, but I wanted to go."

It was Callie's turn to feel relieved. They were more alike than she would have ever guessed.

Danger stuck to their bodies like sweat. The butterflies in Callie's stomach, along with her hunger and stress from pain, added dizziness to her queasy feeling. Becca turned the drawstring on her jacket into a frayed and frazzled mess with her fidgeting. She reached inside the backpack out of boredom and felt around in the dark for something interesting. If only she could turn on the light! Her hand landed on the little gift box that Callie had never opened.

"Callie! I found Mrs. Jennie's gift for you. Come on—open it," she said, full of curiosity.

Callie had forgotten about the gift. She pushed up with her left arm to try to re-position herself, but the pain was too much. "You open it. Hand me the flashlight," she whispered.

Callie held the flashlight only inches above the ground and flicked it on. The circle of light was about as big as a little baby swimming pool. Both girls visually inhaled everything the light touched, feeling like two divers coming up for air. Becca removed the loosened wrapping paper and lifted the lid. A small object was inside. It felt like metal, but she couldn't tell what it was. She held it under the light for a better look.

"Is it a baby shoe?" she asked, puzzled.

"A baby shoe charm. That's strange. Read the note," Callie replied.

Becca opened a neatly folded piece of notebook paper with delicate cursive handwriting on it. "It was written eight years ago," she said. After adjusting the paper for better access to the light, she began to read...

"Sweet Callie,

You may be wondering why I've saved this little shoe for you..."

The girls looked at each other, amazed.

"I haven't seen you in a few years, so I hope you'll at least get this sometime after I die. You're a sweet little angel, such a blessing to me. I hope that what I'm about to tell you will make sense someday. I'm saving this in a special place so that your mother can give it to you for your Necklace of Honor. Hopefully you'll receive it for your thirteenth birthday."

"What's a Necklace of Honor?" Becca asked.

"You'll find out later." Callie said, thinking for the first time that she might want Becca to be at the ceremony. Callie shook her head. "I don't know how Mrs. Jennie knew."

Becca continued, caught up in the mystery...

"You knew me as an old mountain lady who doted over you. You may not remember me at all now. I wish we could've had more time together. The Good Lord's been kind. I've had a lot of things happen to me, but He always saw me through. He promised in the Good Book that He'd never leave us nor forsake us. I believe that, even though I've been married three times. Each time ended in heartache.

Callie, no matter where you are or what you're doing when you read this, you can rest assured that the Good Lord'll be with you. The little shoe was a gift I bought for my third husband's daughter. Her baby boy was the second apple of my eye. You were the first, of course. His mother took him out of my life the day of my husband's funeral. I never got to give it to her. I've never seen nor heard from any of his family again.

I'm giving this little baby shoe to you because it is made of pewter, a very strong metal that will not tarnish. The shoe will remind you to run the race of your life for the Lord. Hebrews 12:1 says, we must "run with endurance the race that lies before us, keeping our eyes on Jesus..." Callie, you can endure any trial with the Good Lord by your side.

All my Love, Jennie Townsend"

Callie held the little charm tightly, moved by Mrs. Jennie's letter. It was almost as if the dear old woman knew what she was going through at that very moment. Callie felt like she knew her so much better now. The hardships that the mountain woman had faced were hard to imagine! Mrs. Jennie's gentle smile was all that Callie remembered. She couldn't recall any complaining or unhappiness in the women's life. She thought about her own injury, Mr. Creepy, and having to stay the night in the cave. Her loving family and friends were waiting at home for her, praying, and longing for her to return. *Surely if the Lord helped Mrs. Jennie through all her hard times, He'll help me through this night, and all the days of my life, too.* The little shoe was a solid reminder of God's loving care and strength. It was a great gift, and Callie cherished it as part of her Necklace of Honor.

The old woman's gift impressed Becca. She was happy for Callie but felt a little envious of the Necklace of Honor thing, hoping Callie would tell her about it soon. She wondered about how the "Good Lord" could really help anyone through difficult times. God and Jesus had always seemed distant, maybe nonexistent. During the past year, she had decided several times that God was just for sentimental fools. She had been working out her new "scientific" position that God was maybe even a myth. Mrs. Jennie's letter was just one more thing that poked holes in her disbelief. It made her a little irritable.

The girls became quiet, off in their own worlds...until they heard something else moving outside!

Chapter 24
THE MYSTERIOUS MESSAGE

The new sound startled the girls to anxious attention. They clicked off the flashlight and sat frozen, afraid to breathe. This was not the sound of a small animal. It sounded nothing like Huckleberry's scritch-scratch foraging. It sounded like footsteps, but they couldn't be sure. They could see absolutely nothing in the dark, so they huddled together in breathless suspense.

Becca leaned in close to Callie's ear. "What do we do?" she whispered.

"Quiet," Callie answered.

They waited—dangling in time, uncertain of their fate. After what seemed like an hour, they relaxed a little. The noise had stopped. Whatever it was had either gone another way, or was frozen too, listening for them and ready to pounce.

Becca wondered about mountain lions. She had read somewhere that they could live in an area for many years without anyone knowing about them. Maybe the cave belonged to one of them. Of course, the bear was a threat. She didn't even want to think about Mr. Creepy. She leaned in again. "Callie, you're moaning."

"Sorry." Callie hadn't realized she was making any noise. *If only the pain would stop...*

Moments passed. The unusual noise was gone.

"This night is a test of my faith," Callie mumbled, loud enough for Becca to hear.

"How strong is it? Your faith, I mean." Becca really wanted to know. *Isn't it God's policy to protect people according to their faith?* She wanted to make sure Callie was well equipped.

"Not sure." She tried to take a deep breath, needing more oxygen. "He won't leave us. He promised. Folks are praying for us right now. I just know it." *Do*

136

I even believe what I'm saying? It was a difficult test for even an experienced Christian.

"Maybe you should pray again. Out loud this time so He'll be sure and hear you," Becca offered. She hoped that hearing Callie's prayer would make her feel better.

Callie felt awkward. She had only prayed aloud in front of somebody when she was a little girl saying bedtime prayers. She started slowly, "Jesus, we're scared and..." she paused.

"Are you allowed to talk to Him that way?" Becca asked. She had heard more formal prayers with fancy words; Callie was talking to God like He was sitting right there!

"Jake does," Callie replied. Her prayer continued, "Without You...we're dead. You know everything. Protect us. We need you. Amen."

"Do you think He heard you?" Becca asked.

"You want me to yell it?" Callie said, irritable from her pain.

"Nope. We're good." Becca said, deciding not to mess with her injured companion.

Still, Callie felt herself relaxing a little. Talking to God had taken some of the fear away.

"I don't want to die," Becca said after a moment.

Callie waited before answering. "We might. Who knows?" She adjusted her position once more, looking for anything that would make her more comfortable. "Dying ain't scary if you belong to Jesus. I believe that." Callie couldn't believe she had said all that. She had always been so nervous when she thought about talking to her friends about God before. That night, it just came out of her mouth. "You can decide to follow Jesus tonight if you want."

"No, thanks," Becca said softly.

"Okay," Callie answered simply. "I need rest." Her pain surged again. Her whole body and mind felt like it was powering down. It was all she could do to keep from moaning loudly. It was even hard to breathe.

Becca was deep in thought about their conversation. She wasn't sure how she felt about all that God stuff. She wished He would come in riding on a white stallion and rescue them. Then she could believe. Exhaustion and frustration threatened to overpower her mind, and her thoughts skipped from one scary scenario to another. She reached for the flashlight once more, turning it on at ground level. She could faintly see Callie's closed eyes in the dim light. Making sure to hold the light low, she scanned the walls of the cave once more. She didn't dare point it toward the outside, lest she draw attention. She examined the rocks for anything interesting she could focus her thoughts on—trickles of water, flora, or unique formations.

The light finally reached a debris-covered boulder. It looked like it had some sort of marking on it. Becca eased over toward the rock and quietly brushed off the old leaves and dirt to reveal a message. It was hard to read, but she finally deciphered four letters: "T-R-U-S." She looked all over the rock for more words but saw nothing else. She wondered how long it had been there. *Who wrote this? Maybe somebody was goofing around. What could "T-R-U-S" mean? Most people have only three initials. How strange. Why would someone put all that effort into carving a word like that?* She looked around the walls of the cave for more clues. *I wish I had more light.* Thinking of herself as a detective took her mind off her fears for a while.

"T-R-U-S," she said to herself aloud. She chuckled. "Two Raccoons Under Siege... The Red Underwear Society... Tomatoes Ruin Ugly Salads..."

"What?" Callie stirred.

"It's just this rock. It has 'T-R-U-S' scratched in it," Becca replied.

Callie was in too much pain to find anything interesting. "Maybe Jake wrote it. He ran away. He hid in here," she whispered.

"When did he run away?" Becca asked. There were so many things she didn't know about her brother.

Callie paused. She really didn't feel like talking. "When your grandpa died. Your father started throwing everything away and selling off stuff. He got rid of a bunch of family heirlooms and your grandmother's quilts." She paused to breathe. "Jake was so angry that he ran away." Callie struggled to get comfortable. "I can't talk anymore."

Becca continued to study the carved rock from where she sat, while considering what Callie had just told her. *Did Jake write it? What was he trying to spell?* "Oh, well, I'll just have to ask him about it later," she resigned.

She crawled back over to Callie's side, fascinated by the mystery; it was like a writing prompt that launched her into all kinds of potential stories behind the message. She couldn't stand it. She had to search again for more words or clues.

Darting back over to the rock and positioning the light a couple of inches from the surface, she brushed away some dirt she had missed before. Still nothing.

Becca looked around for something to clean off the last little bit of dusty dirt. Her eyes landed on a little puddle of water on the cave floor. She crawled over to it, staying close to the ground so the flashlight wouldn't shine too far. After scooping up as much as she could with one hand, she did her best one-handed crawl, flashlight still in tow. The rough ground scraped and poked her bare knees. By the time she got back to the rock, she only had a little water left—most of it had trickled out of her cupped hand. She used what little water she had to dampen the rock around the letters, but nothing more was revealed. Disappointed, she rested back on her knees. *That's it. I'll just have to figure out how to fetch more water.*

Becca propped the flashlight between a smaller rock and the mysterious one so that a slice of light shone toward the little puddle. She walked to the puddle, scooped the water with both hands, and hurried back to the mystery rock, carefully pouring the water down the front. At first, she didn't notice the new letters appearing, but when her hands were empty and she held the flashlight once more, she saw it: TRUST ME. There was nothing else.

"Trust WHO?" she said aloud. Callie didn't hear.

The discovery of the two new words did nothing to satisfy her curiosity about the message. In fact, it made it worse. The message made no sense at all.

"Callie? Did Jake stay out here alone?" Becca asked.

"Yes," Callie groaned. "No more questions."

"Sorry." *'Trust me.' What a stupid thing to write.* Becca frowned. Carrying the flashlight, she crawled back over to Callie, turned off the light, and folded her arms—grumpy.

Chapter 25
THE SIGNAL

Becca awoke to the sound of birds singing. Yesterday's rain clouds were miles away and a fresh, hazy mist hovered in the forest. Her stomach growled its loud objection to its emptiness. After putting on her mostly dry socks and boots, she stood and stretched. The morning brought hope. She could imagine Jake's team spreading out and combing the mountains for them at that very moment.

Callie was awake as well. She hadn't slept the whole night. She had never been so stiff and sore, and her stomach had never felt so sick. The pain in her back and arm had brought her to her breaking point. Despite the warm summer air, she was freezing. She shivered, and her quaking muscles only brought more agony.

Becca heard Callie's teeth chattering and ran to her aid. She removed her own jacket and placed it over her sickly companion. Supporting Callie's head, she helped her take a few sips of water. "I'm going to take a look around," she said, hoping to see the rescue team.

Callie nodded, still shaking.

Becca left the cave for the bright sunlight. She stayed close to the rocks, watching all the time for any sign of Mr. Creepy. She cautioned herself to watch her step; a sprained ankle was the last thing they needed.

There was no easy way to climb to the top of the rock embankment. Slimy mud and slippery leaves filled the narrow space between School Bus Rock and the side of the hill. Her legs slipped out from under her about halfway up the steep slope. She scraped her hands as she helplessly skidded to the bottom. She cussed under her breath. Before she met Callie, she cussed all the time without caring about it. Now it sounded strange. "Sorry, God," she said, unsure how she felt about apologizing to a God she wasn't sure she believed in. She eventually found her footing and made her way back up to the top of the cliff above the cave.

Callie had never been in so much pain her entire life. Her whole body ached, and her thirst was unquenchable. *Why can't I pass out from pain? That's what they do in the movies.* She tried to focus as she whispered, "Please, God," over and over. Her whole being longed to feel His comforting presence.

Becca stood on her perch and surveyed the area. She was so high above the cave that it made her woozy to look down. Green leafy limbs blocked her view of the trail that led back to Callie's house, so Becca squatted down to get a better view. She was surprised that she could see all the way to The Bridge from there. Sunlight dappled through the trees, teasing light into the woods. Becca felt a sore spot on her head that she'd not noticed before, so she retrieved the mirror from her pocket to check it out. Dirt and blood covered her freshly skinned forehead. *Funny, I didn't notice hitting my head when I fell.* Her light skin accentuated the purple circles under her eyes. Her hair was all over the place, so she laid the mirror down so she could make a fresh ponytail. Just as she was finishing up, a bright sunray reflected off the mirror into her face. An idea energized her. *Maybe I can use the mirror as a signal for the rescuers!*

Suddenly, she heard the unmistakable sound of a helicopter off in the distance. *Someone's coming this way—maybe they'll see me if I use the mirror to signal them!* Her stomach lurched and her palms sweated as she recalled her stumble on The Bridge. She pushed away a limb to get a better view, only to watch helplessly as the helicopter zoomed over without slowing down.

Great. There went that chance. She looked back toward the narrow ridge and saw something moving. She crouched down, still fearing Mr. Creepy—hoping against hope it was a rescue team. *Wait! That looks like two people! Is it...? Is it...? Yes! It's Jake and Emma, and they are coming this way!*

Becca waved her arms wildly and yelled "Jake!" at the top of her lungs. She didn't even care about Mr. Creepy anymore. She let out a happy yelp when it looked like Jake was looking straight at her.

"Thank goodness!" she said as she began her bumpy descent from her post.

Going down was a lot faster than coming up! She heard their voices as she made her last jump to the ground. But, when she turned around, they weren't there. In fact, she couldn't see them at all. Becca was shocked and confused. She hurried up the difficult path as fast as she could.

"Jake!" she yelled. No response. *Why can't they hear me?* She stumbled wildly over the rocky trail, expecting to see them on The Bridge. Once she reached the opening, she careened to a screeching halt at the ridge's dizzying edge. No one was there. Then she heard indistinct voices mumbling behind her.

"JAKE!" she screamed as she wheeled around. *Where are they going and why are they in such a hurry?* "This way!" she shouted toward their direction. *Boy, the wind does strange things to sound up here,* she huffed. "JAKE! HEY!" She ran toward them shouting, but they didn't respond. The constant winds near The Bridge swiped every word and swooshed it up and away. *I might as well be whispering.*

Becca grabbed the mirror in desperation and aimed a ray of sun in their direction, hoping to get their attention. The light bounced wildly as she ran. Finally, she stopped and focused a strong shard of light toward their eyes. No response. She shifted to try again...and she tripped, stumbling into a laurel bush.

Good grief, Becca thought wearily, trying to hold back a flood of tears. *It's hopeless. I've missed them.* She pulled herself from the branches and sat down on the ground. *What do I do now?* She was desperate for an idea but drew a blank.

Suddenly she felt the vice grip of a hand on her arm, pulling her to her feet. She panicked, terrified of Mr. Creepy. She was unable to move and couldn't even raise her eyes to look at him. The man grabbed her by the shoulders. Hard. She cried out as she blindly tried to fight off her captor. Terror filled her, and she was unable to run.

Chapter 26

ROVER

"Becca! Becca! It's me, Becca! It's okay! I'm here." Finally, she recognized Jake's voice through the fog of fear. He gently raised her face to meet his, speaking tender words of encouragement. Tears of relief flooded her eyes and rolled down her dirty cheeks. When he hugged her tightly, she melted into the safety of his strong arms.

"I was screaming your name. Where were you going?" Becca asked, exasperated.

"We saw smoke coming from Mrs. Jennie's house and thought ya'll might have started a fire to keep warm."

"We looked for you until it got too dark last night. There's a whole search team out this morning," Emma added.

"Are you okay? Where's Callie?" Jake asked as he released the hug.

"She's hurt. Mr. Cree...a man shot her. We stayed in the cave. She's in bad shape." Becca noticed that both Jake and Emma were weighed down with large backpacks.

Jake jumped into action.

"Emma," he said, "Radio for Rover to come down here. We'll need the spine board and the two bags. And more hands."

Becca led Jake to Callie. "You're in the cave," he noted.

Becca waited for him to fuss at her for being there after he had specifically told them to stay away, but he said nothing else. When they arrived at the cave, they rushed to Callie's side. She was pale and weak.

Jake ran to her side and began assessing her condition. "Why is her arm wrapped up?" he asked Becca.

"I think she broke it when she fell," Becca said.

"Go to Emma and tell her to come down here. You wait for Rover," Jake said, all business.

"Jake, no! I want to stay! I can help. Please!" Becca wasn't about to leave Callie's side after all they had been through together.

"Okay, but you'll have to help me and do exactly as I say. Go tell Emma where we are and then come back," he ordered.

"Callie, you with me?" he asked the injured girl.

Callie's eyelids fluttered as she tried to focus on his face. "Yeah," she managed weakly, only vaguely aware of what was going on. *Am I dreaming?*

"Becca said that a man shot you. Did you recognize him?"

Callie started to explain, but she was too weak to talk much. "Sort of," she said, seeing stars. The cave walls began to spin, and she struggled to remain conscious.

"Stay with me, Callie."

No response.

Jake shook her gently, raising his voice. "Callie. Callie—stay with me. Can you hear me?"

She nodded almost imperceptibly, closing her eyes against the roller coaster walls.

"Okay, I need you to work with me on this. Ok? Callie?"

She opened her eyes halfway and nodded, giving him a drunken smile.

In the meantime, Becca ran up the trail to Emma, telling her everything Jake had said. She had forgotten all about Mr. Creepy. In a flash, she was back at Callie's side.

Becca found Jake removing a metal canister from his backpack. It looked heavy. He quickly took out a mask and put it over Callie's face.

"Oxygen," he told Becca. "I just about left this at home. Something told me to bring it. God works in mysterious ways."

Becca knelt beside Callie, facing Jake. "Do you usually carry oxygen?" she asked.

"Nope, not on me" he said as he gently pulled up Callie's eyelids to check her pupils. Then, he skillfully assessed Callie's fingernails and felt the bones of her uninjured arm and both legs for fractures. He turned his attention toward Callie's feet. "Wiggle your toes," he told Callie.

She did.

Becca was relieved.

"Wiggle your fingers," he said, cradling the wrist of Callie's injured arm in his hand. Becca became nervous. It hadn't occurred to her to check to see if Callie could move her fingers.

Callie barely moved the fingers on her injured side.

As Becca helped Jake remove Callie's makeshift sling and splint, Callie cried out. But Jake didn't stop. He worked carefully and confidently.

Next, Jake pulled a stethoscope from his backpack and quickly put it around his neck. "We need to raise her up a little so I can listen to her lungs," he said. He frowned as he listened to her right side of her upper back and just below her right collarbone.

Becca remained silent. The longer and harder he listened, the more afraid she became. *Why is he listening so long? Doesn't he understand that her shoulder is what's hurt?*

"I have to cut your shirt," Jake told Callie. She barely nodded her head. He used a large jack knife from his pocket to cut the sleeve off Callie's shirt, leaving enough fabric to hold the shirt on. The bullet wound was a small, deep red hole, puffy around the edges. The skin around it was pale. Callie's upper arm had a strange, gray-blue discoloration going deep into the tissue.

"How ya' doing, Cal?" Jake asked her tenderly.

"It ain't fun," she answered weakly, feeling a bit better with the oxygen.

Jake pulled his jacket from his backpack and folded it into a pillow for Callie. "It's the best I can do for now. Hang in there—we're going to get you out of here."

Callie was dazed and afraid. It took every shred of mental and physical strength for her not to scream. She couldn't think clearly at all.

"What can I do?" Becca asked Jake. She wasn't sure that she wanted to hear his answer. She was a little queasy and a lot scared.

"You'll have to be my assistant," he said.

I was afraid you'd say that. I hope I don't pass out. "Okay," Becca answered.

"Put these gloves on," Jake told her. "Don't touch anything after they're on unless I tell you to."

"Are...are you going to...operate?" Becca asked, not able to think of a smarter question. *Don't pass out. Don't pass out,* she told herself.

"No, just wrapping her up good so we can transport her out of here," he replied, still working. "We'll bandage her and put her on a spine board. Hopefully the team will get here soon, and they can help us carry her up the hill. We'll start her IV when we get to Rover. Okay?" He glanced at his frightened sister briefly, then returned to his work. "You can do this, Becca. Even if something gross happens, you must follow my instructions."

A very nervous Becca remained quiet, not knowing what to say.

Jake glanced up at Becca when she didn't respond. "Just take a deep breath and think about how much you're helping Callie. You are a great help to me, you know."

A great help. The words sank into her very being like a soaking rain on the parched ground. *I've never really helped anyone before. He's actually depending on me,* thought the girl who had always depended on others. "Thanks, Jake. I'm ready to do whatever you need," she said aloud, feeling stronger.

"I know you can do it," he replied with a loving wink.

Becca averted her gaze, suddenly feeling self-conscious. Both she and Jake were snapped to attention by Callie's next words.

"Jake?" Callie spoke with urgency in her voice. "I can't stand it anymore. It's really hurting, and I think I'm going to throw up."

Becca looked at her green friend. *Great. If she throws up, I will, too.*

Callie did throw up, and the heaving made her cry. Somehow, Becca managed to look away to avoid being sick herself. When Callie was finished, Becca tossed some leaves over the mess so she didn't have to look at it. Then, Becca looked away to regain her composure. It was upsetting to see her friend suffer so much.

"Hang in there, Callie. We'll get you out of here as quick as we can. You okay, Becca?" Jake said with more cheerfulness in his voice than his face showed.

"I'm okay," she replied shakily. She was thankful for his strength. She turned her attention back to the task at hand.

Jake pulled out a long, narrow packet that looked like a little pillow. He opened the outer wrapping, shook it, then handed it to Becca.

"Put this on her forehead. It might help," he said. Becca was impressed—it was as cold as an ice pack! She positioned it on Callie's head and waited for her next orders.

Jake told Becca to spread the opening of his backpack wide. Inside were all sorts of medical supplies. She couldn't believe all the bandaging items! Jake squirted some alcohol on his hands and on Becca's, then he donned some gloves.

"You'll have to open everything up," he said to her. He instructed her to find several specific items and told her that she was to open the packages only when he asked for them. "Never touch what is inside the packages—it must stay sterile. Callie's life depends on it."

Becca nodded, wide-eyed.

"Look for the bandage pack that has 'Occlusive Dressing' on it," he instructed.

Becca found it quite easily.

"Now, open it up, but don't touch the bandage. Can you do that?"

"I'll try." Becca nervously fumbled with the resistant wrapping. She thought about using her teeth to tear the packaging but decided against it. It finally opened on its own. The gauze-type pad was slimy. It looked like it had Vaseline all over it. Jake took it and placed it over the bullet wound.

"Why's it so slimy?" Becca asked.

"Just being careful in case of pneumothorax," Jake replied, working quickly. "Can't be totally sure. Not taking chances."

Becca wanted to ask him to explain but didn't have time. She could barely keep up with his requests to hand him things. Finally, he used a sling that wrapped around Callie's whole chest, strapping the right arm to her body.

"What is 'noo-mo-thor-ax'?" she asked finally.

"Suck-in chest wound... punctured lung. The slimy bandage helps to seal the air in," Jake replied quietly. "Just being careful in case Callie's lung was nicked by the bullet." He continued to wrap, bandage, and prepare Callie for transport.

Suddenly Becca thought about Emma. "Oh, no! Mr. Creepy's out there somewhere and Emma's standing out in the open!" She started to run and warn Emma but stopped when she heard voices coming toward the cave.

"That's Emma and the crew now. Rover must be here," Jake said.

Just then, Emma came around the tree, followed by the cutest guy Becca had ever seen. "This is Tim," Emma said, noticing the silly grin on Becca's face. He was carrying a long, hard wooden board with oval holes on both sides, along with a large blue bag. Becca figured that he was about seventeen or eighteen years old.

"Hi," he said with a smile, revealing his dimples. His gorgeous blue eyes showed real concern when he took one look at Callie. He brushed his wavy blonde hair away from his eyes as he knelt by her side. Becca noticed his tan, muscled arms when he reached down to help Jake.

"Put the spine board right beside her and we'll secure her," Jake directed, and Tim did.

Spine board. The words hit Becca. She didn't realize until that moment how critical the situation might be.

"We'll do the rest when we get her to Rover," he told Tim.

Emma and Becca helped to move Callie to the spine board. Tim quickly put a neck collar on Callie and secured two firm cushions on either side of her head. Jake strapped her firmly to the board. It all happened quickly, considering how much they had to do. Their efficiency and training made short work of the important—perhaps critical—process.

Two middle-aged men entered the cave to help carry Callie up the hill. Becca backed away as the much stronger men took over.

Emma offered some water and some peanut-butter crackers to Becca, but she declined them.

Jake, Tim, and the two men lifted Callie carefully off the ground and began to carry her out of the cave. Jake was one of the first ones out. He stopped suddenly. "Look," he said to the others, nodding his head in the direction of something on the ground.

"What?" Becca asked.

"Someone was here last night. A man by the size of the prints—a smoker," he added, using his foot to point out a cigarette butt. "It looks like he went up the trail toward home and then turned around and came back." Then he paused once more and looked around on the ground, frowning.

"Jake. Tell me," Becca implored. "What do you see?"

"Well, God was obviously watching out for you two. There are also fresh bear prints leading into the cave and all around the outside," Jake said.

"A big bear, too!" Tim added with astonishment.

Becca and Callie looked at each other. Not only had Mr. Creepy come within 50 yards of them, but the bear was there too, and they never knew it!

Callie knew it was God's protection, and Becca couldn't think of any other way to explain it.

Just then, the radio beeped, and a man's voice said, "The Townsend house is engulfed in flames. It looks like someone was trying to burn it down. We found a gasoline can."

"That's one of the reasons we were taking a shortcut and didn't come this way," Jake said.

Both girls knew the other reason why Jake didn't go to the cave at first—they weren't supposed to be there.

The climb to the top of the hill was obviously a strain on the four men. The muddy, rocky path was treacherous even for one person to climb. Becca carried all that her arms would hold. Emma brought up the rear of the procession with the confidence of a seasoned hiker.

They all walked toward the black jeep in front of them.

"Where's Rover?" Becca asked Tim, expecting to see a rescue dog like Biscuit run toward them at any moment.

"Right in front of you," he said simply. She looked around again, puzzled. The truth dawned on her when she saw the words "Mountain Rover" on the side of the rescue vehicle. *Great. Now he'll think I'm stupid.* She was totally embarrassed.

The jeep was low, with chunky tires with a storage area behind the seats. It pulled an open bed made of welded metal that had a funny seat sticking out on the end. Becca had never seen anything like it before.

The team worked efficiently to prepare Callie for the journey home. Jake started Callie's IV for fluids and added a syringe of medicine to the tubing.

"Callie, this is a little something to knock the edge off the pain. You can't have anything stronger until we find out for sure the condition of your lung."

"Granola bars are in the glove compartment," he told Becca as he worked.

"Try to eat something—you need the energy," Emma encouraged, opening a granola bar and a canteen of water. Becca took a few bites and her hunger and thirst returned. She felt much safer with all the people around her.

One of the men radioed the sheriff with an update while Becca told the rescuers what had happened. As she shared the details about the man who shot Callie, the radioman relayed the information. Eventually, the man handed the radio to Becca so she could talk to the sheriff herself.

The rescue group listened as she told the sheriff all about how they had discovered Mr. Creepy at Mrs. Jennie's and how she and Callie had taken some of the loot so they could show it to the police. She added that the newspaper clippings he had left on the table were further proof that he was, in fact, the thief in the Longfellow heist.

Becca heard the sheriff contact one of the police officers who were at the burning house to keep an eye out for the man. Soon, she was involved in describing Mr. Creepy to the police officer, leaving nothing out—even the bad smell of his breath. Then the radio went silent.

Tim shook his head in amazement at the detailed description.

"You would think he was standing right here," he said. "You should be a detective." He smiled, showing his dimples again.

"I'm a writer," Becca stammered ridiculously, in awe of his attention.

The radio beeped a few minutes later.

"I think we've found the guy," a voice said. "He was on a ledge below a cliff near the Townsend property. He said he jumped over the side to hide but broke his leg when he landed. He has cash, jewels, and silver on him. He wouldn't say why he burned the house, but he confessed that he did it."

"Evidence," Becca said.

"He's a jerk," Callie mumbled with closed eyes—too quietly to be heard.

The radio beeped again. "This is the sheriff. Are the two heroines still there?"

"Affirmative," Jake replied in the mic.

"Good job, girls," the sheriff said loudly. Becca and Callie glanced at each other, smiling.

"Thank you, sir," Becca said for both of them.

Jake grinned from ear to ear after hearing the sheriff's report.

"I'll want an autograph later from you two," he said with a teasing smile while packing up.

Becca rode beside Jake, exhausted. Callie lay in the mobile bed behind the Rover while Emma sat in the chair at her head. Tim and the other men walked ahead of them, leading the rescue parade through the woods.

"Thank you," Callie said to everyone softly.

It wasn't long before an open field became visible through trees and a glint of sunlight bounced off a reflective surface, making Becca blink. Soon they heard a rhythmic patt-patt-patt through the woods and Becca realized that their real transportation was waiting for them.

"The helicopter!" she exclaimed. Jake and Emma chuckled at her excitement.

Callie stirred. "Cooool."

Chapter 27

BOTH TIMES

A wonderful smell wafted through the air, teasing Callie out of her sleep. *Hamburgers...grilling...*she faded off again, longing to return to her napping. Just as she was about to doze off, the tempting aroma charmed her to attention once more. She blinked her heavy eyelids as she tried to figure out where she was. Something wet and cold touched her hand.

"Shadow! Down!" she heard her mother say.

"She's waking up," Becca exclaimed as she ran to Callie's side. "Happy Birthday, Callie!"

Callie was so groggy that she wondered if she was dreaming. She looked around at the faces smiling at her—Mom, Becca, Emma, Grandpa, Jake, and Tim.

A horrible pain ripped through her right side. She reached over and pulled at her bandages, fighting the air as if there was a heavy object pushing against her.

"Whoa, Callie. Let me help you get more comfortable," her mother said, running to help her daughter.

Becca knelt beside Callie's lounge chair. "Callie, don't you remember? You had surgery yesterday."

"You've been conked out since we brought you home this morning. I fixed the chair for you. Did a pretty good job if I say so myself," Grandpa chimed in.

Kate brought Callie some sweet tea with a straw and helped her take a sip.

"You're gonna be sore for a while," Jake said while turning the burgers over. "The bullet was lodged in your shoulder, and it took over an hour just to dig it out. It missed your lungs by only a little bit. God was really watching over you."

Tim spoke up, "Your upper arm's broken in three places. You'll have to have physical therapy later. The doc said you could have the bullet as a souvenir if you want."

"Sure," Callie said, interested.

"You've had quite an adventure, young lady," said a voice from behind her.

Callie squinted her eyes against the evening sun. She looked over her shoulder at the people gathered on their back deck. All of them were familiar—police officers, rescue team members, some church members.

"Becca's been filling us in on all the details of your adventure. You were very brave to stand up to an armed criminal," the sheriff said. "What did you call him? Mr. Meanie?" He took a huge bite of his juicy, overstuffed hamburger and ketchup plopped on his shirt.

"Mr. Creepy," Becca replied, shuttering as she recalled the nastiness of the villain.

"What is his real name?" Grandpa asked.

"Dylan Smith, Howard Jones, or any number of other aliases," the sheriff replied with his mouth still full. "He has a long criminal record."

"And how old is he?" Grandpa asked with a frown. Kate was frowning, too.

"Mid-thirties," the sheriff answered, as he licked a blob of mustard off his finger. Grandpa's and Kate's eyes met for a moment; they looked away quickly.

Callie noticed it. "What is it, Grandpa?"

Becca also noticed it. *There's something funny going on here.*

Grandpa started to say something but stopped himself.

"You both could have been killed," Kate said quietly.

"Not only that—they slept in the cave all night, even though a bad ole' bear was on the loose. There were tracks everywhere," Tim added with admiration. He took a big swig of lemonade and winked at Becca.

She blushed.

"Callie checked both times for tracks but never saw ..." Becca stopped short, realizing that she had said "both times." She quickly picked up her cup and dashed back to the drink table for a refill.

"What were you saying, Becca?" Tim inquired, not noticing that her run for a refill was a retreat.

"Yes—what were you saying, Becca?" Jake asked slowly, his voice raised ever so slightly.

"I, uh..." Becca fumbled. She didn't want to add to Callie's lie. "Well..." she said as she over-shot her cup, pouring the sticky drink on her hand. Becca was caught between wanting to defend Callie and wanting to please Jake. Her respect for Callie had grown so much overnight—she didn't want her new friend to get into trouble.

"Yes," Callie intercepted. "We went inside the cave before we reached the falls." She watched the suspicion in Jake's eyes melt into anger.

Silence. He turned back to the grill and began firmly scraping the hamburger drippings into the coals with his long spatula. Callie looked down, wishing the audience was gone so she could talk to Jake alone.

Kate, Grandpa, Emma, and Becca understood the significance of Callie's statement, but the others didn't know the story; they drifted off into their own conversations. Some had more questions for Becca, but the joy of being the center of attention had faded. She assured everyone that she would write the events down in story form so that everyone could read it.

Callie wasn't hungry anymore. She wished that everyone would leave so she could apologize to her family.

It wasn't long before Emma had to leave. She said goodbye and wished Callie a happy birthday. Only a few moments later, Emma returned to ask if someone could move a vehicle that was blocking her in. After that, it was as if a logjam had been released by moving one log. Well-wishers and congratulators filed by to give their regards to Callie and Becca. In only a couple of minutes, the family was alone.

Jake was distant, avoiding Callie completely.

"Jake, can I talk to you?" Callie said, too immobilized by her pain and bandages to move from her chair.

"Need something?" he responded with a definite chill in his voice.

"I lied to you. I know that. I never intended to avoid the cave," Callie admitted.

"I wanted to go to the cave too, Jake." Becca said, pleading Callie's case. "Callie made sure it was safe and..."

But Jake cut her off, "This is between Callie and me."

Becca backed up a little and cast a worried look at Callie, but Kate and Grandpa drew closer.

"I'm sorry, Jake," broken-hearted Callie said softly.

"Okay," Jake said with a shrug as he turned to walk away, looking disappointed. He never looked at her.

She knew it wasn't okay. "Jake. I was miserable about it all that day." Tears formed in Callie's eyes. She wanted to catch him by the arm so he would stop and listen, but it would have taken forever to get up on her own.

"I know you were trying to protect us. I just wanted to go so bad," she continued, wishing he would turn and give her his charming smile. But she received no response. "Will you forgive me?"

All eyes were on Jake except Becca's. She stood and watched as her new best friend told the truth and asked forgiveness even when a lie would have probably worked. Callie had done what she had promised, and now she faced the consequences bravely. Becca was amazed that Callie seemed to care more about how Jake felt than about her own punishment. Becca's thoughts retreated into her own sad realization: *I would have lied to him again instead of telling the truth.*

Jake turned back slowly and pulled a chair up next to Callie. He ran his fingers through his hair, seemingly deep in thought. Then he leaned forward and looked her straight in the eye. Even though he was mad at her, Callie found comfort in his quiet strength and in the familiar scent of his clean-smelling cologne.

"Callie, I have never lied to you. Ever. Don't plan to. You know it's not right—I don't have to tell you all that. It's about respect, you know? Respect for me, for God. And for yourself. Do I forgive you? Yes, of course. Am I disappointed? Definitely. You didn't trust me. Bottom line. We both know that the bear came within a few feet of you." Kate and Grandpa were visibly shocked at this new revelation. "But it's not about getting caught, is it?"

His brotherly gaze was powerful. She shook her head. "No, Jake, it's not."

Becca wasn't sure she understood what they meant. She'd always thought it was exactly about not getting caught. She walked over behind Jake and hesitantly hugged him around the neck. She loved him now more than ever.

Callie wasn't sure what to say. She felt good about doing the right thing and was satisfied that he had forgiven her, but now it was awkward. She could almost feel the tension in the air.

Finally, Jake cradled Callie's head in his strong, gentle hands and softly kissed her on the forehead.

"You know what we'll have to do now," his stern look was betrayed by his sparkling eyes. "We celebrate your birthday!" And with that, his contagious smile returned.

Chapter 28

MY BROTHER

Birthdays were very special at Callie's house for every family member—including Jake, Callie's pretend brother. Kate presented a luscious made-from-scratch chocolate cake to her with a smile. It was rare for Kate to have a full day off with her family, and Callie could see that she was enjoying it. The flames of thirteen candles danced in the warm summer breeze. Callie was radiant, basking in the cake's illuminating glow.

They sang the birthday song in unison.

Becca tried to sing, faking more enthusiasm than she felt. She stepped backward, feeling like an outsider. Her parents had always given her an expensive party for her and her friends, but there was no love shown. Callie's family was very different.

"Happy Birthday!" The adults were involved and engaged—everyone took part in making Callie's day special. Becca watched her own brother laughing as Callie struggled with her awkward bandaging to blow out the candles. He was not only a part of the day's festivities, but he was also an integral part of the family...like a brother to Callie.

Kate cut the cake, swatting at Grandpa as he snatched the candles off to lick the icing. Suddenly, Becca felt alone. Envy and a mix of other emotions welled up inside of her. She had to get away from everybody. She had to leave Callie's little close circle alone so they could have a family party. Becca tried to hide the bitterness. "Excuse me," she said as she left the porch toward the yard, heading nowhere in particular.

"Where's Becca going?" Callie asked, concerned.

"I'll see," Jake said. He took one piece of cake for Becca and one for himself and headed toward the creek to join her.

"Hey, YOU!" he hollered with a teasing voice when he saw Becca sitting on a rock by the mountain stream. "I brought you some cake."

"Hey, thanks," she said, taking the cake she wasn't hungry for.

"What's up?" he asked casually.

She thought about saying, "Nothing," but decided to go ahead and tell him. She knew he wouldn't leave her alone until she did. "You're more like a brother to Callie than you are to me."

He started to speak once, then paused. It was as if he didn't know where to begin. "Do you know why I moved away?" he asked.

"You wanted to live in the mountains and not be a doctor," Becca replied, reciting what her parents had told her.

"Sort of. Mother and Dad kept trying to make me something I wasn't. It was Granna and Gramps who led me to Jesus. It was a whole different world here—no yelling, screaming, or putting me down. They believed in me, Becca. They showed me the joy of living. Mother and Dad refused to let me get baptized after I became a Christian." He stopped talking long enough to take a couple of big bites of cake.

"Delicious. Kate can really cook." He licked his fork. "It's a matter of the heart, Becca. It was the best thing that's ever happened to me. Moving here was the only way I could be myself and pursue my own dreams. Do you think I wanted to leave you?"

Becca shrugged her shoulders, truly not knowing the answer.

Jake put his hand on her shoulder. "Look at me. No way! I have always loved you and prayed for you. I'm glad you came this summer. Yes, I'm more involved in Callie's life right now—that's natural since I live here. But you and I are blood kin, and I'll always be your brother." He hugged her shoulders and then tousled her hair. "We okay? Here. Eat your cake." He forced a piece in her mouth, getting icing everywhere.

"JAKE!" She ran after him, feeling much better.

CALLIE STRUGGLED TO keep her eyes open. Her latest pain pill, necessary despite her determination to avoid it, pulled her toward a deep sleep. Half of a piece of delicious cake remained untouched beside her. Her last bite clung to the fork still in her hand. By the time Jake and Becca returned from their talk, Callie was out. It took all of them to carefully lift and settle her into her mother's bed. Kate stayed to tuck her in and make sure she would be as comfortable as possible. Shadow curled up on the bed at her feet; his soulful brown eyes looking up at Kate for assurance. She patted him gently on the head and left the room, leaving a small crack in the door. Becca, Jake, and Grandpa had returned to their favorite chairs on the back porch by the time Kate came back.

"I can make pancakes for everyone in the morning," Grandpa offered.

"We can give her the necklace then," Kate said.

Becca was extremely disappointed. The suspense about the necklace was almost unbearable. "Maybe she'll wake up again," she ventured.

"She'll feel better in the morning," Kate said.

Becca couldn't decide whether she wanted to stay with Callie or spend her last night in Halo Notch with Jake.

"Let's go home and make s'mores," he said.

It was an offer Becca couldn't refuse.

Chapter 29

THE SPECIAL DAY

"Wake up, Sleeping Beauty!" Grandpa called. Bright sunlight poured through the curtains and hit Callie in the face.

"Your pancakes are almost ready!" he called again. The sizzle of bacon teased Callie's senses—she loved Grandpa's crispy bacon!

Just then, Kate entered the room and kissed Callie on the forehead. "I'll help you up," she said. "I think I heard the Necklace of Honor calling your name." She helped Callie to the bathroom to freshen up and get dressed. When they came downstairs, Jake and Becca were at the table.

"You missed the first one, girlie!" Grandpa said. "Jake inhaled it before it hit the plate."

Callie sat down at the head of the table, relieved but embarrassed that her mother cut up her pancake for her. It was necessary, though. Callie knew she couldn't have cut anything with her right arm so wrapped up. She ate quickly, enjoying the light conversation. It was almost impossible to ignore the beautifully wrapped box beside her plate.

"Guess what, Callie," Becca said excitedly. "Ms. Hogg will be in jail for a while for assault and battery and theft. I guess her housekeeping days are over."

"What about Mr. Creepy?" Callie asked, sinking her fork into another bite of pancake.

"He's in jail until his hearing next month," Becca said as she helped clean off the table. "He's gonna be locked up for a long time I guess."

"Attempted murder...theft...arson... I can't imagine what all the charges will be," Callie responded, hoping for more information from anyone who knew anything. *He deserves all the time in jail he can get.*

The room was strangely quiet. She looked at Grandpa, then her mother, then Jake. They didn't look at her.

She asked, "Does anybody know what all the charges are against Mr. Creepy?"

Again, awkward silence. Becca and Callie looked at each other.

Becca was curious, wondering what was going on. *Adults are weird—why doesn't anyone answer Callie's question?*

Jake spoke up at last, "Aw, Callie, let's not talk about all that stuff today—it's your ceremony day. I'm sure..." he stopped and ran his fingers through his hair. "I'm sure we'll find out more than we ever wanted to know later." He looked at Grandpa as if to ask for his approval.

"What do you mean, 'more later'? Is something wrong?" Callie asked, becoming impatient.

"Did he escape or something?" Becca asked, starting to worry.

"No, girls," Grandpa said softly, "Your..." he started, then corrected himself, "The man who shot Callie is safely in prison." He choked up like he was going to cry but didn't.

The girls relaxed a little.

Callie looked lovingly at Grandpa. *Maybe he's emotional about all that happened. I bet that's why Jake and Mom are trying not to talk about it.*

"Let's get on with the ceremony," Kate said quickly, then turned toward Grandpa. "We'll have plenty of time to talk about things another day."

Callie smiled and nodded.

"Becca, will you do the honors?" Kate said as she took away Callie's empty plate.

Becca picked up the long box and carefully removed the light blue paper and the poufy white bow. She stuck the bow onto Callie's head. Callie rolled her eyes but didn't remove it. "Are you sure you want it?" Becca asked, prolonging the suspense. Callie glared at her playfully. Becca slowly removed the lid, revealing the beautifully handcrafted necklace inside. Callie and Becca were mesmerized. The golden necklace was the most unusual either girl had ever seen.

"There's not another one like it in the world," Grandpa said with pride.

"Like you, Callie—one of a kind," Kate added softly. The feminine necklace was just long enough to encircle Callie's neck and rest on her collarbones.

It was truly unique. It looked like tiny golden dots all connected—layer upon layer—creating a multi-dimensional effect. Seven circles, each about a finger-width apart along the chain, provided special places for Callie's charms.

"It must have been very expensive!" Callie exclaimed, awed by its beauty.

"Let's just say that I did a little bartering," Grandpa replied with a smile. He and Kate cast knowing looks at each other.

Callie wondered how many carved animals Grandpa had to give up.

"Let's begin," Grandpa said.

Kate spread the necklace out on the table in front of Callie as Grandpa continued, "As I've said, this tradition was started many years ago by your great grandmother, Callie. She wanted a way to pass down spiritual truths to your grandmother, my wife. Your great grandfather had died before your grandmother was born, so your great grandmother thought it was very important for her daughter to understand how special she was to God, and what a crucial role she would play in the lives of those around her. Family members and close friends gathered beads, charms, and a hand-me-down necklace to make the first Necklace of Honor. The necklace was given on the eve of your grandmother's thirteenth birthday. Only two weeks after her birthday, your great grandmother died. The Necklace of Honor became a source of comfort and strength to your grandmother. When your mother was born, your grandmother decided that she would continue the tradition on your mother's thirteenth birthday." Grandpa paused and nodded to his daughter.

Callie thought she saw a tear in her strong mother's eye.

"Your mother asked me to do the speaking, even though she designed the necklace and brought everything together for you," he added.

Kate smiled shyly.

"She designed the necklace using a pattern of tiny beads welded together because she believes that you have many facets to your personality and many talents to offer." He spoke slowly, ceremoniously. "The number seven is thought to represent completeness in the Bible, and you'll have seven charms like your mother and grandmother did. Your necklace is perfect for you because we give it to you with all our hearts. Every charm means something special to the person giving it to you—something he or she wants you to know as you cross over into a new stage of your life. No two necklaces can ever be the same. Your Necklace of Honor is unique. Like you. Our hope is that you will cherish it and let it remind you of our love, support, and prayers for you as you experience God each day."

He stopped and looked at each person, one by one, seeming to wait for comments or questions. Everyone was quiet. Kate stroked her daughter's hair gently. Becca couldn't remember her own mother ever showing love to her like that.

"I'm glad you're here, Cal," Jake said to Callie. He cleared his throat uncomfortably. "You tried to get yourself killed, but it didn't work." Everyone laughed.

"I thought I was using your necklace," Callie said to her mother with sudden realization.

"I hope it's okay that we're giving you a new one. Mine brought up bad memories," she answered. A shadow passed over her face. Kate brushed a tear away quickly and straightened up tall. Callie nodded.

Becca wanted to help make the occasion special. "Let's light some candles!" she said suddenly, looking around the room for some. "It will be cool!" She grabbed Jake's elbow to get him to help her. She pulled a little harder when he didn't catch on. "It's okay, right?" she asked Grandpa.

"That's a good idea," he said, going to the kitchen to get the matches.

Callie looked at her mom. "I'm sorry about what happened to your necklace, Mom" she offered.

"It's in the past. Today's about you, honey," her mother replied gently.

The three candle hunters returned with a handful of mismatched candles and a box of matches. While Becca arranged them on the table, Jake lit them, and Grandpa closed the curtains. Callie felt Shadow's warm body brush by her leg under the table and curl up at her feet.

"Are we ready now?" Grandpa said as he came to the table, feigning exasperation.

"Yes. It's perfect." Becca replied.

Grandpa began again. "Okay. We have all the gifts here. Except one." Callie tried not to look disappointed. That meant there wouldn't be seven after all. She was concerned that her blessing would be incomplete.

"Only six total gifts have surfaced for your Necklace of Honor. Your mother and I have discussed it at length, and we feel certain that God already knows where the seventh will come from. It wasn't our plan for it not to be complete today..." he sighed a little.

"It wasn't our plan for you to get shot, either" Kate added as she bonked Callie lightly on the head.

"God knows what He's doing, even if we don't." Grandpa added. "And we sure don't sometimes," Becca heard him say under his breath.

"When you can't see His hand, trust His heart," Jake said. It was one of his favorite phrases.

"We have all the charms this morning—even if you've already seen them—so that everyone else can know what they stand for. Since Jake and Becca's Granny couldn't leave the nursing home today, I'd like for Becca to do her part," Grandpa said as he handed a dainty handkerchief to Becca, along with a piece of paper.

Becca's eyes sparkled. It felt good to be included. *It's too bad Granna couldn't come.*

A knock at the door interrupted her thoughts as Grandpa said, "Maybe that's Emma. I was hoping she'd make it."

Jake dashed to the door, almost running over a chair in the process. Becca and Callie exchanged smiles—it had become clear to them that Jake and Emma were sweet on each other.

"Hey, Emma!" Jake said as he flung open the door. He then backed away a little, taking a more relaxed pose.

"Sorry I'm late," Emma said, passing Jake with a special smile; she headed straight for the birthday girl and gave her a hug. Everyone greeted her warmly—except Becca, who still wasn't sure how she felt about this charming woman who had held her captive at the vineyard just a few weeks before. Emma deposited her purse and a shopping bag on the couch and found a seat.

Chapter 30
CEREMONY

The soft candlelight warmed the breakfast table as sunlight tugged at the curtains, eager to join the celebration. Callie gazed at her grandfather's sweet face. Crow's-feet wrinkles accented his smiling eyes like quotation marks. His thick hair was salt-and-pepper gray. He had the muscled and worn hands of a carpenter and a deep commitment to the Lord. His tender, strong leadership was exactly what Callie needed for this special moment.

"Jake, would you like to go first?" Grandpa asked. Jake stood, holding a piece of paper he really didn't need. He, too, was strong—his relationship with God glowed like hot embers. He saw God's hand in everything and exclaimed the wonder of creation in his pencil sketches and custom parables. Pulling something out of his pocket, he cleared his throat and began.

"The charm I have for Callie is made of cave limestone. See?" he said, holding a stone out between his thumb and finger for all to see, "it has white Caltrate with iron running through it. I found this piece along the side of the cave where a part of a stalactite had broken off. One of my friends at work put it in his rock tumbler and fixed it for the necklace. Callie knows about the time when I ran away, and I stayed all night alone in the cave. I admit it—I was scared out of my wits!" Everyone chuckled. "I started praying and realized that I needed to trust God to be with me or I was going to freak out in that pitch-black cave. I'll bet I spent an hour or more trying to remember Psalm 28:7: 'The Lord is my strength and my shield; my heart trusts in Him and I am helped.' Callie, every time you see this rock, let it remind you of God's trustworthiness." He laid the rock charm beside one of the seven round circles on the necklace and moved back to his place.

Callie and Becca recalled their night in the cave, events flashing in their minds.

"Thanks, Jake. Trust is a good thing." Callie was at a loss for fancy words, but it didn't matter.

Becca remembered the "Trust Me" that was carved on the rock. "Did you carve some words on a rock in the cave?" Becca asked.

"Yep. It helped keep my mind off being scared. I wrote 'Trust Me' because it was what God was telling me at the time."

"Finally, an answer! That message on the rock was driving me crazy!" Becca exclaimed.

Callie looked at Becca and Jake, eyes wide—the Two Words! *That's exactly what God told me at the beginning of summer. Strange. God told Jake the same thing, and now Becca has seen the message!*

"Hmmm. Seems like I heard that same thing earlier this summer from someone else I know," Grandpa said with a wink at Callie. "Who wants to go next?"

"Since I really have two, I'll do mine next." Kate moved to face Callie, again holding the moonstone charm in her hand. "Callie, you're a bearer of God's image. He created you to reflect His beauty—just like the moon reflects the sun. Your grandmother gave me the moonstone for the same reason that I am giving to you. The world's beauty passes away, but you are radiant if you reflect Him. The Bible says in Psalms: 'Those who look to the Lord are radiant.'" Kate laid the moonstone next to Jake's rock on the table and lined it up with another circle on the necklace. She kissed Callie on the forehead and took her place once again, behind her precious daughter.

"Becca?" Grandpa said with a nod. Becca stepped forward, holding her piece of paper. She spoke clearly.

"Granna wrote this out. It says, "Callie, you and I have spoken many times about the grace of God and how Jesus' death on the cross paid for our sins. We have riches in Christ—even though we don't deserve it. Remember what GRACE stands for: God's Riches at Christ's Expense. I asked your grandfather to carve this little cross from the old cherry tree on the windy hill above my house. God's grace provides new life and hope for every day and eternal life with Him in heaven when we die. Second Corinthians 12:9 says: 'My grace is sufficient for you, for power is perfected in weakness.' We are the strongest, Callie, when we are weak and rely on Him."

Callie and Becca both remembered the "Wind Blows, Tree Grows" story from The Bridge and how it helped them on their hike. Becca looked at the little wooden cross in her hand and thought about her grandmother's words. She didn't understand why an innocent man would willingly die for people he didn't know. *It doesn't make sense. How can I be strong when I am weak?* Her mind was drawn to thinking about it, but she didn't really want to. When she caught herself daydreaming, she quickly put the cross by the third circle and returned to her seat.

Grandpa addressed Emma next, "I'm glad you joined us today, Emma. You're practically family." He handed her the little box from Mrs. Jennie.

"Oh, yes...this one's very special," she said enthusiastically.

Becca felt her jealousy rise again as she noticed how Emma's presence lit up in the room. *Yet another person is added to the happy not-my-family huddle. Everyone except me.* Just as her heart began to grow cold, though, Emma drew her back in with Mrs. Jennie's story.

"Mrs. Jennie was a very special lady. Her knowledge of these mountains and the traditions, customs and ancient herbal remedies has impacted more lives than we'll ever know. Callie, the fact that she saved this special gift for you is remarkable. She was very generous even though she never had much herself. She was always thinking of others first. This pewter shoe stands for endurance. Her favorite verse was Hebrews 12:1-2: '...let us lay aside every weight and the sin that so easily ensnares us. Let us run with endurance the race that lies before us, keeping our eyes on Jesus, the source and perfecter of our faith.' For you, Callie, the gift of Endurance." She nodded to the honoree and placed the shoe on the table. A spontaneous moment of silence washed over the room—an offering of respect for the dear woman.

"Thank you," Callie said with dignity.

Grandpa cleared his throat and held up the cedar dogwood charm he had so carefully created for his beloved granddaughter. "Callie, my gift to you is craftsmanship. You are worth a great deal to your Heavenly Father and to all of us. Psalm 139 says that you are 'remarkably and wonderfully made.' Ephesians 2:10 says that you are God's 'creation,' which means 'masterpiece' or 'poem' in the original language. Your life has meaning and purpose, Callie. Just as God gave His very best in creating you, you should also remember to give your very best in everything you do. You should cherish your body and guard yourself against anything that might take away from the value and dignity God has given. I crafted your charm out of sweet-smelling cedar. The dogwood blossoms—common around here—symbolize Christ's death. For you, Callie, the gift of craftsmanship." Grandpa took Callie by the hand and kissed it gently.

"Thanks, Grandpa," she said humbly.

"I guess I'm last," Kate said, stepping forward once again. Only she and Grandpa knew what the last one was. A hush filled the room, except for Shadow's jingling nametags as he scratched an itch.

"This one's from your dad, Callie," she began, holding a wrapped ring box in her hand.

Everyone gathered closer to see the opening of the mysterious sixth gift. Those who had been standing pulled up a chair and sat down at the table. Callie awkwardly leaned forward, despite her soreness. Only Grandpa and Kate stood.

"The gift in this box is very special." Kate said as she laid it in Callie's hands.

She helped Callie remove the paper and little bow from the tiny velvet box. Callie opened the lid slowly, feeling the resistance of the box's hinge. Wonder filled her eyes as she lifted a tiny golden ring from its white satin bed and held it up.

"It was yours when you were a baby, Callie," Kate said lovingly. "Your Daddy bought it for you the same week you were born." Callie tried to put it on her pinkie finger, but it was too small.

"I can't believe it ever fit me!" Callie exclaimed, wishing her father was still alive.

"It's engraved on the inside—'Pride and Joy.' It was your father's nickname for you when you were little," Mother explained.

"Only he said it like it was one word: Prydanjoy," Grandpa added. He laughed. "Come to think of it, I never heard him call you anything else."

"You never told me," Callie said. She read the tiny letters. Becca moved in closer for a better look, and Jake brought a lamp closer so that everyone could see it better.

Mother continued, "Callie, this ring stands for love. Your father deeply loved you all the days of his life. It's hard to believe, but God's love is even stronger—and it lasts forever. Romans 8:38-39 tells us that nothing can separate us from the love of God that is in Christ."

Callie thought about how God had been with her even when she didn't feel Him. She fingered the tiny ring while she looked at her father's photo on the wall, trying to remember him.

"Thank you, Mom. Thank you, everyone," Callie said gratefully. She leaned forward to put the ring on the table beside the other five charms. It was Emma that noticed this time that she was having trouble reaching the table because of her shoulder. She gently took the ring from Callie and laid it by the necklace. Then, as if something had just occurred to her, she positioned the other charms so that the ring from Callie's father would be right in the middle circle of the necklace.

"Well, I guess that's everything. God will supply the seventh charm when the time is right," Grandpa said.

Callie could hardly wait.

Chapter 31
SECRETS

"I have to tell you something about your uncle" Grandpa said softly.

"My uncle?" Callie said with excitement, finally glad to be hearing more about the family.

Grandpa lifted his finger to his lips to tell Callie to keep her voice down. It was after the ceremony, and everyone had headed outside to enjoy the fresh, fragrant summer air.

Grandpa waited for everyone to settle in the various chairs and benches before casting a solemn look in Kate's direction. She avoided his gaze, looking rather toward the creek. It was clear to Callie that Grandpa had decided to tell something important.

"Travis was—is—two years older than your mother." Grandpa said just above a whisper. He sighed slowly, suddenly looking very weary. "He tended to be rebellious, and we weren't consistent in giving him boundaries. It got to the point where he was out of control. It's still hard to admit, but nothing we tried after that would work. He became angry and violent—even as a child."

Callie's emotions rose in her throat. *Why is this such a secret?* Her mind repeated the question again and again.

Jake, Becca, and Emma drew closer. Grandpa continued in a normal tone, "It only got worse as he grew older. He was in trouble with the law by the time he was your age. He was cruel to us all—especially to your mother. He broke her things and threatened her every day. One day, he hit your grandmother, and I hit him. One thing led to another, and your mother called the sheriff. Travis ran out the door and disappeared, never to be seen again. Until..." his voice drifted off. He took a long sip of his coffee and swallowed hard.

"We didn't talk about Travis much after that," he continued, "it upset your grandmother and your mother. In fact, your grandmother was never the same.

She died two years later. But," he paused for emphasis, "we've never stopped praying for him." Grandpa stopped again and sighed deeply. "We didn't even know if he was alive or dead." His lips quivered as he fought back the tears. "I still love him. He's still my boy, no matter what's happened."

Callie and Becca sensed the misery Grandpa felt. Becca stood and moved in closer, leaning against the porch rail just inches from Callie's chair. Kate looked like she was going to cry. She went over to him and sat on the floor at his feet, leaning against his chair. Becca noticed that she seemed more like a little girl in need of her father's assurance than a grown woman. Grandpa lovingly fingered a curl of his daughter's hair. Emma picked up Shadow and moved to sit by Jake, rubbing the little dog's ears. Becca noticed that Jake stretched and leaned back against the picnic table, draping his arm across Emma's shoulders. Emma didn't look at him, but didn't move away, either.

"But that's in the past, Grandpa. You said it yourself," Callie whispered.

Grandpa's lip quivered more noticeably. He was clearly broken-hearted.

Becca let her eyes wander from Grandpa to Kate, who sat as still as a statue. She thought she saw Kate's jaw muscles tense. *There's something going on here that no one is saying.*

"It's in the past, Grandpa," Callie said again, pleading for him to be happy. "We have each other now."

But Becca had the insight of a good writer. She knew that there was an important truth yet to be revealed. "It's not in the past, is it?" she asked. It sounded more like a statement than a question.

Grandpa patted the air toward Becca as if to push the question away.

"It's time," Jake said gently to his dear old friend.

Grandpa nodded, still unable to speak due to the sobs that threatened to overtake him.

"Kate?" Jake said, seeming to ask for Kate's permission to tell more. Kate gave an almost imperceptible nod.

Jake hesitated a little and then said, "Your uncle is..."

"Mr. Creepy!" Becca practically shouted, feeling smart that she had solved the mystery.

"No!" Callie said firmly. *Shut up, Becca—let Jake talk,* her heart screamed. "That's impossible!" She looked to Grandpa, Jake and her mother for anyone to take her side. No one said a word. "Tell her! Tell her it's not him!"

"I had a feeling when the sheriff told us his aliases, Callie. Dylan was the name of Travis' best friend. Howard was the name of that mean dog he had," Grandpa explained as he fiddled with a small splinter of wood that he just pulled from the arm of the chair. The gurgling of the river penetrated Callie's awareness, as if trying to anchor her in the present—to her secure, beloved mountains. She reeled at the possibilities, wanting desperately to deny the revelation that rocked her world.

"He knew about the Townsend house, he knew about the Longfellow treasure..." Becca continued, logically connecting the dots so that Callie could see the big picture.

"What about the cave?" Emma interjected. "Wouldn't he have known about that?"

"Yeah, what about the cave?" said Callie. *Finally, some help with this.* "Mr. Creepy stopped at the fork in the trail and never came to the cave."

"I made a false trail, remember?" Becca replied, pleased with herself that her trail coverage was so effective.

"Travis didn't grow up here—he only lived here for a short time before he ran away. He hated the mountains. All he talked about what getting away from here. We think he may have even gone back to a friend's house in Oak Ridge for a time," Kate said, still staring off into space.

"You mean he never explored the mountains at all? Wonder why he even came back here, then?" Becca said, puzzled.

"It doesn't matter. I don't believe any of you. I mean, I believe I have an Uncle Travis, but I don't believe that he's Mr. Creepy," Callie said firmly, resenting the ever-growing evidence. "Just because this man's alias happens to be the name of some old dog and some friend Travis had doesn't mean that it's the same person."

"Don't you see, Callie? It must be him. It makes perfect sense. He's even the right age and everything. Think about those eyes...they're gold like yours," Becca pressed. "Don't you remember? What about when he told you to open your backpack and you threw the salty peanuts in his eyes? Think back, Callie. Those eyes, staring at you...they looked just like yours."

Callie did remember. She also recalled thinking that he looked familiar. Her memory made her shoulder hurt more and she winced in pain. She also remembered the NOH note signed by "T."

"Whoa... shot by your own uncle," Becca said as two more dots were connected in her mind. Jake gave her a warning look and Becca answered, "Well, it's true."

"It's all true," Grandpa said at last. Callie looked deep into his eyes, now puffy and red with emotion.

"Mom?" Callie asked, looking for some sort of comfort.

Kate reached over and touched Callie's leg. "It's true. I saw him."

It was Callie's turn to fight back her tears. "If... if he had known I was his niece, would he have shot me?"

The question hung in the air like the sticky, damp humidity gathering above the group.

"Let's not let it ruin your special day," Grandpa said. "Just forget about it. There's nothing we can do about it right now, anyway." Standing with effort, he shuffled off to the workshop, looking much older than he had before.

Callie reeled from the news. *Forget it? Really? Not likely! The one new family member I finally learn about just had to be a horrible man.*

Becca meanwhile had decided to do everything she could to salvage her last day with Callie. "Mother and Dad are bringing my gift to you tonight," she said. "I looked around town here, but ..." She started to say that there weren't any good stores in this little nothing of a town, but her earlier opinion didn't seem to fit anymore. So, she finished her sentence by saying, "I didn't find what I was looking for." She hoped that her self-centered mother had understood what she wanted and would bring the right thing.

"Thanks, Becca," said Callie, trying to sound excited.

Jake busied himself by arranging the Necklace of Honor and the charms on the rustic picnic table, and Emma dashed inside to get her camera and the shopping bag she had brought. Kate went into the house and started cleaning the kitchen.

"I'm sorry, Cal," Jake said gently. "This is hard. I know it is."

Callie just nodded.

When Emma returned, she pulled out a picture frame with a wide, white mat inside and presented it to Callie. "This is your present from me. The big mat has enough room to write what each charm means. I'll take pictures of everybody with your necklace, and we'll frame the best."

"Thank you, Emma," Callie replied with a hug.

AFTER EVERYTHING HAD settled down and photos were taken, Callie relaxed in the hypnotic swaying swing. She watched as the branches quivered to the occasional breeze, listened to the squirrels chatter, and breathed in the fragrance of freshly mown grass. Longing to escape the troubling news about her uncle, she gave in to the sights, smells, and sounds of her mountains and drifted off into a much-needed nap.

Only moments later, she was startled awake by a gunshot and the sensation of falling. She gasped and tried to sit up. It was a jarring shock to realize that it was just a dream. But—*could* Mr. Creepy hurt her again?

Chapter 32

THE OTHER CULTURE

That evening, Callie's family went to Jake's cabin for a farewell cookout. Callie, of course, wore her six-charmed Necklace of Honor.

The McLains were due at any moment.

In the meantime, Callie and Becca occupied themselves at the coffee table with newspaper clippings that hailed their heroism. They sifted through them, putting them in chronological order for their two identical photo albums. Various photographs, thank you notes, and other memorabilia covered the table as well—there were two copies of everything. The girls chatted happily, although Becca was nervous about seeing her parents again. Kate joined them in between her cooking duties, while Grandpa and Jake grilled and talked about football.

The McLains arrived in a huff of dust. The unfriendly couple had just paid a dutiful but insincere visit to Granna in the nursing home and were both cranky. Becca heard them fighting even before they got out of the car. She looked around for Jake, but he had disappeared. Silently and motionlessly, she watched as they got out of their new sports car and stepped onto the gravel driveway. Both her parents were dressed in the latest fashions as expected. She had never noticed before that their behavior, their words, and even the way they carried themselves showed their wealth and status. Becca wondered if Callie had seen the disgusted looks on her parents' faces when they entered the cabin.

Where is Jake? Becca wondered. *He's probably hiding from them.* She felt like hiding from them herself. They didn't even greet her. They just brushed by without acknowledging her presence. *They'd better not say one mean word to this sweet family.*

The adults greeted each other, but it was very tense. Kate said a quick "hello" and then hurried off again. Callie had never seen her mother act so strained around anyone. *Maybe she went to school with Mr. McLain, and he treated her the same way those bullies treated me.*

Callie could only think of one word to describe Becca's mother: uptight. She had flour-white feet crammed tightly into very high heels, slick legs poking from a tight pencil-skirt, snug blouse, downturned blood-red lips, hard brown marble eyes, and bleached blonde hair choked tightly into a bun. *She doesn't even look real,* thought Callie, who wasn't sure whether to chuckle or feel sorry for the woman. She marveled at the contrast when her own mother eased back into the room. Kate's easy gait, her minimal makeup and her touchable hair seemed so natural. Callie weighed Dr. McLain's harsh demeanor against her mother's open and carefree style and found Dr. McLain lacking.

Becca's father was unapproachable. His starched jeans stretched tautly over his muscled legs, his wide belt anchored his barrel chest, and his pressed button-down shirt barely covered his huge arms. Callie thought that he'd crush Becca if the thought of hugging her ever occurred to him. Even his short, expertly groomed beard looked prickly and hard like it had been hair sprayed. His edgy scowl seemed permanent. Callie shuddered at the thought of having to live with this callous rock of a man. *He's nothing like Jake or Grandpa!* She would have never exchanged the comfy jeans, soft shirts, easy smiles, natural hair, and hearty hugs from the men in her life for the stingy riches of the unyielding Russell McLain.

Callie admitted that she was blessed with a great family, but she still felt poor. Somehow the presence of Becca's parents made her insecure. She watched Becca closely, waiting for her to transform back into the snob she had met earlier in the summer. *Did Becca really change at all this summer? Did I? Maybe both of us changed a little, but it doesn't matter now. Jesus, please show your love to these people,* she prayed earnestly.

Becca leaned against the doorway that divided the kitchen and the living room so that she could see the men outside and the women inside the house. She listened as Grandpa carried on a strange, very formal conversation with her father about local property taxes. Although Grandpa knew more about the subject, her father clearly considered himself the expert. Inside, Dr. McLain occupied herself reading medical journals she had brought with her. She haughtily raised her gaze only a few times, only to be ignored by everyone. Callie's and Becca's eyes met, and they exchanged exasperated looks.

Becca checked the porch again and saw Jake back at the grill. She noticed that he stayed quiet and uninvolved in the conversation. It was clear to see how strained the father-son relationship was. Jake's face remained tense and unsmiling, while Mr. McLain's eyes darted continuously from person to person as if paranoid that someone would snatch the center of attention away from him.

Callie joined Becca in the doorway. "What are you doing?"

Becca turned to Callie. "I'm sorry about my parents—they're horrible."

"You acted just like them when you first got here," Callie replied simply.

Becca thought about her mother and father for a moment. *Did I really act that way?* "I'm sorry, Callie. I shouldn't have."

"It's okay. I wasn't so great myself."

It wasn't long before Dr. McLain's contemptuous gaze landed on the Necklace of Honor. She asked a few questions about it and sniffed at the answers. The unfriendly physician raised her pointed nose in the air so often that Callie grew tired of looking up her nostrils. Callie thought she was mean and rude—and almost said so but held her tongue for Becca's sake.

Becca wasn't happy at all with her mother's behavior and tried many times to change the subject. Finally, Kate began to take drink orders and Dr. McLain became sullen.

Suddenly Becca remembered Callie's gift. "Wait here. I'll get your birthday present—if my mother remembered to get it." *Which she probably didn't.* She trotted to her parents' new car and opened the back door. It took only one glance inside to see that the car was empty. Becca suspected that her mother never intended to get the gift for her. "Can't you think of someone besides yourself just once in your life?" she yelled into the vacant vehicle. Pressing the button to open the trunk, she backed out of the car and slammed the door behind her. She found the trunk empty as well.

"I hate her," Becca mumbled as she slapped the trunk closed and headed for a large rock on the side of the yard to cool off. She sat down to think, her back to the house. Not wanting to start a fight with her mother, she decided to sit there until she could calm down. Taking a deep breath, she inhaled the sweet smell of the mountains and tried to relax. A light tap on her shoulder startled her.

"Lookin' for this?" Jake asked as he handed her a wrapped box.

"Where did you find it?" she asked, puzzled. I know it wasn't in the car—I looked everywhere. "Did Mother give it to you?"

"Not hardly. I bought it for you. I overheard you telling her that you wanted it, so I picked one up just in case."

"Oh, Jake! Thank you! Have I told you that I love you?" Becca said, wrapping her arms around her big brother's neck.

"No, you haven't. But you can tell me now," he said with a grin.

"I love you, Jake," she said warmly.

"I know. You told me a minute ago," he teased.

She swatted at him, but he had already dashed away and back onto the wrap-around porch to his silent post at the grill.

Becca waved a thank you to him, wishing with all her heart that she could live with him forever. Then she looked down at the tastefully wrapped present that she held in her hand. *Not bad,* she thought as she admired the attractive color combination he had chosen. *Not too flowery, not too baby-fied. Callie will love it!* Satisfied, she climbed the steps to the cabin and summoned Callie to join her on the couch.

"You were gone a long time," Callie said curiously. "I thought you got lost."

"Nope. I found everything I was looking for." Becca cast a disgusted look at her sourpuss mother, then turned toward Callie to watch her open the perfect gift.

Callie unwrapped the paper and opened the box. Reaching inside, she felt something furry and squishy and pulled out a plush skunk with great big eyes. "Huckleberry!" she laughed. "It looks like him!" Callie hugged it close, admiring its softness. "Thanks, Becca. I love it!"

Becca quoted the only words she could remember from their cave-night poem. Callie joined her, and they pieced together almost the whole thing. It had been a special moment for the two friends. No one else would ever understand what mixture of emotions and experiences they had shared during their long, scary night together. They were both sad that Becca had to leave that night.

But—even though the sun was beginning its retreat—the evening wasn't over yet. Not by a long shot.

Chapter 33
BISCUIT

It wasn't long before the two families sat down to eat together.

Becca's father smirked, "Two cultures at the same table." He gave a wise-guy smile to Becca, and she looked away.

He just can't wait to see me fail, she thought angrily. Yet, as she considered the remark, she had to admit: *We are from two different worlds.* Callie and Becca couldn't have been more different at the beginning of the summer. But the summer—the summer had changed everything! At first, she thought it would never end. Now she dreaded saying "Goodbye" to Halo Notch. There was much to write. Much to think about.

At the beginning of summer, Becca thought the Christian life was just an act. She had even hoped that Callie, her family, or Jake would drop their guard and really mess up. However, the closer she got to them, the more she saw that they were sincere. They had never claimed to be perfect and were always eager to be helpful and supportive. The thought of becoming a Christian herself had even crossed her mind.

Callie, too, looked around the table at all the different characters in her summer drama. There was such a contrast between the two worlds! She knew the time had come to pull away from Becca. Her new friend was leaving, and Callie wondered if she would ever see her again. *Maybe she never really liked me but was just using me to get the information for her paper.* But something in her heart told her that the friendship was real. She wished she had more time to spend with Becca. It seemed so...unfinished.

As the meal ended, the adults migrated to the porch to suffer through a civil conversation, and Callie and Becca joined them. Jake said very little and his parents barely spoke to each other at all. Negative, snide remarks about Jake's choice of career and lifestyle flowed freely from his parents, as did degrading comments about Becca's desire to be a writer. Kate sat close to Grandpa and didn't say a word.

The evening promised a deep orange sunset over the Smoky Mountains, and even the McLains noticed it. The sky grew peach and azure, accentuating the majesty of the mountains. For a moment, everything was quiet.

When the McLains' unpleasantness resumed, Callie and Becca escaped to the front porch swing. Lazy old Biscuit lopped slowly behind them, flopping down on the doormat. Becca promised to write. Callie admitted she wasn't much of a writer but said she would try. Maybe they could get together on Fall Break or at Christmas. Becca believed they would see each other again soon and rattled on about the special story she planned to write. Callie wasn't sure.

They tried once or twice to write the words down to their silly poem about Huckleberry but couldn't remember as many words as they had earlier.

Suddenly, a low growl interrupted them. It took a minute for them to realize that it was Biscuit, the unbelievably motionless dog. The hair stood up on his neck as he issued a rumbly warning toward something unseen on the driveway.

Callie and Becca looked at each other, and then back at Biscuit.

"I've never heard him make a sound!" Becca exclaimed. "Do you think he's okay?"

"Might be a bear. Jake!?"

Biscuit stood and woofed just as Jake appeared, followed by the others. They all looked toward the road but saw nothing.

"Maybe a bear," he offered, "Or a mountain lion."

They waited. The old dog stood frozen, ready to pounce. His deep voice "whuff-whoofed" a couple times.

Everyone was quiet, listening. A low, almost imperceptible hum appeared between the whoofs. Finally, they saw it: a car floating gracefully up the driveway. Speculations flew back and forth about who it could be.

"Sheriff?"

"No. He has a loud, old station wagon."

"Mayor?"

"Mayor's on vacation. Not likely."

"Emma?"

"Biscuit knows her."

"Someone from work?" even Dr. McLain wondered aloud.

Thereafter, no one spoke.

Jake's cabin was way out in the woods. He didn't have many visitors, except for buddies that Biscuit knew.

Gradually, the candy-apple-red sedan eased to a halt and the door opened.

"Why, it's Betty in her new car!" Grandpa exclaimed. He seemed giddy with delight. "So—she decided on the red one."

"They like each other," Callie whispered to Becca. She had suspected it before, but it was obvious now.

Ms. Betty scanned the crowd until her eyes met Grandpa's. "Hello, everyone. I'm glad I found y'all all here." It was only after the greeting that she broke eye contact with her dear craftsman. "I've come to extend a special invitation, and I hope y'all can oblige," she purred, seeming to enjoy her place center-stage. Her graceful gestures were enhanced by her well-manicured hands.

"I'm sure we don't have time to accept your offer. We are leaving tonight," Mr. McLain answered curtly.

"Oh, but this invitation is for tonight. I think this might even interest you, Rusty," Ms. Betty replied with a smile.

Becca saw the mighty Russell McLain flinch at being called Rusty.

"Rusty?" Callie whispered to Becca, amused.

Becca just rolled her eyes. *I keep forgetting Dad's from here. I wonder how he was when he was younger.*

"It is getting quite late," Kate added sweetly.

Ms. Betty smiled, peeking around the corner of the house at the sunset that was transforming the sky on the other side.

There was an awkward silence while the group waited to hear more. Callie noticed that the adults appeared more eager for their evening to be over than to entertain thoughts of prolonging it.

"Mrs. Longfellow has invited y'all all to her house tonight," Ms. Betty continued at last.

"Mrs. Longfellow?" Jake asked with amazement.

"I thought you said she wouldn't even go to the hospital when she was pushed into the curio cabinet," Becca said to him.

Jake started to respond, but Ms. Betty broke in, "Honey, the only way Mrs. Longfellow's gonna leave that house is in a casket."

"Why does she want us to come tonight?" Jake asked.

"We don't have time for this nonsense," Dr. McLain clipped. "We have to get back."

Ms. Betty's smile to Dr. McLain was disarming. "Oh, Honey, I haven't met you." She paused and let her eyes float from Dr. McLain's head to her feet and back up, sizing her up. "But you seem to be well-suited to our dear Rusty," she said a flatly. Ms. Betty was clearly not intimidated by either of the McLains.

"I like her, Callie," Becca whispered.

"Me, too."

Then, as if to get back to her mission, Ms. Betty turned on her charm again and continued her invitation. "Mrs. Longfellow is old and feeble and she has no living relative to pass her riches on to. She made it clear to me that I was to fetch the two young heroines who caught that awful criminal and bring them—with their families—to her home tonight. She'd like to properly thank them. You might oughta strongly consider her invitation."

"Well," Mr. McLain perked up, "This is different. Perhaps we should give the old...elderly woman a visit."

Becca nudged Callie. "See that?"

"I don't see anything."

"Look—in his eyes: dollar signs," Becca said firmly. "If there's a way for him to get his hands on some inheritance money, he's all in," she said with disgust.

Mr. and Dr. McLain huddled over to one side of the porch so they could have a whispered argument.

Jake, Grandpa, Kate, Callie, and Becca drew closer together as well.

"What's she like, Grandpa?" Callie asked, eager to know more about the mysterious woman.

"Mrs. Longfellow? Can't say that I've ever seen her. Only a few people have. She is truly a recluse."

"Jake?" Becca asked, "What about you?"

"I haven't set one foot in the house. She was specific about which doctor could treat her in her home when she was hurt, even though her injuries were severe. No one else could come in. Only the sheriff and the doctor saw her. Oh, and I guess Ms. Betty." Jake replied.

"I think we should go," Kate said. "It's a rare opportunity."

Grandpa looked at each person in the little circle to see if everyone agreed. Every head nodded.

"We accept," said Grandpa and the smug Mr. McLain at the very same time.

"Good. I'll see you at her front door in an hour," Ms. Betty said with a lilt. "Come as you are—no need to dress up."

The adults instinctively checked their watches while both girls rejoiced that they could wear their comfy shorts and flip-flops.

The graceful lady slipped back into her gleaming vehicle and drove away.

And Biscuit, tired from standing so long, turned his worn body around three times and flopped back down, satisfied that he had carried out his watchdog duties.

Chapter 34

MRS. LONGFELLOW

It was already dark when two vehicles entered the rarely disturbed driveway belonging to Mrs. Amelia Longfellow. The McLains exited their own car in silence; everyone else tumbled out of Kate's jeep with sounds of laughter and excitement.

The two parties merged on the sidewalk. Suspense filled the air. It was a marvel that anyone would be granted access to the secluded citizen behind the grand home's well-appointed facade. Even frequently bored Dr. McLain seemed interested.

Callie tried to imagine what was behind the ornate front door. She'd heard stories all her life about the old, eccentric woman. Even ghost stories were abundant. It wouldn't surprise her if the towering house truly was haunted. She imagined a bitter woman with a grumpy scowl and a big black wart on her nose. Who would ever guess that such a dark, miserable human being could live in such an impressive house! Of course, Callie's version of Mrs. Longfellow hated children and shunned all goodness and happiness in the world—what else could Callie have thought? She gazed at every window, expecting to see Mrs. Longfellow glaring from behind the dark curtains.

Becca, on the other hand, not having had the benefit of years of folklore, imagined Mrs. Longfellow very differently. She was certain that she would find an elegant lady, gliding regally across the room in her satin evening gown. She could even see the hostess dripping with jewels and carrying a spoiled pet cat. In her version of the story, the house would be flooded with light from crystal chandeliers behind those heavy curtains.

The outer appearance of the house added plausibility to either of the girls' imaginations, for every window was fully covered. No light from inside the house penetrated the ever-darkening yard.

As the party walked slowly toward the door, Callie hung back so she could slip off her flip-flops and sink her toes into the lush grass carpet. It felt as good as she had thought it would.

"Coming, Callie?" Kate asked, concerned that her still-injured daughter might not be feeling well.

"Coming," Callie said quickly as she poked her feet back into her sandals and shuffled to catch up.

Ms. Betty greeted them warmly on the porch.

Callie and Becca surveyed the clean, geranium-decorated porch and tried to make its appearance fit with what they had imagined. Mr. McLain reached out with self-appointed authority and rang the echoing doorbell. Everyone took a step back from the heavy oak door, staring at the large doorknobs with bated breath.

I'll bet there's a gardener who keeps the outside looking nice to disguise the spooky insides, Callie thought.

Becca had expected something a little more formal, like concrete planters with poofy green shrubs—or maybe marble lion statues on either side of the door.

The wait was almost unbearable! Seconds ticked away like minutes, but there was no sound coming from inside.

"I'll bet Ms. Hogg murdered her and buried her in the basement," Callie said with conviction. Once she had said it out loud, it didn't sound as smart as it had in her head. She was relieved that no one acted like they heard her say it, until she saw Becca gazing at her with a far-away look in her eyes, considering her theory.

Just then, the door latch clicked, followed by a rustling sound. Slowly, slowly, the heavy wooden door squeaked open to reveal not a servant, but the elderly Mrs. Longfellow herself!

She was a frail woman, easily over 90 years old—nothing like what either girl had imagined. She was small and bent, her wispy white hair peeking out around the edges of the knit turban on her head. Her thin, long arms seemed barely connected to the sleeves of her pale pink dress. Her soft eyes blinked often as she surveyed her curious guests.

Kate broke the silence, greeting their hostess with a warm smile. "You must be Mrs. Longfellow! What a pleasure to meet you!"

The reclusive lady smiled graciously, keeping her thin lips closed. Becca noted later that several of her teeth were missing. A large flesh-colored bandage crinkled on her paper-thin forehead. Callie noticed her bandaged arm as well, evidence of her run-in with Ms. Hogg.

The elfin woman turned without a word and hobbled slowly through the large foyer, toward the double French doors to her sitting room on the right. A faint smell of roses lingered in the air. The seven visitors and Ms. Betty followed her, studying the details. Although the lighting was somewhat dim, it was easy to see that the house was clean and tidy. Old antiques, lamps, and pictures lined the large foyer area, and a grand staircase led to the darkened second floor.

"It's like stepping back in time!" Becca whispered to Callie.

"Not what I expected," Callie mumbled, a little disappointed. "I'd hate to live in this huge house all alone."

"It's no fun," Becca replied with dismay, thinking of her own experience.

The fragile hostess finally entered her parlor and sat down with effort in a plush velvet chair. The guests took seats in various places, except for Ms. Betty, who stood behind the woman.

"I wonder how ole' Uncle Travis got in here," Becca whispered to Callie, thinking how easy it would be to break in, grab the loot and leave.

"Mr. Creepy," Callie hissed, loud enough for all to hear. She lowered her voice then, but stressed every word when she said to Becca, "He'll never be Uncle Travis to me. Never." Even the words "Uncle Travis" tasted terrible in her mouth.

"Sorry," Becca replied, making a mental note not to call him Uncle Travis again.

Mrs. Longfellow settled into her chair and spoke softly, "I understand that there are two heroines nearby. Do you know where I might find them?" Her eyes sparkled as she looked at Callie and Becca.

"Mrs. Longfellow, may I introduce you to my granddaughter, Callie, and her dear friend, Becca?" Grandpa said with pride. The two girls stood and stepped forward.

"Oh, my! That horrid man *did* hurt you!" Mrs. Longfellow shook her head as she looked at Callie's bandaging.

"I'm okay," Callie said. She shot a look at Becca, hoping she had heard the "horrid man" comment. Callie didn't know what to say next but felt like she should say something. "I'm glad you got your things back."

"Yes, dear. I am, too. That's why I've invited you here. I understand that you've had a very special birthday, and I have something for you." She motioned to Ms. Betty.

Ms. Betty glided over to a nearby table and retrieved a deep green satin bag, which she presented to Mrs. Longfellow.

"This piece has been in my family for hundreds of years," the elderly woman explained as she weakly reached out, handing the pouch to Callie. "I regret that I don't remember how we came about it—girls, you should write down your memories before you get too old and forget."

Mr. McLain shifted to the front of his seated greedily.

Callie fumbled to open the elegant drawstring pouch. Becca saw Callie's struggle and opened it for her. The audience watched with suspense.

When the opening was large enough, a large, dark-red charm fell into her hand.

"It's beautiful!" Becca whispered. "It looks like a ruby!"

"It is a ruby of very high quality," Mrs. Longfellow said proudly. "That much I do remember."

Mr. McLain leapt from his seat and took the charm out of Callie's hand, examining the large, square ruby in its ornate gold setting. "This is very old. They don't cut them like this anymore." He studied it carefully.

Jake stood quickly, marched over to his father, took the charm, and returned it to Callie. Mr. McLain gave him a harsh look, but Jake looked him in the eye and didn't budge.

"Thank you, Mrs. Longfellow, but I can't accept this," Callie said sadly.

"Oh, but you must my dear," she insisted. "I chose this one specifically for you. It's red, which reminds me of bold courage. Moreover, it's priceless, which reminds me of you and your friend. It will hurt me terribly if you don't accept it." She nodded at Ms. Betty once more.

Everyone was surprised when Ms. Betty gently lifted a tattered old Bible from the same table and opened it to a ribboned passage. She lightly cleared her throat and read in her velvet tone: 'Joshua 1:9 Haven't I commanded you: be strong and courageous? Do not be afraid or discouraged, for the Lord your God is with you wherever you go." She closed the Bible reverently and embraced it in front of her before returning it to the table. Although her face remained very serious, her eyes were soft and warm.

Mrs. Longfellow continued, "You see my dear? Courage is a very good thing. Courage backed up by an Almighty God is even better. Enjoy your charm. Perhaps you will think of this night and remember."

She turned to Becca. "And for you, young lady—I've heard that you're a writer. An old friend of mine is a book publisher. She's agreed to meet with you for a whole day, so you can tell her about your writing. Your parents will have to agree, of course." Mrs. Longfellow looked at Mr. and Dr. McLain. Becca looked at them as well, eager for their approval, but doubtful she would get it.

"Of...of course," Mr. McLain finally managed to spit out as if embarrassed to say "no" to the wealthy Mrs. Longfellow. But, in an almost scolding tone, countered Becca's excitement with, "This in no way means that you'll end up being a writer. A day learning about the realities of getting a book published could be quite...enlightening." He looked over at his ill-tempered wife. "It might even give our daughter a more practical perspective."

Becca smiled. Callie noticed that she didn't hug her father or run to him.

"Good. I'll tell my friend to contact you to arrange a date." Mrs. Longfellow smiled knowingly and nodded to the girls. "It was a pleasure to meet all of you," she said, standing slowly.

Everyone stood, pausing to listen as the generous old woman spoke once more. "By the way, I've made a sizeable donation to the town library for a new young people's wing in honor of both of my heroines."

With this, Mr. McLain rushed forward as if to make sure his interests were considered. After all, having the McLain name on a public building—even in Halo Notch—was no small matter. Jake stepped in once again, taking him by the elbow and drawing him away. Becca thought for a moment that they were about to scuffle, but Jake was unwavering. Mr. McLain snarled, starting to speak, but Grandpa added his strength to Jake's and the mighty Russell McLain backed down.

Callie felt very special. "Mrs. Longfellow? I'll never forget this for as long as I live. Thank you."

"Me neither," Becca added.

"Come closer, girls." Together they walked over to the generous woman. She took their hands. "You young ladies risked your lives to bring a dangerous criminal to justice and restore my precious belongings to me. I'll never forget that for as long as *I* live. At least," she added with a tinge of sadness, "I'll try hard not to forget."

Once again Mr. McLain stepped forward, "There's a lot we need to discuss about the library..." He began.

But Ms. Betty cut him off as she gestured toward the door, "Thank you for coming, everyone. I'm sure there will be time to learn more later."

Mr. McLain started to object, but Ms. Betty stared him down and he turned and left, Jake's grasp firmly on his elbow. Dr. McLain sniffed haughtily, turned on her heels, and stomped out of the house.

"Ms. Betty could whoop him," Callie whispered to Becca. Becca agreed.

While walking back to the jeep, Callie passed the charm around for everyone to see; Becca chattered excitedly about the visit with the publisher and the new library wing.

It was Jake who made the connection: "Callie. Your seventh charm." Everyone was amazed. The Necklace was finally complete.

Becca's father impatiently pressed the girls to say their goodbyes once they reached the driveway. He was determined to leave as soon as possible and became irritable at any sign of stalling. But when Callie moved closer to Becca to hug her, Mr. and Dr. McLain shuffled Becca away and into their car. Becca and Jake objected to their rudeness, but the message was clear: "Get away—we're leaving." Becca took her seat as Dr. McLain slammed her door shut, and sorrowfully waved goodbye through the window as the car sped down the quiet little Main Street.

Reluctantly, Callie climbed into the jeep to go back to her life without Becca.

Becca watched longingly as the dear family she had come to love faded into the distance. *There's something special about them beyond just being nice. They have happiness...or joy or something. Something that stays the same no matter what they're going through. Maybe there's more to being a Christian than I thought.* She looked up in the rearview mirror at her father and noticed his cold eyes and permanent frown. She could just barely see part of her mother's scowl in the passenger side view mirror. She sighed. *I wish I could have stayed with Jake.*

"I wish she could stay," Callie said sadly as the jeep slowly pulled onto Main Street and headed for home.

"Me, too, Callie," Jake replied as he ran his fingers through his hair and looked out the window. "Me, too."

Chapter 35
HOPE

A few months later, Callie stepped lightly up her rocky driveway. In her backpack was a great report card—all A's and B's. Even the icy rain of a blustery October afternoon couldn't squelch the warmth she felt inside. *I can't wait for Mom and Grandpa to see this!* She patted the zippered pouch that held her prized document. *First, dry clothes.* She quickened her pace at the thought of a warm, crackling fireplace.

Shadow barked happily from the porch as soon as she rounded the last corner. "You're such a baby, Shadow, the rain won't melt you," she called out fondly. She kicked off her muddy shoes on the front porch and dropped her heavy backpack just inside the door. It was hard to keep her balance with all the nudges from her affectionate dog.

The fireplace glowed as aromatic cedar logs crackled and hissed. Grandpa rarely burned this wood because he used almost every scrap of it for his carvings.

"Thanks for the fire, Grandpa," she said as she headed straight for the bathroom to strip off her wet clothes. "I have a great surprise for you: my report card!" She squeezed the cold rain from her hair and reached for a towel.

"That's wonderful, Callie—you've worked really hard! Need anything?" he called.

"Clothes, please—everything." Her teeth chattered as she towel-dried her hair and combed it.

As he climbed the stairs to her bedroom, Grandpa called out, "You have another letter from Becca." She never tired of getting mail from her friend.

Grandpa brought down Callie's favorite flannel pants and a sweatshirt. He squeezed them through the slightly opened bathroom door.

"Thanks, Grandpa," Callie said, still shivering. *He knows these are my favorite clothes.*

Grandpa was waiting for her with a cup of hot chocolate and a blanket when she came to the couch. He returned to the kitchen to pour himself some coffee and then joined her, Becca's letter in hand. Callie couldn't decide what to do first—show him the report card or read the letter from Becca.

"Let me see that report card, Callie," he smiled and held out his hand. They exchanged envelopes. Shadow curled up beside her and nudged her hand with his cold nose. She stroked his head and opened the envelope.

"This is great, Callie! A's and B's! We need to celebrate!" Grandpa exclaimed.

"My math teacher's great. He's helped me a lot," Callie said. "He's always saying funny things and playing this crazy music when we come into the room. He makes school more bearable."

Callie unfolded Becca's letter. She was surprised when a gray slip of paper fell out and landed on the floor.

Grandpa bent over to pick it up, and Callie saw that it was a check. Perplexed, she read Becca's big handwriting on her signature purple paper:

"Dear Callie,

I learned a lot from you this summer, and it really paid off. I'm sorry that I ever made you feel like a freak or just a project. I admit that I felt that way at first, but you are far from either! You may not believe it, but our essay was in the newspaper! Better yet, Mrs. Longfellow's friend, the book publisher, printed it in a collection of stories written by young people.

I'm happy to tell you that we won the contest!"

"Our essay," Callie repeated, smiling.

"They sent me a check for $1,000 and a $1,000 scholarship for college. Since the scholarship is in my name, you get the money. I insist. The story wouldn't exist without you and our adventure together. It's only fair. Can you believe it? Enjoy!

By the way, I've been going to church with one of my friends here—they have a fun youth group. I'm still thinking about all this Jesus stuff.

Luvyabye, Bec"

It was great news! Callie was happy that the essay had won, and that Becca was thinking about becoming a Christian.

The check, however, presented a problem. Her family didn't like to take charity, and she knew that Mom and Grandpa would view it that way. Callie figured she would have to give it back. She quietly handed the letter to Grandpa. *Will he be mad about the check? What will I tell Becca if I have to give it back?*

Grandpa read over the letter silently, never touching the check.

"Sounds like Becca may want to accept Christ as her Savior soon," he said. "That's very good news."

"What's taking her so long?" Callie wondered aloud.

"I don't know, Honey. It's a very personal, important decision. We just need to pray that her heart will be open to Him."

The subject of the check didn't come up just then. It just hung in the air begging for attention.

Just then, Kate came in from work, dripping with icy rain. She tossed her purse to the floor and battled with her broken black umbrella. It looked like a big buzzard flapping around. Finally, it submitted to her, and she tossed it out the front door and onto the porch.

Callie bounced over to her and showed her the great report card. "Thank you for not punishing me the last time," Callie said quietly.

"Honey, I'm so proud of you. You're a smart girl, and I'm glad the school took care of the bullying situation." Mother gave her a quick, wet hug. "Let me get out of these clothes. I'm glad we have a fire."

"Look here," Grandpa said to Kate as he held up the check, "Becca sent Callie some money."

Callie started to object to how he said that. It wasn't the whole story. She wondered what Grandpa was thinking and couldn't tell if he disapproved or not. Kate came over and scanned the check briefly. She frowned slightly. Callie noticed that Grandpa was watching for his daughter's reaction. *Oh, great, Mom and Grandpa are mad now, and if I give it back, Becca and maybe Jake will be mad at me, too.*

Callie eased down to the floor to play with Shadow, wishing she wasn't in this situation. *It's not even charity, so I don't know what the problem is.*

Kate put the check on the table and went to her room.

"I'm gonna change clothes. Is there some coffee?" she asked.

"Just made some," Grandpa replied.

She turned to Callie. "We'll talk in a minute."

Callie didn't want to talk about it. She was certain she'd have to return it. She sighed. *I guess I need to find an envelope and a stamp. But we could do so much with $1,000—mom's room has a broken window, the jeep has bald tires, Grandpa's chair is falling apart. Maybe we could even use some of it for Christmas presents. It just isn't fair.*

Kate was back in no time, pouring herself a steaming cup of Grandpa's freshly brewed coffee. She sat down by Callie and traced the top edge of her cup, looking at the floor. Callie didn't see her look to Grandpa for his opinion.

After a long time of silence, Kate spoke.

"You can keep the money to start a college fund. "You're doing well in school—you'll want a degree to do better in life than I have," she said at last.

"You've done fine," Callie objected.

"Callie, I'm not a waitress because I want to be. I simply don't have a lot of options. I've even thought about going to college myself."

Callie tried to imagine her mother going to college with a bunch of 18-year-olds. It was hard to imagine. She was glad she didn't have to give the check back, but quite disappointed that it was going into some fund for the future. Still, Jake had mentioned a Forestry degree. She liked the idea of being able to work in the mountains. A thousand dollars might even pay for a year or so of classes.

"I'll send Becca a letter to tell her!" Callie said, running up the stairs. Halfway up, she turned and ran back down. "Thanks, Mom," she said with a hug.

LATER THAT NIGHT, CALLIE put on her Necklace of Honor and her father's sweatshirt. She opened her window and dried off the windowsill so she could sit on it. A crisp October breeze zipped through Callie's hair, chilling her. She lowered herself to sit and survey her yard.

Nothing moved but the leaves on the autumn-painted trees. A swirling breeze whipped around a big yellow maple, and an armful of golden leaves trembled and surrendered, falling to the ground. The sky was deep purply blue, like a sapphire under a purple light. The bright moon blinked through the clouds. One cloud that looked like a handlebar moustache stretched across the moon's full face.

Callie gave a long, satisfied sigh as she thought about her time with Becca. What had started as a disaster had turned out to be the best summer ever. She recalled their first meeting—how she despised the rich stranger from the city. The Becca she knew now seemed like a whole different person. She missed her and longed to see her again. She smiled. *I wonder what other adventures we could have...*

She touched her Necklace. The baby ring for Love, the dogwood charm for Craftsmanship, the moonstone for Radiance, the ruby for Courage, the cave rock for Trust, the pewter shoe for Endurance, and the wooden cross for Grace. She smiled as she remembered the moment that she received each charm and smiled.

She shifted uncomfortably as the memory of Mr. Creepy—her own uncle—invaded her thoughts. Those hateful, gold eyes pierced her very being. *Lord, will the anger ever go away? I still can't believe all he did to me—to all of us. I wonder what he did with Mom's charms? Maybe some of the pieces are hidden somewhere.* She halfway wanted to confront him and ask about the charms but was afraid to. Bad dreams still haunted her. *Someday I'm going to search for those charms no matter what and give them back to Mom!*

The words of Jesus that she had heard earlier in the summer, "Trust Me," lingered in her mind. "Lord, I really want to trust You in all this. Grandpa says that I need to forgive... that man... but... I'll need your help to do it."

Callie hopped off the windowsill and into her cozy room. As the curtain swooshed together, she flung back her covers and dove into her warm bed. Shadow didn't even move when she snuggled her cold feet up next to his warm body. She tenderly removed her necklace and placed it on the nightstand.

"Jesus, I see how you worked through this summer. I was lonely and You were there for me. You turned an enemy into a friend. I longed for adventure, and You gave me the adventure of a lifetime! I was hurt and I didn't understand how you could let it happen, but You protected us in the cave. You helped Becca win the essay contest. You gave me a great teacher. You've done so much! I felt poor—and I may be poor compared to some people, but I'm not poor in the important way. Not at all. I have Mom, Grandpa, Jake, Becca, Emma...and You! And Shadow! Thank you for being there for me. Thank you for everything!"

Patting the bed to summon her faithful companion to her side, she took a deep breath and felt her mind and body relax. Happy and satisfied, the young woman and the fluffy, warm Shadow curled up together and fell fast asleep.

The End.

www.ingramcontent.com/pod-product-compliance
Lightning Source LLC
Chambersburg PA
CBHW070826180626
46818CB00001B/412